THE
OF MURDER

A totally gripping British crime mystery

BRIAN BATTISON

Detective Jim Ashworth Book 6

Originally published as
Poetic Justice

JOFFE
BOOKS

Revised edition 2021
Joffe Books, London
www.joffebooks.com

First published by Constable in Great Britain in 1996
as *Poetic Justice*

Cover art by Nick Castle

ISBN: 978-1-78931-861-6

For Tutty,

a loyal and much-loved companion who passed away
on 7 April 1996.

Julie Wilson } Mother & Daughter
Tracy Wilson 18 mnths

PROLOGUE

If the cat hadn't overturned the coffee mug, Julie Wilson would have noticed the shards of glass in her baby's food when she emptied the contents of the jar into a dish. As it was, she turned in time to see the cat scampering away while a tidal wave of coffee washed over the worktop and trickled down the front of her newly fitted kitchen units. Her eighteen-month-old daughter, Tracey, chuckling merrily at the mess, reached out a hand towards her mother, eager to taste the prettily coloured rhubarb and custard. Julie banged the dish onto the tray of Tracey's high chair then, shaking a fist and threatening the cat's life, she rushed into the hall where he was bounding to safety up the stairs.

Bright sunlight poured through the kitchen window and picked out the sharp edges of glass as Tracey grasped her spoon and plunged it into the puréed mixture, her eyes still fixed on the coffee dripping relentlessly to the floor. Gurgling and giggling, she placed the spoon to her mouth and immediately a spike pricked her tender upper lip, drawing a spot of blood and causing her to cry out. Recoiling in her chair at the unexpected discomfort, the baby flicked the spoonful of food across the room where it spattered onto the rust-coloured carpet tiles.

Her mother came storming back, muttering under her breath, and was busy mopping up the coffee when Tracey once again returned her attention to the dish. Raising the spoon to her mouth, oblivious to the shiny fragment balancing on its edge, the baby sucked contentedly, all the while bringing the glass closer until it tumbled from the spoon and landed in the dish with a slight plop. She ate with a slow, awkward determination, all the time watching her mother with a puzzled expression for, although too young to distinguish the words, the baby found her scolding tone unsettling.

'Oh, Tracey,' Julie wailed, spotting the pink blob on the carpet. 'Keep it on your dish, darling.'

Grabbing another handful of kitchen towel, she scooped up the mess. 'God, I can't stand much more of this. It's all right for Patrick, out at work all day, and then when he . . .'

Her words trailed off when she noticed small pieces of glass on the towel. Looking to where her baby was sitting with the tip of the spoon between her lips she saw, even from that distance, jagged edges protruding from the dessert. Her first instinct was to dash to her daughter and snatch the spoon away but she hesitated, remembering the game her husband always played when the baby refused to eat. He would advance on her slowly, saying, 'Give that to Daddy. Come on, Tracey, give it to Daddy,' and the girl would chuckle heartily and wolf the food down.

Julie could only watch in horror as the glass was sucked towards her daughter's mouth. There seemed to be so much of it; she could have swallowed some already. In desperation, she rushed to the worktop and grabbed the baby's rattle. Turning quickly, she started to shake it.

'Tracey, darling, look at Mummy,' she called, her voice quavering. 'Tracey, look at Mummy.'

CHAPTER 1

Chief Inspector Jim Ashworth of Bridgetown CID ambled along the aisles in the Save U Supermarket, glancing at the shelves. He was a large man in his fifties, and his movements were slow and ponderous because he was deep in thought. The supermarket manager, Kevin Davenport, stopped in front of the empty baby food rack and looked anxiously around the store, worried no doubt about the effect the incident and the police presence would have on trade.

'As you can see, Chief Inspector, I've had the display cleared. Your lot are examining the jars now.'

'Yes . . . good,' Ashworth mused, running a hand through his thick black hair which was finely peppered with grey. 'Tell me, Mr Davenport, the glass was in a baby food product made by Arnolds . . . they also manufacture soft drinks, don't they?'

'That's right,' he said, his agitation deepening. 'I've had those displays cleared as well.'

'Good man,' Ashworth said softly, taking time to survey the store.

'How long do you think this will take? I mean, we're losing a lot of trade and—'

'It'll take as long as it takes, Mr Davenport. I'm sure I don't have to remind you that if her mother hadn't noticed the glass, a very young child could have lost her life.'

'I know . . . I mean, of course . . . but it's Head Office, you see, they'll want trading back to normal as quickly as possible.'

'They'll just have to wait until we've cleared this up,' Ashworth told him bluntly.

Further discussion was curtailed by the sight of Detective Sergeant Holly Bedford weaving her way towards them through the displays. She was twenty-eight years old and her enviable figure, further enhanced by a well-tailored navy blue skirt and matching jacket, was attracting a fair number of surreptitious glances from the many bored men trailing the store behind their wives. It was rumoured that Holly's tour of duty in Bridgetown would end as soon as she had worked her way through the town's male population, and although this view was rather uncharitable, it was not wholly devoid of the truth. Her marriage had ended some years before with the death of her husband and her still-tangled emotions shunned any form of permanent attachment, yet Holly was a highly-sexed girl who found it hard to resist an attractive male. Her high-heeled shoes clattered noisily on the tiled floor as she approached the two men.

'All done here, guv,' she announced chirpily.

'Good.'

Ashworth, turning to speak to the manager, found Davenport studying Holly with open interest. He sighed loudly and gave an impatient cough, causing the man to jump and look from one to the other, their expressions telling him clearly that his presence was no longer required.

'Oh, right . . . okay,' he blustered. 'Well then, if you'll excuse me . . .'

'Surely,' Ashworth said, grunting with disdain as he watched the man sidle away. 'Any news of the little girl, Holly?'

'They think she's all right, guv, but they're still waiting for the results of the X-rays to come through.'

'That's something, I suppose. Right, tell me what you've found out so far.'

Holly fished a note pad from her shoulder bag and flicked hurriedly through its pages.

'All the baby food and soft drinks manufactured by Arnolds have been taken away for examination. At first glance it doesn't look like anything else has been tampered with. Local radio are issuing warnings about any baby food and soft drinks purchased recently. The local press have been informed, and the directors of Arnolds are having breakdowns, as are the directors of the supermarket.'

'Hmm,' Ashworth said, exhaling sharply.

The two detectives were attracting considerable attention from the early afternoon shoppers and were about to move to a more discreet position when an elderly lady brought her trolley to a halt in front of them.

'Excuse me,' she said, looking up at the chief inspector. 'Can you tell me where the soup is?'

Holly had to hide a smile as Ashworth frowned thoughtfully, and said, 'Soup . . . oh yes, if you go to the end of this aisle then turn left, it's a little way along on your right.'

The woman trundled away, the rusting wheels of her trolley screeching periodically.

'We shop here sometimes,' Ashworth explained, catching the mischievous glint in Holly's large green eyes. 'Now, shall we leave before some young housewife expects me to offer her two packets of her old washing powder for the one she's just bought?'

Holly chuckled and fell in beside him, lengthening her stride to keep in step.

'Something else, guv — it seems there was enough glass in the jar of baby food for it to be very noticeable, but the mother's attention was diverted just as she was putting it in the dish.'

'A shot across the bow,' Ashworth remarked, as the automatic doors slid back and they emerged into the car park.

'I don't follow,' Holly said, picking her way through the vehicles to where Ashworth's Ford Scorpio was parked.

'The extortionist didn't want to injure a child; he was just showing the company how easy it would be to ruin their business.'

'What do we do now, then, guv?'

'We wait for someone to demand some money.'

At the car Ashworth gallantly opened the passenger door for Holly before climbing into the driver's seat.

'You've put out a nationwide alert on this, I take it?'

'Of course, guv. We can't just assume that it's a local thing, can we?'

'Has anybody started a check of the security tapes?' he asked, steering the car towards the exit.

'Yes, at the supermarket and the ones from Arnolds's factory. They're all being analysed.'

'Good,' he grunted. 'And now we wait and try to dodge the flak while we're doing so.'

Centuries before the surrounding estates were built, bringing with them town status, the centre of Bridgetown had formed the heart of the village and it still retained a rural look, with its thatched cottages now turned into shops. As Ashworth negotiated the Scorpio along the narrow high street, Holly turned to study his profile. Although twice her age, he was fitter than most younger men and Holly felt a strong physical attraction towards him, but knew that, despite the fact that he had strayed once during his thirty years of marriage, Ashworth was happy with his wife, Sarah, and she would never allow herself to jeopardize their relationship. Even so, there were times such as now while he sat lost in his own thoughts, excluding her entirely, when she wondered how he might react should she offer the bait. That interesting avenue of thought was interrupted, however, by the car turning into the police station car park.

Ashworth bounded up the steps and into reception with Holly in tow. Martin Dutton, the bald-headed duty sergeant, was behind the desk.

'Jim,' he said, 'the little girl's all right. The X-rays showed she hadn't swallowed any glass.'

'Thank God for that, Martin.'

'Newton's doing his nut,' Dutton whispered, nodding towards the ceiling. 'And Councillor Cowper's been in, doing her nut. They're upstairs together now—'

'Doing their nuts in unison, no doubt,' Ashworth intoned, with a trace of humour.

Dutton laughed. 'That's about it, Jim.'

'What do they expect?' he muttered, making his way towards the stairs. 'The case has only just broken.'

'Instant results, Jim,' the sergeant called after him. 'They expect instant results.'

'Councillor Cowper?' Holly queried, as they climbed the steps to CID at the top of the building.

'Emma Cowper. She's a Conservative councillor, makes a lot of noise and many people's lives uncomfortable. No doubt, she sees pushing the police around as a vote winner. This is going to be a high-profile case, so she'll be sticking her nose into it whenever possible.'

In the office, Detective Constable Josh Abraham was settled in front of the computer with his back to the door, and when Holly walked past him en route to her desk she playfully ran her fingernails across his neck.

'Get off,' he muttered, slapping out at her.

'Can't keep my hands off you, lover boy.' She bent towards him, whispering, 'One of these days I'm going to have you, I promise.'

'All right, you two, cut it out,' Ashworth said, shifting his weight about in his chair until he was comfortable. 'Right, then, Josh, what have you got?'

'Not much at the moment,' he said, swivelling round to face the chief inspector. 'I've checked records, and none of our local villains have any form in this direction, so I've started on the nationals.'

'I see.' Ashworth seemed unimpressed as he stared into space, drumming his fingers on his blotter.

Holly perched on the edge of her desk and winked at Josh who in turn stuck out his tongue. They had become very good friends over the years, but their relationship would go no further for, despite his masculine appearance and the steely grey eyes that women found so attractive, Josh was in fact homosexual. He turned back to Ashworth and grinned.

'Forensic are still checking the jars of baby food, guv. The office is stacked high with them. They're doing their nuts.'

'It seems to be in vogue today,' Ashworth remarked.

He was about to say more when the office door swung open and a woman breezed into the room. She was forty-one years old; her two-piece cashmere suit was expensive if a little sombre, and her manner oozed authority.

'Right, Chief Inspector,' she said, pulling up a chair and sitting before his desk. 'Where are you getting with this baby food case?'

'Please take a seat, Councillor Cowper,' Ashworth said, pointedly.

'Never mind the sarcasm — where are you getting with this baby food case?'

'Emma, Emma,' Ashworth said, sitting back and smiling. 'This brag-and-bluster act of yours may work with most people, but this is Jim Ashworth you're talking to — remember?'

The woman's face flushed. 'You're a public servant, don't forget—'

'I'm not *your* servant,' he replied, stabbing a finger. 'It's the same rules as with every other encounter I've had with you — if you want a civil answer, you'll have to ask your questions in a civil manner.'

For a moment it seemed that the councillor would explode, but then she regained her composure and grinned.

'He's still the same, then?' she said, turning to Holly, who gave a noncommittal smile. 'Oh, come on, Jim, there's a lot of public concern about this case.'

'And a lot of votes in it for you if you can claim you had to kick-start the police.'

Once again Ashworth's direct manner brought a high colour to the woman's cheeks. She said, 'Superintendent Newton promised me his full cooperation.' And when

Ashworth merely shrugged, she added, shrilly, 'The baby could have died, you know.'

'I'm well aware of that,' he said, 'and no one's more concerned about it than I am, but I'm not the Lone Ranger, Emma.'

The councillor rose abruptly and smoothed down her skirt. 'Right, I just thought I'd check that everything possible was being done. You'll keep me informed at all times?'

'As and when you need to be informed, Emma, you shall be . . . as and when.'

The two locked eyes and then the woman grinned again, but her anger was betrayed by the forceful way in which she closed the door behind her.

Ashworth shook his head. 'I don't know, when some people are elected to the council, they seem to think they hold the same powers as those sitting at God's right hand. That's always puzzled me.'

* * *

It was 6 p.m. on a glorious autumn evening, and sunlight was flooding onto the driveway of his large four-bedroomed detached house as Ashworth brought the Scorpio to a stop just short of the garage doors. He stood for a moment and gazed at the front garden, still ablaze with roses and a sprinkling of late summer flowers, then went inside to be greeted by Sarah, a handsome woman who favoured light-blue twin sets and tweed skirts.

'Everything all right, dear?' she asked, while he hung up his waxed cotton jacket.

'Yes, I think so.'

At the sound of his voice Peanuts, their Jack Russell, came bounding out of the lounge to meet him.

'Hello, girl,' he said, bending down to stroke her. 'You've only just woken up, you lazy thing.'

Sarah picked a path around the dog, who was running about in tight circles, barking excitedly, and on her way to the kitchen she asked, 'Is the little girl all right?'

'Yes, she's fine, thank God,' Ashworth replied, drawn to the doorway by the smell of lamb chops and mint sauce.

As they ate, Sarah sensed that her husband wanted to talk about the case so, after topping up his wineglass, she said, 'Tell me what's happening, dear.'

'Not much to tell, really. I've left Holly and Josh at the station going through the files — I'm hoping they'll come up with some likely suspects — and we're still waiting for the results from Forensic . . .' He took a long sip of wine and licked his lips appreciatively. 'After that, it's a matter of waiting; a process which I'm sure will be made increasingly more difficult by the involvement of Councillor Emma Cowper,' he added, almost to himself.

'Oh, I ran into her sister, Meg, today while I was shopping,' Sarah said, as she started to clear the plates. Ashworth's still held a couple of pieces of meat, so she left it.

'Meg?' he said, frowning. 'I don't think I know her, do I?'

Sarah was filling the washing-up bowl and waited long enough for her husband to slip the scraps to the dog, who was supposed to be on a diet, before she turned.

'She restores furniture. Such a pretty girl, and she's got a lovely personality.'

Ashworth simply shrugged his shoulders.

'Actually,' Sarah continued with enthusiasm, 'the gossip at the Women's Institute suggests that there's more than a little friction between Emma and Meg at the moment. More friction than there usually is, I should say.'

'Really?' Ashworth muttered, trying to sound interested.

She folded her arms and leant against the sink, the dirty dishes forgotten. 'Yes. You know Emma had an affair with Jean Churchman's husband some five years ago . . .'

Ashworth's eyes widened. 'Someone had an affair with Emma Cowper?'

'Oh, it didn't last very long. He did actually leave Jean and move in with Emma, but after about six weeks, he left the district.'

'So, the swine collected his medal and vanished, eh?'

Sarah laughed. 'Jim, you really are developing an acid sense of humour. But, you see, that means Emma and Jean Churchman are arch enemies — they hate the sight of each other. Well, Emma was forever going on at Meg about restoring furniture at the house so Meg started to look for premises and guess what . . . she's rented a workshop from Jean Churchman.'

She waited for some reaction to this startling revelation, but all she got from her husband was a puzzled expression.

'Can't you see how difficult that could be, Jim?'

'I suppose it could be awkward, yes.'

'Anyway, when I saw Meg today, I asked her about a telephone table for the hall. The one we've got is much too big — don't you think? — and I said you'd call in and have a look at some.'

But Ashworth had stopped listening, for mention of the telephone had directed his thoughts back to Holly and Josh at the station.

CHAPTER 2

Emma Cowper arrived home in a foul mood, the effects of the confrontation with Ashworth still visible on her flushed face. Her apparent inability to have him kowtowing before her like the rest of the senior officers filled her with an impotent rage. That man had always been a thorn in her side and every time the opportunity had arisen, she had attempted to have him removed from office; the fact that those attempts had always failed only intensified her dislike for him.

She threw her briefcase onto the hall table and hung up her coat before retiring to the lounge, a large room with light-blue decor and quality furniture as befitted a local councillor and successful travel agent. Her sister, Meg, sitting in an elegant floral armchair beside the fireplace, failed to look up at her bustling entrance. The younger by three years, Meg was the complete opposite of the immaculate Emma. She was dressed in faded blue jeans and a shabby white shirt; her face, framed by short fair hair, was freckled, with small perfect features and an angelic expression.

'I can smell varnish,' Emma huffed, as she crossed to the drinks cabinet and poured herself a liberal gin and bitter lemon.

'That's because I've still got my work things on,' Meg replied coldly.

'I wish you'd have a bath and a change of clothes when you finish work,' Emma snapped. 'How many times do I have to tell you?'

'Oh, for God's sake, don't keep on at me.'

'I'm not going on at you. We agreed that you'd stop painting that furniture of yours in the garage because of the smell, and now you bring it home with you . . .'

'We didn't agree,' Meg flared, jumping to her feet. 'You made such a fuss that I had to find alternative premises. And I don't paint furniture, I restore it — there's a big difference, you know.'

'Is there really?' Emma spat, slamming her glass on to the cabinet. 'And didn't you for one minute think that the premises you'd chosen might cause problems?'

A sly smile touched Meg's lips. 'With Jean Churchman, you mean? Well, I happen to like Jean; she's become a very good friend to me.'

'And she'd stab me in the back as soon as look at me.'

'A lot of people would,' Meg replied tartly.

'You did it on purpose, to get at me. Father always said the only way you could better me was to go behind my back.'

Meg's face took on a hurt expression at the mention of their late father, and in a petulant tone, she said, 'Someone's upset you, haven't they?'

'Oh yes, Jim Ashworth has most definitely upset me. That man doesn't have an ounce of respect for my position in this town.'

'The Chief Inspector?' Meg said brightly. 'He's coming to see me about some furniture.'

'I'm not surprised. Second-hand furniture would be right up Ashworth's street.'

That insulting remark wounded Meg but not wishing to prolong the argument, she elected to leave the room. Emma shouted at her back, 'I'm having some people in tonight.'

'And you want me to keep out of the way, I suppose.'

'Yes,' she replied bluntly.

'Okay, I'll stay in my room, then.'

* * *

'Here it is,' Holly said, hurrying into the CID office, clutching the newly finished Forensic report.

Josh turned away from the computer screen and looked up expectantly while she scrutinized the pages for several minutes.

'It says here that they've found four other jars of baby food with glass in them.'

'Were the seals broken?'

'Yes and no . . . that's the clever bit, lover boy; it says they'd been opened and then re-sealed using four minute dabs of super glue to hold the thing in place. It's virtually undetectable to the human eye.'

'Very clever,' Josh said, leaning back in his chair.

'And dangerous,' Holly pointed out. 'That bastard could plant the stuff anywhere, and it wouldn't be noticeable.'

'Anything else?'

'Yes, the glass was from a milk bottle,' she said, studying the report. 'The Co-Op, apparently, so that narrows it down nicely to a few million suspects nationwide. The security tapes at the supermarket haven't come up with anything, and neither have the ones from Arnolds's factory.'

'Those cameras are a waste of money, Holly. What's the point in having them if they don't cover the whole area all of the time?'

'I know. So, whoever we're looking for could have some knowledge of security.'

'That reminds me,' Josh said. 'You're seeing the head of security at Arnolds in the morning. His name's Jerry Townsend.'

'Oh, right. Have you come up with any likely candidates?' she asked, pointing to the computer.

Josh shook his head. 'The trouble with this sort of crime is that they either get away with it, or they're caught and get twenty-five years.'

He pressed a button and information flooded the screen. 'The only one who looks anywhere near likely is a bloke called Vincent Blakewell. He's a small-time villain, forty-two years old, has a string of convictions for confidence tricks, mostly. He once tried to extort money from a group of Indian shops in Birmingham by threatening to set fire to them if the owners didn't pay up.'

'What is this, lover boy — desperation?' she laughed, pushing herself off the desk to scrutinize the computer screen.

'Not much, is it?' he said, pulling a face. 'But like I say, there's not a huge pool of suspects to draw from.'

'Is there anything that puts him remotely in the frame?'

'Well, I rang the Birmingham police, and they said he's got a hankering for the good life — fast cars and the rest — but he's falling well short of it at the moment: he's unemployed and living in bed and breakfast accommodation, so he could have done it out of necessity.'

'It's possible he could have been going for the big one, I suppose. How long has he been in Bridgetown?'

'About six weeks.'

'And with his form, he'd never expect us to connect him with this sort of job. Hmm, very well done, my little detective constable,' she said, patting his shoulder. 'Right, then, I'd better ring the guv'nor, and pass on what we've got.'

* * *

The drinks party at Emma Cowper's house was drawing to its close, and a line of taxis pulled up in the drive to ferry away the happily inebriated guests. Emma, positioned at the front door, was adopting the pose of a royal personage, clasping hands and chatting benevolently with each of her departing friends.

'Shirley, darling,' she gushed, embracing the woman and planting a dutiful kiss on both of her cheeks. 'Thank you for coming, and I'm so sorry I hogged Richard all evening, but we had such a lot to talk about.'

She smiled serenely and turned to the woman's husband. 'Now, you're not to worry, Richard, I'm using my influence with the police to get this wretched supermarket business sorted out as quickly as possible. So do tell the other Save U directors not to worry, either.'

Richard Samuels's concerned look lifted marginally as he thanked Emma and ushered his wife to the waiting cab.

Petrol fumes hung heavily over the front garden as the last of the vehicles finally drew away and Emma closed the door, sighing contentedly, for the evening had been a resounding success.

* * *

Ashworth arrived at the police station next morning to find Martin Dutton pointing an ominous finger towards the ceiling.

'I take it I've been summoned,' he said wearily, leaning an elbow on the reception desk.

'That you have, Jim.'

Dutton paused while Bobby Adams, his uniformed assistant, appeared with two mugs of tea and, after taking a sip, he went on, 'I reckon this is the first time we've ever had anything like this in Bridgetown.'

'You're right. Villains are getting more devious, Martin.'

'And dangerous,' Dutton said, shaking his head and tutting. 'Fancy planting glass in baby food. What sort of person does that?'

Ashworth shrugged, and glanced towards the stairs. 'Oh, well, I suppose I'd better get this over with.'

He nodded to the sergeant and smiled encouragingly at Bobby, the young constable who, while doing a short stint in CID, had made a good impression on the chief inspector.

Approaching the door to Superintendent Newton's office with a good deal of reluctance, Ashworth steeled himself for a heated confrontation. Newton had only been in the job for a matter of months and the two officers had crossed swords almost from day one; and although an uneasy peace reigned at the present time, it was extremely fragile and the slightest disagreement was likely to shatter it. At the door, Ashworth resigned himself to the inevitable, and made his knock forceful.

'Come in.'

The chief inspector let himself into the neat room to find Newton attempting to look busy at his desk. He was a small man, around five feet eight, with a receding hairline and a fierce passion for orderly discipline.

'Good morning, Chief Inspector,' Newton said, forcing his lips into a smile.

Ashworth nodded stiffly. 'Good morning, sir.'

'Take a seat.'

Settling into a chair facing the desk, Ashworth watched the superintendent, who was intent on tidying a stack of reports.

'I won't ask you for an update,' Newton began, as he re-aligned his ruler with the blotter. 'I know it's far too early for that. To be honest, all I really want to say is that I'm well aware of Councillor Cowper's interest in this and I'll try to draw her fire, leaving you and your team free to get on with the job.'

Ashworth, hoping that surprise did not show on his face, said, 'Thank you, sir. I must say, the woman does seem to be taking a lot of interest in the case.'

'Yes, and I think I know why — it's the local elections next spring, and I've an idea Miss Cowper's already started her campaign.' The superintendent let out a chortle, his throat muscles appearing to contract at the unfamiliar action, and in response Ashworth gave a polite laugh.

'You've no leads at the moment, then?' Newton ventured, after a pause.

'None, I'm afraid, sir. I believe DC Abraham has come up with a con-man who's recently moved into the district, but it's nothing more than a shot in the dark, really.'

'I see. Now, as this is the first case of its kind in Bridgetown, I've taken the liberty of getting in touch with other forces with experience of this kind of crime. It seems there are two types of perpetrator: the amateur who gets caught very quickly trying to collect the money, and the real professional who keeps the campaign going for so long that the company involved is likely to jettison the police and pay up before they go bankrupt.'

'That's helpful, sir, thank you.'

Newton cleared his throat, and added rapidly, 'And if Arnolds do decide to settle with this extortionist, we would be ill-advised to interfere. Their trade has already been hit badly, and if that factory goes down it would be a disaster for the local job scene.'

'Hence the good councillor's concern,' Ashworth put in.

'Quite, Chief Inspector. I believe her heart is in the right place, but as far as this case goes she'll have to accept that the impossible we do immediately, miracles take just a fraction longer.'

Realizing that the banal joke was the termination of the meeting, Ashworth got to his feet.

'Well, sir, if that's all, I'll get on.'

'Of course; keep me posted.'

Marching towards CID, Ashworth pondered that the interview had gone a lot better than expected, with Newton even attempting some humour; but what he failed to see, in his rather modest way, was the fact that once having done battle with him, very few clamoured for an instant rematch.

* * *

Meg Cowper flounced into the kitchen, wearing nothing but a set of flimsy white underwear. Emma was settled at the breakfast bar, already neatly dressed and fully made-up. She sipped her coffee and studied her sister's visible cleavage with contempt.

'I do wish you wouldn't walk about half naked, Meg.'

'Why not?' she laughed, pouring herself a coffee. 'It gets the milkman going.'

'Any of my friends could call in,' Emma continued frostily. 'Goodness knows what they'd think . . .'

'You took some of the booze out of my wardrobe for your little bash last night,' Meg accused.

'I borrowed two bottles of gin, that's all. I'm going to replace them.'

'You're always doing it. I practically live in my bedroom, while you have the run of the whole house. Why can't you just stay out of my room?'

'Meg, I was going to buy two bottles today and put them back . . . honestly.'

'You're always stealing my booze — the money you make, as well. God, you must think I'm thick.'

Emma smiled, making no attempt to refute that last remark, and Meg slammed down her coffee cup and stormed out of the room. That smile had hurt her far more than any words her sister could have uttered; it was a cruel talent that Emma had mastered very early in life.

The years which stood between them in age were the crux of the matter. When Meg was born, Emma, at the tender, impressionable age of three, had suddenly found that she was no longer the focus of attention; all at once her parents were fawning over the new baby. The resentment which built up because of this stayed with her and grew, still deeper, when Meg developed into a pretty, sociable child. Emma was plain and inhibited but possessed a superior intellect and she used this constantly to convince her younger sister that she was stupid. When both eventually grew into adults of equal attraction, all was forgiven and forgotten . . . but only on the surface, for the jealousy and the sibling rivalry still lingered deep in the subconscious minds of both women. Those emotions affected them differently, and whereas Emma was driven to succeed in everything she tackled, Meg seemed capable only of ambling through life, afraid to accept its challenges.

When the door to Meg's bedroom slammed shut, Emma settled back to enjoy her coffee, her smile becoming a superior grin.

CHAPTER 3

Ashworth viewed the shabby building with genuine disgust. It was an inner terraced Victorian house which stood on an estate to the north of Bridgetown. Any semblance of splendour had long since departed from the tree-lined street. The houses which had once been gracious had fallen into disrepair and the road and pavements, littered with dog filth and rubbish, were badly in need of resurfacing. Holly climbed out of the car and waited while Ashworth took the precaution of ensuring that the central locking device had indeed secured all doors.

'Nice place,' she said wryly, as they negotiated the wide stone steps leading to the front door. Ashworth merely grunted and banged on the peeling wood. A fair-haired young man opened up, immediately letting out the strong smell of fried food.

'Yeah?' he said, none too politely.

'Is this the Regency Bed and Breakfast Hotel?' Ashworth asked.

The man's upper lip curled suspiciously. 'Who wants to know? You from the Social?'

'No, we're the police.' Ashworth produced his warrant card and pushed past the man into the hall.

'Oh, Christ . . . filth.'

'Just what I was thinking,' Ashworth murmured, staring into the dirty kitchen where an ancient cooker stood, thick with grease. 'Tell me, are you in charge of this . . . establishment?'

'Yeah, that's right.'

'We're looking for a man called Vincent Blakewell.'

'Oh, Lord Bloody Blakewell. You'll find him at the top of the stairs, first door on the left. But you'd better be quick, everybody has to be out by half past.'

'And why is that?'

'It's only bed and breakfast, mate. They kip in the beds, have their breakfast, and then they're out on the street. This ain't the bloody Ritz.'

'At last we agree on something,' Ashworth remarked drily.

Holly followed him up the stairs, and they had almost reached the top when the man shouted, 'Don't forget, I want everybody out of the building in five minutes . . .' He smirked when Ashworth glared down at him, and added, 'Well, I've got my snooker to practise. Hoping to turn professional, ain't I?'

'Son, you're getting up my nose. Now, if you don't get back into that cesspit you call a kitchen and keep quiet until after we've gone, I'll have the health and hygiene people in here to close you down in five minutes flat.'

The man glowered but kept his mouth shut and then scuttled out of sight.

'I don't know what's happened to respect for the law,' Ashworth muttered, above the sound of their shoes on the bare boards of the stairs. Holly simply smiled.

The door on the left of the landing was opened by a well-groomed man. He wore a fashionable grey suit, and his brown hair was cut short around a tanned, good-looking face.

'Yes?' he asked pleasantly, his eyes travelling over Holly's figure.

'Chief Inspector Ashworth of Bridgetown CID,' he announced, thrusting forward his warrant card. 'And this is Detective Sergeant Bedford.'

Holly noticed some of the colour draining away beneath the man's tan, and straight away asked, 'Are you Mr Vincent Blakewell?'

'Yes, I am.'

'May we come in, sir?' Ashworth asked.

'I suppose so.' Blakewell stood aside and allowed them to enter.

The man's smart appearance contrasted sharply with the room's squalor. There was a single bed in one corner, the grubby red mat at its side clashing badly with the pocked, plum-coloured linoleum; two straight-backed wooden chairs stood on either side of a chipped chest of drawers which had a primus stove resting on its top; and the window was grimy and without curtains.

'This is purely a temporary arrangement,' Blakewell assured them in a cultured voice while they surveyed the room.

'Really, sir? Our colleagues in Birmingham informed us that you were in Bridgetown.'

'And why would they do that?' the man asked, his eyes flicking nervously between the two detectives.

'We had some glass turn up in jars of baby food at a local supermarket, and we wondered if you knew anything about it.'

'Why should I?' he said, his laugh too loud.

'You do have a conviction for extortion,' Holly cut in.

'That was a long time ago,' Blakewell retorted. 'I haven't been in trouble for three years.'

Holly shrugged. 'That's one way of putting it, I suppose, but we could just as easily claim that the police hadn't caught up with you for three years.'

'Are you seriously accusing me of planting the glass?'

'No, sir,' Ashworth said mildly. 'We're just asking questions.'

Blakewell looked relieved. 'Well, all I can tell you is that I had nothing to do with it.'

'Thank you, sir,' the chief inspector said, already at the door.

Once outside, he turned to Holly. 'I don't know whether it's due to Government policy, but I don't believe people should have to live like this.'

'No, guv,' Holly said, pretending to stifle a yawn. This was one of her guv'nor's pet subjects and, if allowed, he would go on at some length.

He shot her a sideways glance, and chuckled. 'All right, young lady, don't get cheeky. Anyway, what do you think of our Mr Blakewell?'

'Very smooth, and he was definitely worried until he knew we hadn't got anything on him.'

'Yes,' he mused, opening the passenger door. 'I think we'll be keeping an eye on Mr Blakewell.'

* * *

Vincent Blakewell fidgeted on the landing of the bed and breakfast establishment as he listened to the sound of the Scorpio pulling away. He began to pace, one hand wiping sweat from his forehead, the other loosening the knot of his tie, and he jumped when the payphone in the ground floor passage started to ring. Quickly vaulting down to it, he grabbed the receiver.

'Yes, it's Blakewell.' He was silent for a few seconds, then whispered savagely, 'Now, you listen to me, I've had the law here asking about the supermarket job . . .'

* * *

Ashworth was expertly handling the Scorpio on the narrow twisting lanes leading towards Arnolds's factory, when he said, 'I'm going to be a bit naughty . . .'

'All right, then, guv, pull over somewhere quiet and let's get it over with.'

He laughed, and when Holly remained quiet, he glanced at her. 'You're not your usual chirpy self.'

'I know. I keep thinking about that little girl . . . she could easily have died, guv. This isn't like our usual cases, is it? I mean, whoever's doing this is quite prepared to kill innocent people, even babies. He doesn't care how many he kills, as long as he gets what he wants.'

'I'm finding it more than a little disconcerting myself, and what makes it worse is the fact that we've nowhere to go because we don't know where this lunatic is going to strike next.'

'I don't suppose we could persuade Arnolds to close the factory down?'

'No, I don't think so, Holly, and in any case, that wouldn't solve anything. The goods that are going on supermarket shelves today were produced months ago. Anyway, don't forget that whoever is doing this is probably buying the goods, impregnating them with glass, and then putting them back on the shelves.'

'I suppose so,' she said, sighing. 'Unless it's somebody at the factory.'

'That's an avenue we'll have to check out, but to me it seems unlikely.'

'You were going to be naughty,' she said, changing the subject.

'Oh, yes, I want to call in at Jean Churchman's place to see Emma Cowper's sister about a table Sarah wants to buy. She lives just around the next corner.'

'Okay, guv.'

Ashworth brought the car to a halt outside a large Tudor house which had white walls criss-crossed with black beams, and a thatched roof that actually shone in the autumn sunlight. He made his way through the central archway leading to the gardens, then crossed a paved courtyard where strong scents of roses and harvested fruit filled his nostrils, and stood gazing at the two acres of land with its sweeping lawns and large orchard in the distance.

'Well, if it isn't Jim Ashworth. What brings you here?' Jean Churchman asked, as she came along the path towards him.

He turned to smile warmly at the woman. She was forty years old, quite tall, and possessed an elegance which could not be hidden, even when dressed as she was now in an old corduroy skirt, huge navy sweater and sage-green body warmer.

'Hello . . . I'm looking for Meg Cowper.'

The wind caught and tousled her short black hair as she stopped to scrape mud from her Wellington boots with a small stick.

'You'll find her in the old stables,' she said, pointing the stick to his left.

'Thanks. You know, I don't envy you with all this land.'

'It keeps me busy. I've just been trying to thin out the rhubarb patch. The stuff spreads like wildfire.'

They chatted about mutual friends for a while then, with a wave of his hand, Ashworth approached the outbuilding. Once through the original stable door his steps echoed on the flagstones while his nose wrinkled sharply at the pungent smells of varnish and paint which hung heavily in the air. Meg immediately emerged from one of the stalls, clutching a small brush.

'Hello, I'm Jim Ashworth,' he said.

She gave him an open smile. 'Oh good, just give me a minute to wash this stuff off my hands. It really is lethal.'

'Of course. My wife wanted me to look at a table,' he said, as she crossed to an enamel sink and turned on the tap.

'I know.' Her back was towards him while she washed her hands, and when she turned there was a huge grin on her face as she said, 'My sister doesn't like you.'

'I don't like her,' Ashworth replied with a chuckle.

'You stand up to her, that's what she can't stomach.'

'She'll get used to it.' He paused, then added mischievously, 'But then again, maybe she won't.'

'Well, I must say, I like you.'

'It's not escaping my notice that you're attempting to butter me up,' he warned playfully. 'Hoping for an easy sale, no doubt.'

Meg was still smiling when she ushered him into one of the stalls and removed the cover from a light teak-coloured table.

'Now, that is nice,' he mused, drawing his fingertips along its surface.

'I had to do a lot of work, bleaching it back to the wood,' she said. 'Mrs Ashworth and I discussed one hundred and forty pounds, and I'm to take your old table away.'

'To do up and sell on, I suppose?'

'Well, yes, but once again I'd have to go back to the wood. Not many people want dark oak nowadays, so it's not as if I'd be getting something for nothing.'

'Even so, one hundred and forty pounds is still a bit steep. What if we say one hundred?'

'Sorry, no,' she said, shaking her head. 'I couldn't possibly make a profit at that price.'

'All right, then, if this is what Sarah wants, we'll say one hundred and forty.'

* * *

Ashworth was clearly taken with Meg Cowper for he talked about her all the way to Arnolds's factory. When he described her as a 'Cadbury's Flake' type of girl, jealousy rose up in Holly as she pictured all of the beautiful women who had appeared in the chocolate commercial. On arrival at the factory they were shown the way by the head of security, Jerry Townsend, and Holly's ego was rapidly restored for the man obviously had difficulty in keeping his eyes off her.

The office was as small as Townsend was large and, after clearing files from two upright chairs, he invited them to sit down. The man addressed most of his remarks to Ashworth, but his gaze kept straying towards Holly. His bulk matched that of the chief inspector, and she put his age at around forty. He was very attractive and ordinarily his dark looks would have brought a tingle to her spine but she found his continual leering a definite turn-off.

Townsend sniffed the air. 'Have you been to Meg Cowper's workshop?'

'Yes,' Ashworth said, shifting his weight uncomfortably in the small chair.

'I'd know that smell anywhere — varnish, and all that other stuff she uses. I'm a good friend of Jean Churchman's so I see quite a bit of Meg.'

'Really?' Ashworth said, clearly uninterested.

'But, of course, that's not why you're here.' Townsend reached for some papers on his desk. 'Now, yesterday I saw the security tapes from the Save U Supermarket. I was invited by the directors,' he added swiftly, when Holly and Ashworth exchanged a puzzled look. 'Your officers were clearing the shelves, and the directors asked me to look at the tapes; they wanted to know if I could identify any personnel from the factory . . .'

'And?' Holly urged.

Townsend shook his head. 'There was no one from here on them.'

'Is there anyone here who might be disgruntled enough to want the factory to suffer?' Ashworth asked.

The security guard gave a humourless laugh. 'We've got two hundred people working on the factory floor, and I'd say that on any given day one hundred and ninety-eight of them are disgruntled, unhappy, and thoroughly pi—' He glanced at Holly. '—peed off. But then, that's Britain in the nineties, isn't it? They're all too worried about losing their jobs to do anything that might ruin the factory, though.'

'How about someone from here who's just trying to work a scam?' Holly ventured.

Townsend pursed his lips. 'I don't think so. I mean, something like this would suggest more brains than you'd find in the average factory floor worker.'

'I've known some very intelligent people working in factories,' Ashworth retorted.

The man shrugged and fished another sheet of paper from his desk. 'Of course, like most companies nowadays we hire some ex-cons as part of a rehabilitation system.'

Ashworth's eyebrows rose. 'And how many have you got on the payroll at the moment?'

'Two. Jason Brent: he's twenty-two, has a history of petty crime, and he's been here for six months. He comes across as Jack the Lad, very popular. Not very clever, but he does have a lot of charm. Then there's Colin Everitt: he's forty-two years old, and he's done time for embezzlement and generally helping himself to other people's cash. He's been here for ten weeks now. Both of them have kept their noses clean, so far.'

'Which department do they work in?' Ashworth asked.

'Despatch.'

'So, they'd be in a perfect position to tamper with goods before they left the factory,' Holly said.

Townsend gave her a hurt look. 'We do keep a close eye on them.'

'I'm sure you do,' Ashworth said, 'but I think we'd better take a look at them.'

'Be my guest.'

They followed him out of the office and along a depressing, green-walled corridor, the throb of machinery in their ears. Presently, Townsend brought them to a halt by large double doors, ushering them to one side while an employee pushed past with a rack laden with soft drinks.

'This is despatch,' he said. 'Do you want to have a word with Brent and Everitt?'

'A very discreet one,' Ashworth replied. 'We've nothing on them, and I don't really want them embarrassed.'

Townsend gave him a quizzical glance as they made their way between the work benches.

'You take Brent,' Ashworth whispered to Holly. 'Just tell him who you are and see how he reacts.'

She nodded and wandered over to the young man pointed out to her by the security guard. He was sealing cartons containing mixer drinks and when she approached, he looked up and gave her a cheeky grin.

'Hi,' she said.

'Hiya,' he replied.

He was a good few inches taller than Holly, with a slim but muscular build. Dark hair fell over his eyes and he kept having to brush it to one side. While thick brown sticky tape squealed from the roll as he sealed another box, Holly stared into his attractive face.

He was still grinning when he said, 'What can I do for you, then?' His accent carried a slight cockney twang.

'I'm DS Bedford, from Bridgetown nick,' she informed him quietly.

'You don't say.' He pushed the box on to a conveyor belt and grabbed the next one.

'We're looking into the glass found in jars of baby food from this factory.'

'So?' The grin had faded from his face, and Holly could feel his eyes piercing her clothes, trying to gauge what was underneath.

She looked away. 'We're just here to ask a few questions.'

'What's a nice bird like you doing in the filth?'

'Keeping an eye on you, at the moment,' she quickly countered.

'I don't mind your eyes on me, darlin'.' He turned to seal another box. 'Bedford, eh? And what comes before that?'

'Detective Sergeant.'

Brent laughed. 'What would you say if I asked you out for a drink?'

She gave him a cynical smile. 'Something vulgar, I should think.'

'Oh, darlin', you can be vulgar with me any day of the week.'

'Watch it,' she warned, before walking away.

Holly glanced to where Ashworth was still casually talking with a studious-looking man in the act of packing a lorry in the loading bay and wandered out into the corridor. Jerry Townsend followed her.

'What do you think of young Jason, then?'

'He makes my flesh crawl,' she said. 'I wouldn't trust him in any direction.'

'I wouldn't mind betting he'll be back inside before long, but having said that, I don't think he's got the brains to execute the type of caper you're looking into.'

'Maybe not.' She leant back against the wall, conscious of his dark eyes roaming over her.

'Now listen, Detective Sergeant Bedford . . .' He rested his palm on the wall a little way above her left shoulder and moved closer. 'I hope we meet in slightly better circumstances next time.'

'Not if I can help it,' she retorted, stepping out of his reach.

Unabashed, the security guard was about to continue his flirting when Ashworth came marching through the swing doors.

'Right, Mr Townsend,' he said, briskly, 'thank you for your help.'

Holly fell in beside Ashworth as he strode along the corridor. 'Well, guv, what about Colin Everitt?'

'He's a former accountant. Just served eight of a twelve-year sentence for embezzlement. He says he just wants to get on with the rest of his life, and he asked me very politely to leave him alone.'

'And are we going to?'

'I don't think so,' Ashworth said, holding open the outer door. Holly strode ahead of him, and their footsteps sounded on the tarmac as he went on, 'The man is very intelligent, obviously well educated . . . somehow I can't see him settling for the kind of lifestyle that comes with working in a factory.'

Holly's radio bleeped, and she stopped to delve for it in her shoulder bag.

‘DS Bedford,’ she said, pressing the button.

Police Constable Alan ‘Gordon’ Bennett’s voice crackled from it. ‘Holly, there’s more glass turned up in baby food purchased at the Save U Supermarket.’

She exchanged a glance with Ashworth.

‘Okay, give me the details, Gordon.’

CHAPTER 4

Richard Samuels was waiting immediately inside the automatic doors at the Save U Supermarket when Ashworth ushered Holly through the large crowd that had gathered in the car park.

'Get this lot shifted,' he growled.

'Uniformed are on their way, guv.'

The doors slid open before them, and Samuels rushed forward.

'Can you tell me what's happened?'

'From the reports we've had, it appears that some glass was found in a jar of Barker's baby food.'

'Barker's? Not Arnolds? Oh God, what the hell's happening?'

'Well, sir,' Ashworth said, his eyes scanning the empty supermarket, 'unless we've got a complete maniac running around with the sole intention of killing babies, I'd say this chain of supermarkets is the extortionist's target, rather than the food manufacturers.'

'This could put us out of business,' Samuels blustered, all colour seeping from his face.

'Have you received any demands for money?' Holly asked.

Samuels shook his head rapidly. 'No, no, we've heard nothing.'

'But you would let us know, if you did?' she persisted.

'Yes, of course we would,' the man snapped. 'Can't you do anything about this?'

'We're doing all we can, sir. Forensic are on their way to remove the baby food, and we'll study the security tapes again.'

'But it's not enough,' Samuels insisted. 'We're going out of business here. Just look at the crowd outside.'

'How come the news travelled so fast?' Ashworth asked, as he watched the gathering which uniformed officers were attempting to disperse.

'Oh, our rivals would see to that,' he said bitterly. 'If we go out of business, they'll pick up our percentage of market share.'

They were disturbed by a secretary poking her head around an office door to their left.

'Councillor Cowper's on the phone for you, Mr Samuels,' she said.

'That bloody woman — she's all I need today.' He stormed into the office, slamming the door behind him.

Ashworth peered around the darkened, deserted store, and said, 'I thank God I don't have to spend all my time thinking about market shares.'

'It does come across as callous, guv.'

'It's certainly a cut-throat business. I read somewhere, Holly, that if the current price wars continue, one of the chains is likely to go bust.'

Even as he spoke, warning bells were starting at the back of their minds, and they looked at each other, their eyebrows raised.

'Guv, you don't think it's likely that one of the other chains is doing this, do you?'

'No, definitely not,' he said with uncertainty in his voice. 'One thing's for sure though, there's not much we can do until somebody makes contact with a demand for money.'

* * *

Meg Cowper briskly agitated the brushes in a jar of turpentine until the clear liquid became a cloudy brown. She was humming a tune and checking her tee shirt and jeans for speckles of varnish when she was startled by a noise from behind. Turning quickly, she found a man standing by the open stable door, watching her.

'Yes? Can I help you?' she asked.

'I'm so sorry,' he said, striding forward. 'I didn't mean to startle you.' The man's voice was cultured, his smile friendly, and Meg relaxed a little.

'It's okay, you just made me jump,' she said, returning his smile. 'I wasn't expecting anyone.'

'Are you Meg Cowper?'

She nodded, quite flustered, for the man possessed a powerful sexual magnetism, and he looked so handsome in his check sports jacket and immaculate grey flannel trousers.

'My name is James Dallington, and I'm looking for some reproduction furniture,' he said, his hazel eyes holding hers.

'I haven't any pieces in stock at the moment, but I'll keep a look-out and if any do come in, I'll let you know.'

They chatted for quite a while about his requirements, and Meg found him charming, easy to talk to, and more attractive with the passing of each minute. She locked the workshop and walked with him through the courtyard.

'I wonder . . .' He hesitated. 'Well, I was wondering whether you'd care to have a drink with me some time.'

'I think I'd like that,' Meg said, smiling shyly.

'Splendid. How about this evening, then? We could continue our discussion about furniture.'

'Yes, all right.'

'Shall I pick you up at your home?'

Meg knew instinctively how Emma would react to her seeing this very good-looking stranger, and said immediately, 'No . . . no, don't do that. Why don't I meet you here, at eight p.m.?'

'I'll look forward to it.'

His car was a dark blue Ford Escort, last year's model, and she watched him until he had driven away. Climbing into her ten-year-old Volkswagen, Meg chided herself for accepting the invitation. Where men were concerned, she was far too eager, far too weak. She fell in love much too easily and once in that sorry, happy state, she would do anything to please the man, regardless of the cost to her self-esteem. Still, there was no harm in meeting Mr Dallington for a drink.

* * *

The chief inspector hardly had time to install himself behind his desk before the telephone buzzed.

'Ashworth,' he barked into the receiver. But then his demeanour changed and he listened intently. Dropping the receiver back into its cradle, he looked decidedly pensive.

'Well, they've made contact with Richard Samuels at the supermarket.'

Holly and Josh looked up attentively.

'A demand for forty thousand pounds has been made . . .'

'That's not much, guv,' Josh ventured. 'Not for the risks they're taking.'

'I agree, it's not much at all, and that's making me wonder whether money is the prime motive in all of this.'

'What's happening, then?' Holly asked.

'Samuels wants to come in and make a statement.'

* * *

He met Richard Samuels down in reception. The man looked tired, and he kept rubbing at his eyes with the back of his hand.

'Would you like to come up to the office,' Ashworth asked briskly.

'Yes, and I hope you don't mind not coming to the supermarket, only we really don't want another police presence there—'

'Bad for trade?' Ashworth interjected cynically.

'Chief Inspector, your tone of voice suggests that you don't think very much of the supermarket business, but there's a very good reason why it would be advisable to keep your officers away.'

They had reached the top of the third flight of stairs, and Ashworth strode along the corridor, saying, 'You can enlighten me in the office. It's just along here.'

Once there, he motioned for Samuels to take the chair in front of his desk while Josh turned off his computer and Holly made herself ready with note pad and pen.

'Right, Mr Samuels,' Ashworth said, 'what have you got to tell us?'

'The telephone call came this morning . . .' Samuels began. 'Shortly before nine a.m. It was a woman's voice, all muffled as if there was a handkerchief over the mouthpiece — you know the kind of thing. Anyway, she ordered me not to say anything, just listen. Then she detailed the number of baby food jars that had been tampered with, and told me she was a member of an organization that wanted forty thousand pounds in exchange for leaving us alone—'

'That's not a great deal of money,' Ashworth cut in. 'Not when you think of the prison sentence they'd face if they were caught.'

'I think I can explain that,' he said. 'She went on to say that after we'd paid up, they were going to target other chains.'

'I see. And how is the money to be handed over?'

'This gets a bit complicated, so I've written it all down.' He reached into his inside pocket for a piece of paper. 'We're to contact all local banks and building societies and instruct them that, as from tomorrow, they're authorized to pay out two thousand pounds to a card with the pin number 2364. Only one payment will be collected from any machine over the next two days.'

'And are you willing to pay that amount?' Ashworth asked.

Samuels gave a resigned sigh. 'Of course. Forty thousand pounds is a drop in the ocean to us.'

'But you're still willing to have us involved?' Holly queried.

'Certainly. But, bottom line, we're willing to pay just to get these people off our backs.'

Ashworth sank back in his chair and thought for a moment. 'Did she say anything else, Mr Samuels?'

'Quite a lot. She said that this phone call would be the only long one. If there was a need for others they'd be kept short to avoid them being traced. She also gave me a message for you . . .' He hesitated and wiped his perspiring palms on a handkerchief. 'She said that if the police become involved, her organization will take out Detective Sergeant Bedford.'

Ashworth frowned. 'That was the term used — take out?'

'Yes, and to underline what she meant, the woman said they were quite prepared to kill either members of the public or police officers in order to get the money.'

Ashworth digested this for a full minute before he spoke. 'All right, Mr Samuels, if you make arrangements with the banks and building societies, we'll endorse them.'

'Good.' Samuels got to his feet. 'I don't mind telling you, Chief Inspector, I shall be glad when this is all over.'

'So shall I,' Ashworth said, rising from his seat and extending a hand. 'Thank you for coming in, Mr Samuels. I'll show you out.'

'There's no need, I can find my own way.'

The door had hardly closed behind the man, when Ashworth said, 'There's two and two here that keep adding up to five.'

'I'm with you, guv,' Holly said. 'I mean, what's forty thousand pounds? If they pulled this scam with ten different supermarket chains, it'd still only add up to four hundred thousand, and that's nothing nowadays.'

'Which just reinforces my view that money is not the main motive,' he murmured, his fingers beating a tattoo on the desk top. 'Either that, or we're dealing with a couple of small-time villains.'

'Not an organization, then?' Josh asked.

Ashworth shook his head. 'It seems unlikely. Even so, Holly, I want you to take this threat they've made against you seriously.'

'Don't worry, guv, I can take care of myself.'

'Maybe you can, but martial arts training is only useful up to a point. Until we know what we're up against, I want you to be very vigilant.'

She nodded. 'But how are we going to watch all of those cash machines?'

'We're not,' he said, wandering across to the glass wall and looking out over the town. 'I'd imagine that's the idea behind the elaborate instructions — they know we haven't got the resources to deal with that.'

'But they're still taking a big chance, guv,' Josh said. 'If we only stake out two—'

'Yes, Josh, but I don't think they'll try to collect the money. They'll just use it to put pressure on the supermarket directors, probably by saying that they didn't get it because they knew we were watching. Then I wouldn't be surprised if they tamper with some other product to pile on more pressure.'

'And by that time the directors should be willing to settle without telling us,' Holly concluded.

'That's it, but we'd better set up a couple of look-out points, just to be on the safe side. Now, this is going to be a twenty-four hour job, so we'll need to recruit someone in. Josh and I can take one location, and Holly and the unknown officer, the other one.' He moved quickly towards the door. 'I'd better go and fill Newton in on this, and then we'll scout around and see whose front bedroom we can commandeer for a couple of days.'

When they were alone, Holly turned to Josh and pulled a face. 'I'm going to end up with Bobby Adams for two days, I just know I am.'

'What's wrong with that?' he asked, switching the computer back on. 'He did some good work on the last case.'

'He's hardly exciting, though, is he?'

'Holly, you'll be there to observe, not to satisfy your sex urge.'

'Yes, but if I'm going to be shacked up with a man for two days, I'd at least like the excitement of knowing he might make a pass at me.'

Josh, shaking his head despairingly, turned his attention to the computer screen.

* * *

Holly's guess proved to be correct; she would be sharing her stint of observation with Bobby Adams. The cash machine allocated to them was in the high street, directly opposite the Bull and Butcher public house, and they would be watching from one of the upstairs bedrooms. She was still unhappy at the prospect of spending forty-eight hours with the naive young policeman, and more than a little miffed by the fact that Josh and her guv'nor would be holed up in a private house where, no doubt, they would be constantly mothered by a fussy woman only too delighted to cater for their every need on the refreshments front.

The machines were programmed to make the cash available from midnight onwards, so they would all have to be in position by 11 p.m.

CHAPTER 5

Meg cut into the remaining piece of steak on her plate and gazed across the candle-lit table at her escort, James Dallington. The restaurant, in a first-class hotel on the edge of Morton, was almost empty and the few diners that were there paid scant attention to the attractive couple occupying a corner table. She placed her cutlery on the plate and reached for her wineglass as Dallington shot her a warm smile.

'Thank you for making the phone call for me,' he said.

She raised her glass in a silent toast and sipped the exquisite burgundy.

'James, I know so little about you . . .'

'You know I'm a company director, here in Morton,' he said, dabbing a napkin to his mouth, and picking up his drink. 'You know that my business often takes me to Bridgetown . . .' He grinned. 'Where I was fortunate enough to meet you.'

'But—'

'Have you changed your mind, Meg?' He paused, then lowered his voice. 'Don't you want to go to bed with me?'

She stared down at the table, and said, quietly, 'I haven't changed my mind, James, no.'

'Would you like a brandy here, or upstairs in my room?'

‘In your room, I think.’ A vivid flush warmed her cheeks, for she feared that her voice had betrayed her eagerness.

Dallington clicked his fingers, and a waiter was immediately at his side with the bill for him to sign.

* * *

It was 10 p.m. when the telephone rang in Holly’s bedroom, and she emerged from the bathroom in bra and pants, cursing vociferously. Scrambling across the bed, she picked up the receiver.

‘Hello?’

‘Hello . . . it’s Bobby Adams . . .’

‘What do you want, Bobby?’ she asked, her eyes rolling with irritation.

‘I’m just ringing to say I’m in place.’

‘Okay,’ she said, keeping her voice even. ‘I’m just getting ready. I’ll be there within an hour.’

‘Right. I’m . . . I’m looking forward to working with you again.’

‘Likewise, Bobby,’ she said without enthusiasm. ‘Likewise.’

‘See you later, then.’ The line went dead.

‘That boy’s a toss-pot,’ she muttered, replacing the receiver. ‘I can just imagine Josh and the guv’nor having a good laugh about this. In fact, everybody at the bloody nick’ll be taking the piss.’

She was scratching her right breast through the flimsy material of her bra, and studying her reflection in the wardrobe mirror, when she giggled, having remembered Josh’s code-name for the job: it was, Operation Bobby Adams Loses His Virginity.

She struggled into a pair of tight blue jeans, pulled on a thick white sweater, then picked up her weekend case and went downstairs. After making sure all the windows were locked, she let herself out of the front door.

There was a definite chill in the air, and a fresh easterly wind stung her cheeks and ruffled her hair. For some reason she felt a slight sense of unease — spider's legs marching along her spine — and stopping by her red Micra parked in the driveway, she glanced along the seemingly empty road. Shadows danced and a discarded drinks can propelled by the wind was rattling along the pavement, but she could see nothing to cause her disquiet. Even so, that sensation came again, and all at once she was certain that something wasn't quite right. With eyes narrowed, she surveyed the road again, but could find nothing out of place.

'You're getting paranoid, girl,' she laughed, throwing the case on to the passenger seat and climbing in.

When the tail lights of Holly's Micra disappeared into the distance, a man emerged from his crouching position behind a parked car. Quickly skirting round to the driver's side he scrambled in, started the engine and set off in pursuit.

* * *

Meg's head was spinning pleasantly by the time she had finished her second brandy. The alcohol was heightening her senses, chasing away her inhibitions, and when Dallington gently took the glass from her hand, she was ready to start their lovemaking.

'Would you like another?' he asked.

'No, thank you,' she said, reaching for her handbag. 'I'd like to use the bathroom.'

He walked her across the room and held open the door.

'Are you going to stay the night?'

She turned to him. 'Yes, please.'

'I want you to do something else for me tomorrow.'

'I'd do anything for you,' she whispered. 'Anything, James.'

'Good.'

* * *

Holly flounced into the darkened room, carrying a double gin and tonic. Bobby was sitting by the window with a pair of binoculars and a camera fitted with a zoom lens beside him on a small table. He looked round when Holly entered.

'Nothing so far.'

'Well, there wouldn't be, would there?' she hissed, throwing her weekend case on to the nearest single bed. 'The machine isn't programmed to pay out until midnight.'

Bobby shrugged and turned back to the window while Holly took a sip of gin and kicked off her high-heeled shoes.

'This is a really shit job — do you know that?'

'I'll take the first watch,' Bobby offered, 'if you want to get some sleep.'

Holly wandered across to him and peered through the net curtain. The cash machine was directly opposite, bathed in the strange orange glow from a nearby street light.

'A really shit job,' she muttered.

'It might help if you didn't drink while you're doing it.'

'Piss off, boy,' she retorted, draining the glass.

Bobby was taken aback. 'Why don't you get some sleep?' he said, remaining polite. 'You might wake up in a better mood.'

'Just leave it, Bobby, I don't need this.'

'And I don't either,' he threw back. 'All I want is for us to do a good job.'

'Yeah, yeah.'

There followed a period of strained silence, punctuated by Holly's frequent tutting sounds, and eventually, Bobby said, 'We'd better get something straight — I know what everybody at the nick thinks about me. And I also know that you don't want to work with me.'

'Oh God, look . . .'

'No, just listen for once. It might interest you to know that I'm not looking forward to spending two days and nights with you either.'

'Oh, come on, Bobby, don't—'

'If you don't like me, ask to have me taken off the case.'

'Don't be so bloody silly, boy. I'm just pissed off,' she said, attempting to cajole.

'But in the meantime,' he continued frostily, 'unless you're anywhere near decent to me, I'll be giving back as good as I get. All right?'

Holly could only gaze at him, her mouth gaping open in surprise.

'Am I making myself plain . . . girl?'

* * *

Josh was finding it difficult to focus his attention on the job because of Ashworth's loud snoring in the background. They were installed in the front bedroom of a quaint thatched cottage and from the window he was watching the cash machine outside a rural branch of the Trustees Savings Bank.

He shifted around in the rattan armchair, which looked more comfortable than it actually was, and strove to quell his irritation at the continuous snorts coming from the bed. His thoughts moved to the owner of the cottage, a pleasant woman in her early fifties, who had fussed over them constantly from the moment they arrived. She was obviously very taken with the chief inspector and Josh, grinning despite himself, wondered what she would think of him now, stretched out on the small bed fully clothed with that hideous sound emerging from his throat.

'Shut up, guv,' he muttered under his breath.

* * *

Holly opened her eyes and waited for recall to acquaint her with the unfamiliar surroundings. Street lighting threw a soft glow into the room, faintly illuminating Bobby, lost in concentration at the window. Having managed but a few hours sleep she was not fully refreshed and there was a vile taste in her mouth. She badly needed a coffee.

Throwing off the quilt, Holly climbed out of bed and stood for a moment, pulling into shape her crumpled sweater, then wandered over to the gas ring — so graciously supplied by the landlord, together with a tiny camping kettle.

'Anything happened?' she asked.

'No,' Bobby said, still decidedly distant. 'I'd have called you if it had.'

She filled two mugs and ambled over to him. 'Peace offering,' she said, passing his across.

He took it from her, smiling hesitantly.

'I'm sorry, Bobby.'

'Forget it.'

'I was in a lousy mood, that's all, but I shouldn't have taken it out on you.'

'Be honest, Holly, you think I'm a plonker just like everybody else at the nick.'

'My guv'nor doesn't, or he wouldn't have you in CID.'

'No, he doesn't, and Sergeant Dutton doesn't either, but to the rest of them I'm a plonker of the first order.' His tone was matter-of-fact, without a trace of self-pity, and he seemed quite relaxed as he sat back to sip his coffee.

Knowing that he had accurately described the general consensus among the uniformed officers, Holly stayed silent and made herself comfortable on the floor beside his chair.

'I don't care, you know. I mean, I look at the others — only half doing the job, trying to make me feel ridiculous for actually caring about people — and I know I don't want to be like them, so it doesn't bother me.'

It was clear that Holly was not required to answer, so she said nothing and waited for him to go on.

'I used to blush and stammer a lot . . .' He grinned then. 'It's very difficult to pretend you don't care, when you're going red all over the place . . .'

Holly was conscious of her mouth gaping again, and she made a conscious effort to keep it closed. 'Yes, I suppose it is,' she said.

'So I took a postal course: How to overcome blushing and shyness.'

She choked on her coffee when he said that, and after a spasm of coughing, she asked, 'Did it work?'

'Yes, I think so.'

'That's good. Right then, do you want to get some sleep?'

'No,' he said, standing up and stretching his legs. 'I wouldn't mind a ciggy, though.'

Holly eased into his chair when Bobby moved away from the window so that the glow from his cigarette wouldn't be spotted from the road, and she was peering at the cash machine across the deserted street while the smoke circulated around the room. As she was an occasional smoker, the smell brought with it a nagging oral craving which did little to help her mood.

Glancing at her watch, she saw that it was 3 a.m. and bored and still tired, she tapped a foot on the carpet and stifled a yawn. The tip of the cigarette showed up red in the semi-darkness when Bobby took his last drag, and as he was stubbing it out he held up the packet. 'Do you want one?'

'Please,' she replied, getting up so they could change places.

Holly sat on the floor, resting her back against the far wall, and lit the cigarette. The first few inhalations brought a spinning to her head and a feeling of lightness to her limbs; the sensations were far from pleasant, but she persevered.

'So, what have we got on the case?' Bobby asked.

'Suspects, you mean?'

He nodded.

'Not many, really. There's a Vincent Blakewell; he's a con-artist, but I don't think he's in this league. Most of his convictions have been for relieving older women of their savings . . .'

'Anybody else?'

'Yes,' she replied doubtfully. 'A couple of guys with previous, working at Arnolds. Jason Brent, who's not bright enough to open a jar, let alone put anything in it; and Colin Everitt, an ex-accountant who's done time for embezzlement. But neither are goers, in my opinion.'

'Hold on, what have we got here?' Bobby said, reaching for the binoculars and training them on the street.

Holly scrambled from the floor and joined him at the window. 'What is it?'

'Somebody was watching the pub. He looked straight up at this window. He's ducked into a doorway two up from the bank.'

Her eyes went immediately to the shop front.

'There he goes,' Bobby said excitedly. 'I can't see what he's like, though; he's wearing a cap and his coat collar's turned up. But he was definitely looking up at this window, Holly.'

CHAPTER 6

The next morning, Meg was a picture of happiness and contentment when she visited the Save U Supermarket, with a rosy glow to her freckled cheeks and a tranquil smile on her lips. Even the usually tedious task of steering a wayward trolley around a crowded store, selecting mundane necessities, failed to dampen her soaring spirits. She was in love with a wonderful man, and he seemed to feel the same way about her. That delicious thought was never far from her mind as she made her way to the checkout.

Her path was momentarily blocked by a pimply youth, employed as a shelf stacker, pushing along a trolley precariously piled high with mixer drinks. His expression was sullen due to the fact that trade, having recently fallen because of the baby food scare, was now brisk. Those days of inactivity had been welcomed by him, if not the supermarket directors, especially as his pay packet had not suffered. He brought the trolley to a halt by the mixer drinks display and his expression turned to one of scorn.

'I thought the old tosser said all the dry ginger was gone,' he grumbled, pushing the two remaining bottles to the back of the display.

Disregarding the customers milling around the drinks section, he continued to mumble and started to stack the shelf.

* * *

Ashworth's mood was light years away from contented happiness. The previous night, he had missed out on his habitual bedtime tipple of malt whisky, causing his sleep to be patchy, and he was now staring out at the cash machine with feelings akin to loathing. Furthermore, the woman of the house had earlier prepared a full English breakfast for them, which Ashworth had consumed with a great deal of zest, but which was now producing a huge amount of discomfort and bubbling wind.

Josh had kept watch throughout the night, and was now preparing for bed, unaware of his guv'nor's embarrassment as he stripped down to his boxer shorts. Before too long, he was snoring lightly, causing Ashworth's scowl to deepen.

'I can't stand people who snore,' he muttered to himself. 'It's all to do with incorrect breathing.'

But his attention was then gripped as an elderly lady dismounted from her bicycle and pushed it on to the pavement next to the cash dispenser. Over thirty years in the police force had taught Ashworth that things were not always as they seemed and therefore he picked up the binoculars and brought the woman into sharp focus. Her movements were ponderous as she retrieved a handbag from the wicker basket attached to the handle-bars and leant against the wall, rummaging amongst its contents. Finally, she took out a cash card and inserted it into the machine. He had hoped to catch her pin number but at the last moment she moved to block his view. He did, however, see her hand reach forward for the money.

'Ten pounds,' he whispered dejectedly. 'She's withdrawn ten pounds.'

Just then Josh let out a prolonged snore.

'Shut up, Josh,' Ashworth called over his shoulder.

* * *

Trade at the Save U Supermarket was at last back to normal. Richard Samuels, the only director to live locally, had personally taken over the day-to-day running of the Bridgetown store, having despatched the manager to another branch.

The shoppers, tempted back by various special offers — ten pence off a bag of sugar, six pence off a loaf of bread, and many more — were reassured by the conspicuous presence of six security guards, and the director's permanent patrol of the aisles.

* * *

By the end of the day takings were way above average and Samuels was moving around the empty shop floor, checking to see which shelves needed restocking. The dry ginger ale had sold well, with only half a dozen bottles left on the display.

* * *

By the second night, Holly was nurturing a hot hatred for the cash machine. Neither she nor Bobby had slept much during the day, and the only food on offer was fish and chips, which they ate straight from the paper. They therefore had to rely on endless cups of coffee and both smoked more cigarettes than was good for them.

Due to the fact that the bank was on the town's main street, the cash machine was busy for the bulk of the day, leaving them little time for conversation. By 9 p.m. the street was much quieter, but the long hours of concentration were taking their toll. Holly, nursing a tight caffeine-induced headache, stretched and yawned in the chair.

'Do you want some kip?' Bobby ventured.

'No, it's okay,' she said, running her fingers through her hair. 'I wouldn't mind a shower, though.'

'Right, I'll just use the loo.' At the door he turned back, and blurted, 'I'm not a virgin, you know.'

'What's brought this on?' she asked, laughing with surprise.

'I know what the others at the station say about me, but I lost my virginity five years ago.' And with that, he went through to the bathroom.

'I don't believe that boy,' she murmured, shaking her head.

Holly was still looking towards the door when the telephone rang and made her start. She glanced at the cash machine and then at the telephone on the bedside table, realizing that if she answered it the bank would be out of her sight for several minutes. Luckily, Bobby must have had the same thought, for he hurried from the lavatory still adjusting his flies.

'Take the window,' she ordered, moving towards the bed and grabbing the receiver. 'Yes?'

There were sounds of disco music, loud voices, the thud of darts hitting a board, and above them the pub's landlord said, 'Sorry to disturb you, but I thought I'd better let you know that someone's been in asking if Holly Bedford's here?'

She frowned. 'Just Holly Bedford? Not Detective Sergeant?'

'No, just that.'

'Did you get a description?'

'Not really. My barmaid said the man was wearing a cap pulled right down over his face, and he had his coat collar turned up, so she couldn't see much.'

An image flashed into her mind of the man Bobby had seen lurking in the shop doorway. Puzzled, she said, 'Thanks for letting me know,' and then hung up.

'Everything all right?' Bobby called from across the darkened room.

'I'm not sure.'

She told him what the landlord had said, and he straight away mentioned the man in the street.

'Does anybody know you're here?'

'Outside CID, no one; not even uniformed know our exact location. No one could know I'm here.'

'Unless he followed you. He could have waited for you to come out, then when you didn't he could have gone in to ask . . .'

Bobby had put her exact thoughts into words. Could the so-called organization have meant their threat?

'Oh well, time will tell,' she said brightly. 'I'll take my shower.'

'Hold on,' Bobby said, in a panic. 'I gave my underwear a wash in the bathroom. I'd better get it out.'

'It's okay, Bobby, I have seen men's knickers before, you know. I'm not a virgin, either.'

Holly was expecting to find some sturdy Y-fronts but hanging over the side of the bath was a pair of jockey trunks made of soft jersey, the sort that manage to hug and cling in all the important places. She undressed, her eyes on the pants, already seeing Bobby in a new light; but one thought clouded her mind . . . the threat to take her out should the police become involved in the case.

* * *

Horace Moore was determined that his secret would never be made public. In Bridgetown he was regarded as a respectable if somewhat ageing solicitor . . . a pillar of the community; and although his mental faculties had deteriorated sharply since the tragic death of his wife, Maisy, less than four months ago, he was still very much in demand at the practice.

After Maisy's death a dreadful loneliness had descended upon him, bringing with it a marked stoop to his shoulders, a grey sheen to the little hair he had left, and a now almost total reliance on the whisky bottle. Most mornings it was eleven thirty before his head was sufficiently cleared for his brain to function properly, yet he was sure no one at the practice had noticed.

Horace was at home, sitting in the comfortable armchair in his study where he now spent most of his free time. As always, he had started the evening determined to cut back on his steadily rising alcohol intake, but with each drink his resolve weakened, as the melancholy brought on by his wife's death deepened, until the best part of a bottle had gone. He held up the last drop to the light, judging that there was enough for one more drink. Moving clumsily to pour it into the glass, his elbow overturned the ginger ale bottle standing on a small table beside his chair. Cursing, he put down the whisky glass and somehow got to his feet, swaying wildly then lurching across the room to the Save U Supermarket carrier bag containing two bottles of dry ginger ale which he had bought in his lunch hour.

Weaving a path back to his desk, Horace fell into the chair and, catching his breath, he took out one of the bottles and tried to break the seal, but it seemed stronger than usual and the cap failed to budge. Gripping the bottle between his knees, he tried again but only succeeded in dropping it, and it landed on the carpet with a thump. Suddenly the effort involved in retrieving the bottle seemed too great and allowing his head to slump forward, Horace fell into a deep, drunken sleep.

* * *

Bobby was obviously opposed to sleeping fully clothed for he stripped off, carefully arranging the garments on the back of a chair, before getting into bed, and therefore Holly was treated to another glimpse of his raunchy underwear. She smiled mischievously, for he did fill them rather well.

Attempting to get her mind back on the job, she focused her eyes and thoughts on the cash machine. In no time at all Bobby was enjoying the sleep of the innocent, and Holly was yawning widely when her radio bleeped.

'DS Bedford,' she whispered into it.

'Hi, Holly.' It was Josh's voice which rose above the crackling static. 'Anything happening?'

'Sod all.' A sound similar to heavy snoring seeped from the radio, and she said, 'What the hell's that noise?'

'It's the guv'nor,' Josh said, with a weary sigh.

'Jesus Christ, you'll get a noise abatement order served on you if he keeps that up.'

'You don't have to tell me. And he had the cheek to wake me up this morning to tell me I was snoring.'

Holly chuckled. 'Why don't you do the same to him?'

'I don't think I fancy that, somehow, not with the mood he's been in all day. Anyway, I thought I'd let you know that I've been on to the nick and they say none of the money's been collected from any of the banks or building societies.'

'Nor will it be, as our dear guv'nor would say. I reckon we're being messed about, Josh.'

'And we've lost our only real suspect, as well. Vincent Blakewell has moved to Kettering in Northamptonshire. It's all open and above board — he's signed on there. We must have frightened him away.'

'Oh, great.'

'Has anything else happened?' Josh asked cryptically.

'What do you mean?'

'You know . . . with you and Bobby. The betting at the nick is, evens you've raped him and you're holding him hostage, or two to one on that he's broken his neck trying to escape from the first-floor window . . .'

'Abraham,' she whispered loudly. 'Bollocks and double bollocks.'

'Tut, tut, Holly, you are a crude girl.'

'I know I am. Now, go on, piss off and catch up with your knitting.'

'Miaow.'

The smile on her face showed a huge amount of affection as she placed the radio on the table.

‘Oh, come on, somebody do something,’ she muttered, staring out of the window. ‘Whatever’s happened to all those dirty old men who’re supposed to expose themselves outside pubs?’

But nobody did do anything and the hours dragged slowly on. All four members of Bridgetown CID were hugely thankful when the observation period came to an end, and while Holly took Josh and Bobby for a celebratory drink, Ashworth headed for the one place on earth which contained everything he needed . . . home.

CHAPTER 7

It was 8 p.m. by the time Holly parked her Micra in her tiny drive. She quickly let herself into the house and went from room to room, checking that everything was all right. She was looking forward to a few drinks and a steaming hot bath — a few hours of steaming hot sex would have been nice too but she couldn't have everything.

In the lounge, she poured a large gin and tonic and took it upstairs to run the bath. Steam was already starting to escape on to the landing when, with drink in hand, she went into the bedroom to undress.

Glimpses of her silhouette could be seen by the man in the car parked opposite her house. He strained his neck to watch the shadow remove its top and take a sip from its drink. Then the outline vanished and what followed was left to his imagination, which ran riot as he continued to watch the lighted window.

'Yes, Holly,' he murmured, 'all I need to do is work out your pattern, and then the rest will be so easy.'

* * *

When Horace Moore emerged from his whisky-sodden sleep that morning, he made a vow not to start drinking until at least nine thirty p.m. and he was determined to stay resolute.

Arriving home from work, he took a beef-dinner-for-one from the freezer and popped it into the oven. The hour it took to warm through was a testing time, and he found himself thinking about the whisky bottle again and again, but forced himself to wait. Finally, he was settled at the kitchen table, the meal before him, and as he forked the uninspiring slithers of beef into his mouth, he looked towards the Dutch dresser where a framed photograph of Maisy took centre place. She seemed to be smiling back at him. Hers was a warm sweet smile, always on her lips, meant for him alone.

With that familiar pain starting deep within his chest, Horace put down his cutlery and set about emptying his plate into the pedal bin. Then he did something he had not done for a long time: he walked around the ground floor of the house, his step sometimes purposeful, sometimes hesitant, for traces of Maisy were in all of the rooms, her laughter all around him. Brief flashes of the past crowded into his mind and he reached out a hand in a vain attempt to capture the love that for over forty years had been the stabilizing force in his life.

But of course his hand came back empty, and Horace stared down at it for many minutes before heading for the stairs and his study . . . and the whisky bottle.

* * *

Holly lay in the bath until the water began to cool on her skin, her pleasure somewhat spoiled by a feeling of tension. She climbed out and roughly dried herself then, pulling on her dressing gown, she wandered into the bedroom. Crossing immediately to the window, she pulled back an edge of the curtain and peered out. The road seemed deserted, and she could identify all of the cars parked in the various drives and at the kerb.

So, why this distinct feeling of being watched? Holly would be the first to admit that she was a down-to-earth, gritty type, not given to fanciful thoughts, and yet she felt certain that someone was out there. Perhaps the threat had set her imagination into overdrive. She shrugged and allowed the curtain to fall back into place.

* * *

Horace's step was heavy as he walked into the study. The bottle of dry ginger which had slipped from his fingers the previous night was still on the floor. He picked it up and placed it on the table, then reached for the Scotch bottle and poured a small amount. The seal on the dry ginger was easy enough to break now that he was sober, and the mixer fizzed and sparkled as it mingled with the whisky in the glass. Positioning the drink in front of him, Horace glanced at his watch. It was 9.25 p.m. Five minutes to go. For all of those five minutes, he kept his eyes on the second hand creeping around the watch face, and when it touched the twelve for the fifth time the minute hand shuddered to the six and Horace reached for the glass, downing the drink in one swallow and swiftly pouring another.

Almost immediately a warm glow began to engulf him, and it was some time before the first searing pain shot through his stomach. It was quickly followed by a second, this one much worse, and his cry was one of discomfort and surprise. The glass fell from his grasp as he stumbled to his feet, but the worsening pain was sapping his strength, making his legs flaccid and unable to support his weight. He pitched forward as a sharp pang raked his body, and he could do nothing but lie face down, fighting for breath.

Fearing a heart attack and suddenly frightened, Horace focused his eyes on the telephone standing on his desk. So often over the past few months he had prayed for death, had begged God for the blessed relief that he would surely find in an afterlife which included his beloved Maisy. But now, with the granting of his wish seemingly imminent, there surfaced within him a strong will to survive. Suddenly, Horace Moore was no longer a broken, tired old man longing to die, but someone who desperately wanted to cling to the spark of life. He managed to crawl towards the desk, even though convulsions repeatedly ravaged the soft muscles of his frail body and his stomach felt on fire with the increasingly violent pains.

The desk was nearer now and he lay for a moment trying to breathe, but with little success for each deep inhalation seemed to provoke the spasms in his middle. Unwilling to give up, Horace dug the toes of his slippers into the carpet and attempted to pull himself along, his arms stretched out in front of him, arthritic fingers gripping the pile. He managed three pulls before his arms collapsed beneath him and his forehead hit the floor with a dull thud. Dry sobs sent shudders through his body as he lay there.

Trying to ignore the pain, he looked up. The desk was just above him, the telephone almost within his reach. Horace was now shaking uncontrollably, sweat pouring down his face, and the desk seemed to oscillate before his eyes but, harnessing the last of his failing strength, he pushed himself up to a kneeling position and swept the telephone to the floor. It landed with a resounding ting at the very moment that a darkness descended. Layer upon layer of black swept over him, but he nevertheless reached out for the telephone receiver and his fingers curled around it as the darkness became impenetrable.

* * *

The telephone rang in Ashworth's hall and Peanuts was straight away on her feet and barking furiously at the lounge door. Sarah was about to get up when Ashworth put out a hand to stop her.

'I'll get it,' he said.

Picking up his glass of whisky and soda he made his way to the door, still with one eye on Kenneth Branagh's *Henry V* flickering from the television screen.

'Don't worry, I'm videoing it,' Sarah said, above the dog's frenzied yapping.

Angered by the disturbance, Ashworth yanked up the receiver and growled, 'Hello.'

'Hello, Jim, I haven't called at an inopportune moment, have I?' It was Alex Ferguson, the pathologist.

'No, it's all right, Alex,' he said, setting his glass on the table delivered by Meg Cowper the previous day. 'I was only watching the television.'

'Only we've had a couple of cases of poisoning admitted to hospital, and I thought you'd want to know right away.'

Ashworth was suddenly alert. 'Is this to do with the Save U Supermarket case?'

'I'm afraid so. The substance was in bottles of dry ginger ale, all bought from there.'

'How bad are the people concerned?'

'Well, the solicitor, Horace Moore, was in fairly bad shape, but he managed to get to the phone and dial 999. The other case is a young chap from one of the estates — he's suffered nothing more than acute discomfort.'

'But Horace is going to be all right . . . ?'

'I should think so, Jim. I've taken both bottles of ginger away for analysis. I'll have the results by morning.'

'Any idea what the poison might be?' Ashworth ventured hopefully.

'Off the top of my head, from the symptoms showing in the patients, I'd say it was oxalic acid. It's a bleach, and about fifteen grammes can be a lethal dose.'

'I see. Well, thanks for telling me, Alex. You'll get back to me as soon as you have further news?'

'Of course, Jim.'

They said their goodbyes and then Ashworth stood staring down at the fine wood-grain in the new table.

'Everything all right, Jim?' Sarah called from the lounge.

Picking up his glass, he wandered over to the doorway, and said, 'No, Sarah, two men have been poisoned by ginger ale that came from the supermarket.'

'Oh no, dear. Are they still alive?'

'Yes, they are, but if we don't get a break soon, whoever's doing this is certain to kill somebody.'

* * *

The atmosphere was frantic at Bridgetown Police Station the following morning. It seemed that everyone was calling for Ashworth, and he had hardly set foot in the building when a summons came from Superintendent Newton's office. For once Newton opened the door in answer to Ashworth's knock and ushered the chief inspector into the room. Emma Cowper was occupying the chair facing his desk and at the sight of her, Ashworth visibly bristled.

'There's no need to look like that,' Newton said, his tone reassuring. 'The councillor is aware of the problems we're facing.'

'Good.'

Ashworth nodded to the woman, and he was pulling up a chair when she said, 'I'm just finding out what the situation is with regard to the supermarket paying the money in order to get these monsters off their backs.'

'I have explained,' Newton said, 'that we would be powerless to stop the directors paying the money if they so wished.'

'But with members of the public suffering from the effects of poisoning, there would still be a case for us to pursue,' Ashworth countered doggedly.

The superintendent gave a diplomatic cough. 'Yes . . . quite. But we couldn't insist on the banknotes being marked, and we couldn't interfere with the money being handed over.'

'I believe,' Emma said, favouring Ashworth with a look of concern, 'that one of your team — DS Bedford — has been threatened if the police involvement continues.'

'That she has,' Ashworth admitted, 'but I don't see that as a reason to drop the investigation.'

There was a knock on the door.

'Come in,' Newton barked.

The door opened and Bobby Adams shuffled in. 'Excuse me, sir,' he said to the superintendent, 'but Doctor Ferguson has delivered the results of his tests on the bottles of dry ginger, and I thought the Chief Inspector should have them right away.'

'Good man,' Ashworth said, taking the report.

After Bobby's hasty exit, all expectant eyes were on the chief inspector.

'Oxalic acid,' he finally said. 'It's a bleach which can be obtained from pharmacists, either as a powder or in crystal form. The tests revealed seven grammes in each bottle.' He looked towards Newton. 'That's half a fatal dose.'

Turning his attention back to the report, he went on, 'Horace Moore reacted badly due to the fact that he's an elderly man and in poor general health, so the acid could easily have killed him by bringing on a heart attack. The other victim, a young chap, suffered a mild form of poisoning. Both are now recovering in hospital.'

'Thank goodness for that,' Emma intoned.

'So, whoever's doing this is extremely dangerous,' Ashworth said. 'Quite prepared to kill to get the desired end result.'

The door was rapped again, and Martin Dutton popped his head into the office.

'Excuse me, Superintendent, but Mr Samuels is here, demanding to see you.'

'Show him in, Sergeant.'

Dutton stood aside, and Richard Samuels marched in. 'Good morning,' he said stiffly. 'I've received another call from the woman representing the organization. She informed me that they didn't attempt to collect any money because of the obvious police presence. The doctored ginger ale was planted in retaliation—'

'Did she make any further demands for money?' Ashworth interjected.

'If you'll allow me to finish, Chief Inspector . . . She also told me that a fatal dose had been put into a product which now stands on a shelf in one of our Midlands supermarkets. She obviously wouldn't say which one.'

Ashworth and Newton exchanged a glance.

'So, I've taken it upon myself to close every branch in the Midlands,' Samuels continued. 'Now, there's to be a directors' meeting this afternoon, and we'll decide then what to do next.'

'What are your choices?' Ashworth asked.

'Has Emma told you that we want to pay the money?'

Ashworth nodded. 'Much as I appreciate your dilemma, Mr Samuels, I think that will only move the problem elsewhere. These people have threatened to target other chains, I seem to remember . . .'

'I know that, but—'

'And if you part with the money, they may well come back to you again, because you'll be regarded as a soft target.'

'I've thought all of that through,' Samuels replied, 'and the last thing I want is for them to get away with it.'

Ashworth's raised eyebrows asked a question.

'What I'm trying to do is persuade the board to hire some private security guards. They wouldn't be known to this organization, whereas the police are.'

'And who might these people be?'

'I don't think you have a right to ask that,' Emma cut in.

Ashworth fixed her with a steady gaze and was about to respond, when Samuels said, 'It's all right, Emma, I don't mind volunteering the information. They'd be headed by Jerry Townsend, the chap in charge of security at Arnolds's factory.'

'I see,' Ashworth said. 'And they would be working with us?'

'No, not exactly,' Samuels said, averting his eyes. 'They'd be working for us, trying to uncover the names of the people behind this. But any information would be passed on to you.'

'That's very decent of them,' Ashworth said with much sarcasm.

'Good, well, that sounds fine,' Newton said. 'Don't you think, Chief Inspector?'

As three pairs of eyes settled upon him, Ashworth reluctantly nodded his agreement.

'There is one thing you can do for me,' Samuels said.

'And what might that be?' Ashworth asked.

'Could one of your officers call at the supermarket around eight p.m. tonight? The board should have come to some decision by then.'

'That can be arranged,' Newton said, smiling broadly.

When the councillor rose to leave, Samuels accompanied her from the room and, as soon as they were alone, Newton turned his attention to the chief inspector.

'Now, I know that you don't like anyone interfering with police business—'

'That I don't, sir. Law enforcement is our job and it shouldn't be handed over to a bunch of cowboys.'

Newton held up his hand for silence. 'But in this instance, we don't have any choice. Tell me, Chief Inspector, have you any idea who could be behind this?'

Ashworth gave a dismal shake of the head. 'None at all, sir. There are only two men in the frame — Jason Brent and Colin Everitt. They both work at Arnolds, but they're so unlikely . . . this thing's just too big for them.'

'I'll let you get back to your office, then, Chief Inspector. There's nothing else we can do for the moment.'

CHAPTER 8

As soon as Ashworth stomped into the office, Holly and Josh could see from his body language that all was not well. Bobby, however, as a recent recruit to CID, was blissfully unaware. The chief inspector, standing in the middle of the room, related the events that had taken place and by the time he had finished, he was positively glowering.

'So we're off the case, then,' Josh said.

'That's about it. Samuels wants one of us to call at the supermarket tonight to find out the result of the board meeting.'

Holly immediately held up her hand and when doubt jostled with the scowl on Ashworth's face, she said, 'Yes, guv, I know a threat's been made against me, but I am a police officer and I'd rather not be regarded as a liability just because you're in a bad mood.'

His glower became a smile, indicating just how much he had mellowed towards his detective sergeant over the past two years.

'Fair enough. Eight p.m., then.'

Settling himself at his desk, he said, 'And now I'd better check with Alex Ferguson about oxalic acid. If we can find out what it's used for, that information could supply us with a lead.'

‘Oxalic acid, sir?’ Bobby said, reddening slightly when all attention was focused on him. He was sitting at a corner of Holly’s desk, not having been allocated one of his own and, in a tone now full of confidence, he said, ‘It’s a bleach used in restoration of wood, metal, that sort of thing . . .’

Still no one spoke, and his self-assurance slipped a little. ‘I took a postal course in Forensic Sciences,’ he explained haltingly.

‘Good,’ Ashworth said. ‘When you say restoration of wood, what do you mean, exactly?’

‘It removes stains, sir.’

‘So it would be used in restoring furniture?’

‘Yes, sir.’

Ashworth wrote the name, Meg Cowper, on his blotter, and said, ‘Can you tell us anything else, Bobby?’

Although uncomfortable at being centre stage, he nevertheless pressed on. ‘You can buy it from chemists, sir, and you can make it yourself by boiling rhubarb leaves. In fact, there have been quite a few accidental deaths caused by people cooking the leaves and eating them as a vegetable.’

‘I know someone who restores furniture,’ Ashworth mused. Then, aware of their expectant glances, he added hastily, ‘Now, don’t get yourselves excited, this lady couldn’t be a suspect in a million years, but she might be able to supply me with some information.’

He sank back in his chair, his mind starting to race. ‘As it looks like being a quiet day, why don’t you all go to the canteen?’

Never needing to be told twice, Josh was the first out of the door, with Bobby a close second. Holly was just as eager, but she held back to collect her shoulder bag.

‘There’s more to that lad than meets the eye,’ Ashworth remarked.

‘Yes, guv, I must admit he’s fitting in okay.’

‘I’m well aware that the rest of the station still regards him as a joke, but I trust that sort of thing won’t get out of hand in this office . . . eh, Holly?’

'Don't worry, guv, I'll take him under my wing.'

'Good. He's a sensitive lad, and I don't want him getting upset.'

* * *

At 8 p.m. on the dot, Holly was pulling into the multi-storey car park directly opposite the Save U Supermarket, its own having closed two hours ago. Despite the late hour the lower tiers were almost full, the majority of vehicles belonging to patrons of a nearby bingo hall. Holly had to cruise up to the fourth floor to find a space, and by the time she parked the Micra her temperamental nature had manifested itself in a number of muttered oaths. Climbing from the car, her mood was made worse by a strong wind almost ruining her carefully combed hairstyle.

'Shit,' she spat, moving quickly to the descending ramp. Her high-heeled shoes echoed loudly on the concrete surface but once on the third floor, away from the blustering breeze, she slowed her step.

The man waited until she was out of sight, then approached her car and peered through the driver's window before stepping lightly to the barrier fence and gazing down at the busy road far below. It was a full two minutes before Holly emerged from the entrance, and the man watched as she waited for a gap in the traffic then dashed across the road and finally disappeared through the supermarket's sliding doors; and all the while his fingers fretted and kneaded the woolly object in his hand.

'When you come back,' he whispered.

* * *

Ashworth stopped off at Jean Churchman's house on the way home with the intention of speaking to Meg. As his own working hours were far from fixed, he expected to find her busily employed in the stable block but the building was securely locked and, glancing at his watch, he realized that she would have left some three hours ago. With a long glance at the enormous garden, he made his way through the arch and back to his car.

* * *

'Sorry to bring you out so late,' was Samuels's greeting to Holly.

'All part of the job,' she said, smiling, as he steered her into his tiny office behind the wines and spirits counter.

'The board have agreed to pay the money once it's demanded and we're to keep all branches closed until it's over.'

'This must be costing you an arm and a leg,' she remarked.

'A fortune.' He motioned for Holly to take a seat and settled himself behind his desk. 'Most of our supermarkets are situated in small town high streets so even at the best of times we only get the passing trade; the majority of shoppers use the new out-of-town superstores . . .' He gave a derisive snort. 'But then, my fellow board members all have corner shop mentalities.'

Holly smiled politely and was trying to formulate an excuse for leaving when a knock came on the door and Jerry Townsend stood framed on the threshold.

'Oh, sorry, I didn't realize you had company.'

'No problem, Jerry. You already know Detective Sergeant Bedford, I think.'

'I do,' he said, his gaze wandering up and down her legs. 'I hear your boss isn't too overjoyed about me being involved in this.'

'He'd rather we were handling it,' she replied, unfolding her legs and pulling down her skirt.

'I hear he's a difficult man,' Townsend remarked.

She smiled fondly. 'Let's just say, if you rub him up the wrong way, he's bloody near impossible.'

'I'll have to make sure I don't do that, then,' he said, his eyes trying unsuccessfully to flirt with hers. 'Anyway, my brief is only to watch and report my findings to your department.'

'Look, if you'll excuse me . . .' she said, standing up.

'Yes, certainly,' Samuels said, rising slightly from his seat. 'Jerry, show DS Bedford out, will you?'

Townsend stood aside, then followed Holly through the empty supermarket. There was something about the man which made her feel ill at ease.

'If I asked you out for a drink, what would you say?' he asked, pressing a button to activate the sliding doors.

Holly gave him a frosty look. 'I'd say no but thank you for asking.'

* * *

'You're going out? Again?'

Meg spun round to find her indignant sister positioned in the bedroom doorway.

'Yes, and what the hell's it got to do with you?'

'Oh, I know what's going on. Don't think you can pull the wool over my eyes.'

'And what exactly do you mean by that?' Meg demanded, pulling on a short mauve dress.

'You're getting yourself screwed.'

'My God, I don't believe this,' she muttered scornfully. 'I'm thirty-eight years old, Emma. Stop treating me like a schoolgirl.'

'Why haven't I been allowed to meet this man?'

Meg turned her back, refusing to reply.

'You don't have to tell me. The answer's obvious, isn't it?'

'You can talk,' Meg snapped back. 'If some of your grand councillor friends knew what you were like when you're flat on your back . . .'

'But there is a difference between us, sister, dear . . . once somebody's making you happy you become the proverbial doormat, you'll do anything for the man. It really is pathetic to watch.'

'It's called love, Emma. Does that word ring a bell?'

'Love,' she scoffed. 'You're only making a fool of yourself. Mother and father always said I was the clever one.'

'The way I remember it, they always said I was the pretty one.'

Stung by that remark Emma left the room, slamming the door, and Meg let out a triumphant laugh.

* * *

Holly decided to use the lift up to the fourth floor of the car park; as the doors slid open the cold wind immediately bit through her clothing. She stepped out and the lift began to descend the moment the doors closed. Having reached the floor by a different route, she temporarily lost her bearings and scanned the lines of vehicles, all of which took on the same neutral colour beneath the harsh fluorescent lighting.

Finally spotting the Micra, Holly hurriedly approached it, vaguely aware of a sound coming from behind. Stopping abruptly, she glanced around. The area was eerily silent, and shadows loomed large across the walls, but there were no movements to betray another presence. Shrugging, she hitched her shoulder bag higher and carried on.

She was at the car, fumbling in her pockets for the keys, when a shuffling began behind her and a sharp object was pressed into the side of her neck. Before she had a chance to turn, a rough hand grabbed a handful of hair and pulled back her head.

'Right, you cow, just do what I say or you're dead.' The words were underlined by the point of the knife digging deeper into her neck.

Holly fought to remain calm. Relaxing her muscles, she took in a deep breath but could still feel the bump bump of her heart as adrenalin raced around her body.

'Turn round . . . turn round really slowly.'

She obeyed and came face to face with the man, his features concealed beneath a brown woollen balaclava, his eyes barely showing through two narrow slits.

'Good, now walk round the car, open the passenger door, and climb over into the driver's seat.' When she hesitated, he yanked her hair, and added menacingly, 'do it, or I'll kill you.'

Pressure from the knife increased until its point punctured her skin. Holly whimpered.

'Do it,' the man hissed.

'All right . . . all right.'

With the knife still at her neck and her hair still in his grip, she began to edge around the car, unaware that in the background the lift was shuddering to a halt, its doors swishing open. But the man heard the sounds and Holly felt him stiffen with a startled panic, but he neither slackened his grip nor lessened the pressure of the knife.

'Don't make a sound,' he whispered close to her ear, his breathing now rapid.

'Just drop the knife, and move away,' Bobby called, his voice echoing loudly. 'I'm a police officer.'

The man's eyes narrowed beneath the mask. 'Keep away,' he warned, 'or I'll kill her.'

Holly heard Bobby's footsteps slow before coming to a halt, and then he said calmly, 'Just put the knife down, and move away.'

With one more vicious jerk on her hair, the man took away the knife and pushed her forward, sending her sprawling. A shoe dug into her ribs, winding her badly, and then there were sounds of running feet pounding down the ramp and finally fading into the distance. Bobby rushed to her side.

'Are you all right, Holly?' he asked, helping her up.

She probed tentatively at her ribs and winced. 'I'm all the better for seeing you, Bobby, boy.'

* * *

Shirley Samuels greeted her husband warmly in the large hallway of their modern detached house. He seemed vaguely preoccupied as he deposited his briefcase on the hall table, and his mind was elsewhere as he stooped to plant a light kiss on his wife's cheek.

'Bad day, Richard?'

'An absolute bitch,' he said, sighing.

'Come on through, I'll get us a drink. You look as though you need one.'

Clasping his hand, she led him into the lounge and made straight for the drinks cabinet where she took out fresh bottles of gin and Scotch. Samuels settled into an armchair and in a defeated tone related the events of the day.

'So all the markets are closed,' she said, frowning worriedly at her husband.

'I'm afraid so.' He accepted the proffered drink and took a sip. 'Unless we can get this sorted out quickly, we'll go broke.'

As Shirley Samuels tasted her gin and tonic, she mused that this was the first time in three weeks that her husband had managed to get home before 11 p.m., and although loath to put her thoughts into words, she was glad that the supermarkets were closed if it meant seeing more of him from time to time.

* * *

'So, what did the doctor say?' Ashworth asked.

'I've got bruised ribs, and a small cut on my neck. Apart from that, there's no harm done.'

Ashworth had returned to the station the moment he was told of the attack on Holly, and he was now standing in the middle of the office while she recovered at her desk with Bobby standing sentinel-like behind her.

'How did you happen on the scene, Bobby?'

'Well, sir, I knew a threat had been made against Holly, and I thought it unwise for her to go to the supermarket alone, so I followed.'

'It's a good job you did. That was a fine piece of work, son. There's a lesson to be learnt from this. During the investigation, Holly, it would be wise for you to have one of us with you at all times.' Catching her devilish grin, he smiled and added, 'You know what I mean, young lady.'

'Oh, damn, and I thought my luck had changed.'

'I don't know if I can swing a fourth permanent member for CID,' he went on, turning his attention to Bobby, 'but I'm going to have a try, son.'

'Could I have a quiet word with you, sir?' Bobby asked.

'Well, yes, of course you can.'

With a nod to Holly, Ashworth strode to the door and Bobby followed him into the corridor, closing the door quietly behind him.

'Sir, I hope you don't mind . . .' he began, his gaze direct, 'but would you stop referring to me as son? It suggests that I'm a kid brought in to gain a bit of experience rather than an equal member of the team . . .'

At the sight of the young constable's ardent expression, Ashworth had to bite down hard on the insides of his cheeks to quell the loud laugh which threatened to erupt, and as soon as he felt it was safe to speak, he said, 'Right, then, if you'd like to call me guv instead of sir, I'll call you Bobby.'

'Bob.'

'Bob?' Ashworth repeated.

'If you wouldn't mind . . . it's more clipped, more manly.'

'Yes, all right . . . fine. And I must say that was a good piece of work you did tonight; it was a very nasty situation, and you dealt with it well.'

'Thank you. Goodnight, guv.'

'Goodnight . . . Bob,' he murmured, finally allowing his amusement to spill over as the young constable marched off along the corridor.

CHAPTER 9

Richard Samuels had a couple of drinks and then went upstairs to run a bath. By the time it was ready he had undressed and was returning to the bathroom, conscious of a mild discomfort in the pit of his stomach.

Halfway along the landing he doubled up and gripped the bannister, a strangled groan on his lips for the pain had suddenly worsened, and it was then that he heard a cry of distress coming from the lounge. His wife was calling his name again and again, her tone almost one of terror and then, as he stumbled down the stairs, her calls became a scream.

* * *

Holly took Bobby for a thank you drink at the Bull and Butcher, and in the crowded bar they were joined by Josh who had only just heard about the attack. Their usual innuendo-ridden banter was temporarily put on hold by his concern, and for the first few minutes he constantly fussed until Holly was close to exasperation.

'For God's sake, Josh, I'm fine,' she laughed. 'I've only got a prick in the neck.'

'Law of averages,' he said with a sly grin.

'What do you mean?'

'It's the only place you haven't had one.'

'Oh, bollocks, Abraham,' she said, giggling. 'Anyway, behave yourself, here's Bobby with the drinks.'

He turned to see their new team member pushing his way through the crowd, the tray of drinks held aloft.

'Nice one, Bobby,' he said. 'In the car park, I mean.'

'Thanks.' He placed the tray on the table and sat beside Holly.

'So, you've no idea who attacked you, then?' Josh ventured.

'None. Like I told the guv'nor, he had a balaclava over his head, with just slits for the eyes.'

'What was his voice like?'

'I couldn't tell, it was muffled.'

'But couldn't you make out an accent, at least?'

She shrugged, then took a sip of her gin. 'I honestly couldn't tell, Josh. It could have been London, could have been local. I mean, a lot of Midlands accents have some London mixed in with them, don't they?'

* * *

The ambulance driver stepped down on the accelerator, pushing the needle of the speedometer to sixty-five miles an hour. A light rain was falling and the road ahead glistened and shone in the glow of the street lamps as the ambulance approached a busy junction choked with traffic. With siren blaring, the driver pulled out from behind the slow-moving line and lurched along on the wrong side of the road, the siren's wail causing oncoming drivers to bring their vehicles to a halt amidst a squeal of tyres. With practised ease he managed to negotiate a path down the centre of the road, then once more leant on the accelerator and the ambulance sped across the junction, taking the first left into the hospital grounds. Orderlies poured out as the vehicle skidded to a stop outside the Accident and Emergency entrance.

The driver jumped from the cab and ran round to open the back doors, shouting, 'The woman's been poisoned. She's in a bad way, and her husband's the same. He's following behind in another ambulance.'

* * *

'One thing puzzles me, Bobby . . .' Josh said, setting down his glass.

'It's Bob, actually . . . would you both call me Bob? I had to ask the guv'nor if he'd do the same.'

'And what did he say?' Josh asked eagerly.

'He said, okay. He's all right. I don't know why everybody goes on about him.'

Josh shot a surprised look at Holly, who was equally as amazed by this remarkable transformation in one who not so long ago was a gauche new recruit.

'Well, Bob,' Josh said, after a pause. 'You haven't got a car, so how did you follow Holly?'

'I went on the bus,' he said, before taking a long pull at his pint.

There followed a stunned silence.

'I knew she wouldn't be in any danger on the way,' he went on. 'The car park and the supermarket were the danger areas.'

'Oh,' Josh said, finishing his drink.

'Do you want me to see you home, Holly? Make sure you're all right?'

'No, it's okay . . . Bob.'

'Right, I'll say goodnight, then.' At the exit, he turned back and waved.

'God, he's bloody beautiful, isn't he?' Holly whispered, lifting her hand in acknowledgement.

'Holly, do I sense . . . ?'

'No, you don't, Abraham. Bobby's getting to be like a kid brother to me. But you, lover . . .'

Josh's eyes rolled towards the ceiling.

'I could convert you, given half a chance,' she grinned. 'Just think about it . . . think about being in bed with me.'

Josh frowned, bit on his lip as if deep in thought, and then mimed being sick in his hand.

'You sod,' she laughed, aiming a playful cuff at his shoulder.

'Seriously, though, Holly, you will be careful . . . ?'

'Josh, I can look after myself.'

'I know that, but it looks like this guy's going to keep coming after you.'

'I'm ready now. Don't you worry, the next time he comes for me, I'm going to put him in hospital.'

* * *

'She's gone,' the doctor said sadly, looking down at the remains of Shirley Samuels.

Her eyes were open and staring, her neck and face a chalky white. The doctor extended a hand and gently pulled the eyelids shut. All around him nurses were removing the equipment that had been used in a vain attempt to pump the poison from her stomach before it had time to enter her bloodstream.

'How's the husband?' the doctor asked.

'I'll check,' a nurse responded, moving quickly to an internal telephone on the wall.

* * *

An air of gloom tinged with impotency descended on Bridgetown Police Station when news of the first fatality came through. Up in CID, Alex Ferguson, fresh from the pathology lab, was perched on the edge of Ashworth's desk.

'It was in the whisky and gin,' he was saying. 'Both bottles contained more than a lethal dose, but Shirley Samuels drank more than her husband.'

'We're lucky we haven't got a double murder, then,' Ashworth remarked, his shoulders slumped.

'Absolutely,' Ferguson agreed. 'As it is, Richard Samuels will be in hospital for a couple of days, and then he should be fine.'

'Apart from the fact that his wife's been murdered,' the chief inspector pointed out.

'Yes,' Ferguson said, looking suitably chastised.

'Isn't it strange that she drank so much more than he did?'

'Not really. At the post-mortem the state of her liver suggested that she had quite a large alcohol intake. It happens a lot, doesn't it? Hubby's a busy man, not at home very often, so the wife turns to the bottle for comfort. Oh, by the way, the whole of the stock was removed from the supermarket for analysis, and three more spirit bottles were found to be contaminated.'

'Oxalic acid?'

'Yes, in all cases.'

'Alex, in your opinion, would you say it was a strange choice of poison?'

'No, Jim, I wouldn't. It's a difficult poison to trace back to its source which, I suppose, would make it attractive.'

'I know someone who uses it,' Ashworth mused. 'Meg Cowper.'

'Meg?' Ferguson exclaimed. 'I wouldn't be surprised if she murdered her sister, but that apart, I can't see her having anything to do with this.'

'I agree. I'll have to see her, though.'

'Well, I'd better be off, Jim.'

'All right, Alex, and thanks for coming round.'

Holly bustled in carrying two mugs and almost collided with the pathologist. After apologizing profusely for spilling tea on his jacket, she crossed to Ashworth's desk and placed one of the mugs before him.

'Everything okay, guv?'

'No,' he grunted. 'I mean, why . . . why do this for forty thousand pounds?'

'You know the answer to that, guv. If they pull this one off, the other supermarkets — the bigger chains — should pay a damn sight more just to remove the threat of it happening to them. I doubt if they'd even report it to us.'

'The Save U company will go out of business, won't it?'

'I reckon it will, guv, yes.'

'I don't know, after all the years I've spent in this job a senseless death can still affect me.' He shook his head as if to chase away the thought. 'And there's something else disturbing me about all this, Holly . . . how the hell did they place those goods on the shelves with such ease?'

'We've run a check on all the staff, guv. And nothing's turned up on the security cameras, yet.'

'You said Jerry Townsend was at the supermarket last night?'

'Yes.'

'And he looked as if he had the run of the place?'

'There didn't seem to be any restrictions on his movements. You don't think he's involved . . . ?'

'I've been finding out about him. He might be head of security at Arnolds, but his role is more of a consultant. He runs his own business, and it was his staff guarding the supermarket.'

'But what could his motive be? If he's a consultant with his own security business, money can't be a problem.'

'No.' He sighed, frustrated by their lack of progress. 'You wouldn't like to get to know him a little better, would you?'

'Definitely not, and please don't ask me to, guv. He gives me the creeps.'

'I see,' he said, drumming his fingers. 'Oh, well, shall we go and see Meg Cowper, then?'

* * *

Meg looked particularly attractive: her blond hair was freshly washed, and her freckled face beneath a white sun hat was lightly tanned. While most other men would have been thinking up ways of getting Meg out of her figure-hugging jeans, Ashworth was wondering how she could possibly squeeze into them.

'Chief Inspector,' she said, smiling. 'You haven't brought the table back, I hope.'

'No, don't worry, we're both very pleased with it,' he said, returning the smile. 'This is my colleague, Detective Sergeant Bedford.'

They immediately eyed each other as rivals in the way that attractive women tend to do. Holly's smile was friendly, however, as she said, 'Hi.'

'And what have you been getting up to, young lady?' Ashworth challenged.

'How do you mean?' Meg asked, more than a little disconcerted.

'Telling Sarah about all the other pieces of furniture you had in stock when you delivered the table,' he replied, in a mildly scolding tone. '*And* suggesting how nice they'd look in our lounge.'

Her sunny smile returned. 'I do have to live, Chief Inspector, and in any case, Mrs Ashworth said you're the one who makes those decisions.'

'That's what she tells everybody,' he said ruefully. 'I just wish it were true.'

'Oxalic acid,' Holly put in, tired of their superficial chatter. 'Do you use it in your work?'

'Yes, of course, all furniture restorers do.'

'And have you heard about the death of Mrs Shirley Samuels?'

'Yes, I have. It was quite a shock. Who would want to do a thing like that?'

'Oxalic acid was the poison used in that case, and also in the earlier cases of poisoning . . . you might have heard about those, too.'

Meg looked up at Ashworth, her eyes widening. 'You don't think I—'

'No, of course not, Meg,' he quickly replied. 'But we do have to check all sources in an effort to establish who has access to the stuff.'

'Who comes in here, you mean?' He nodded. 'Well, my sister, Emma, sometimes ventures into the lion's den . . .' Her voice dropped to a whisper. 'She might well fantasize about killing Jean Churchman, but I can't see her poisoning anyone else.'

Ashworth laughed obligingly while Holly scribbled in her note pad.

'Jean comes in for a coffee from time to time,' Meg continued, 'and so does Jerry Townsend.'

She was distracted momentarily by a sound from outside, and Holly took the opportunity of motioning for Ashworth to leave them alone.

'I'll just have a quick look at the pieces you've got in, Meg,' he said, taking the hint.

Holly waited until he was inspecting a bookcase, well out of earshot, then said to Meg, 'How do you get on with Townsend?'

'I don't,' she replied, pulling a face. 'How can I put this without sounding crude?'

'He's always trying to get inside your knickers?'

'Yes,' she laughed. 'That's it, exactly.'

'Mine too. I'm hard up, but I'm not desperate. Now, Meg, would you be aware if any of the acid went missing?'

'I know it's a poison, and I'm very careful with it . . .' She approached a series of shelves to their left and took down a plastic container. 'But, to be honest, I don't measure it or keep records. If a lot of it went missing, I suppose I'd know . . . I'm not sure.'

'Can you remember if you've left anyone alone here? Jean Churchman, say, or Townsend?'

A look of confusion crossed her face. 'I may have done . . . you know, gone outside for something, but once again it's not the sort of thing I'd notice.'

'Have you ever left your boyfriend in here?' Holly asked, lightly.

'I haven't got a boyfriend,' Meg said, her face flushing beneath the tan.

'Really? I would've thought they'd be queuing.'

'I'm . . . well, I'm sort of in between, at the moment.'

'So am I — frustrating, isn't it? Tell me, Meg, what's the relationship between Townsend and Jean Churchman?'

'They're together.'

'As in living together?'

'No, Jerry still has his own flat.'

'Okay, so they're having sex together?'

'Yes. You know, you're not how I'd imagine a detective sergeant to be.'

'A lot of people tell me that,' Holly said, grinning. 'Anyway, thanks, Meg, you've been a great help.'

On hearing the cue, Ashworth said a warm goodbye and ushered Holly to the car. When the bottom half of the stable door clanged shut, Meg once again studied the container in her hand. Holding it up to the light, she saw that the white powder was well below the ink line she habitually put there to mark its level after use, and there was the hint of a sad smile on her lips when she reached up and returned the container to its shelf.

As they walked back through the arch, Holly got a good look at the cottage. 'How the other half lives,' she remarked, without the slightest hint of envy. 'Guv, I know you told me that Jean Churchman's husband ran off with Emma Cowper, but I can't understand why she would want to harm Jean? I'd have thought it would be the other way round.'

Ashworth chuckled. 'You don't know Councillor Cowper. Once she gets involved in a feud, she always believes she's in the right . . . that's her big problem. And, anyway, the man left her after a few weeks, so it could look to her like Jean had the last laugh. Did you glean much from Meg?'

'Yes, I did. Unlike you, my head's not turned by a pretty woman, so I noticed a lot of things . . .'

'My appreciation of an attractive woman,' Ashworth said, stopping by the Scorpio, 'didn't prevent me from noticing that she jumped when I asked her what she'd been up to.'

'I noticed that, too.' She went on to tell him that Jean Churchman and Townsend were regular visitors to the workshop. 'And there's another thing, guv. When I asked if her boyfriend went there, she denied having one.'

'So?' he said, searching for his car keys.

'Believe me, guv, that woman is head over heels in love — I ought to know the signs — so why should she deny being in a relationship?'

'Could be he's married,' he suggested, opening up the passenger door. 'Meg's about thirty-eight — there aren't many eligible bachelors of that age about.'

Holly got into the car and as soon as Ashworth was comfortable in the driver's seat, she said, 'But that still means that someone completely unknown to us has access to a supply of oxalic acid.'

'Oh, come on, Holly, you don't really think that Meg Cowper would have anything to do with something like this?'

'Look behind the pretty face, guv.'

'And you'll find a sweet person, not capable of harming a fly,' he assured her.

CHAPTER 10

Their next stop was the hospital. Ashworth had doubted whether Richard Samuels would be well enough to see them, but his doubts were quickly dispelled by the hospital administrator who led the two detectives along a maze of narrow corridors.

'Not only is he well enough to see you, Chief Inspector,' the administrator said, 'but he's insisting upon it.'

They had to stop for a moment and make way for a porter pushing an elderly patient along in a wheelchair. The man whisked past them, leaving a hospital smell in his wake.

'How's he taken the death of his wife?' Ashworth asked.

'Badly,' the administrator told him. 'Councillor Cowper was his first visitor this morning, and she found him very distressed. Afterwards, she voiced her concern to me and I arranged for the hospital chaplain to see him. The man's really good at his job which, in these circumstances, is to give Samuels a reason to go on. Anyway, he's a little better, now.'

They stopped by a half-glass door through which Richard Samuels could be seen sitting up in bed, talking to a nurse.

'When is he being discharged?' Ashworth asked.

'Ordinarily, we'd want to keep him here for two to three days, but he's insisting on discharging himself today.' The man shrugged and spread his hands. 'We can't keep him in against his will and, to be honest, with beds in short supply . . .'

'But surely you should be concerned about whether he's well enough to go home,' Holly said sharply.

The administrator fixed her with a defiant glare. 'Young lady, we can't keep him here against his will. As I said, the doctors would like him to stay for two to three days, but he's a fit, healthy man and they've no doubt that he'll make a full recovery.'

'Thank you,' Ashworth said, turning to knock on the door.

They entered the room and introduced themselves to the beautiful Asian nurse who straight away made herself scarce. Holly was already searching for her note pad as Ashworth strode to the bed.

'Mr Samuels, firstly, may I offer you our sincerest condolences . . .'

'Thank you, Chief Inspector. It hasn't quite sunk in yet. To think that this time yesterday, Shirley was . . .' He stopped abruptly and brought a hand to his face, his shoulders shuddering with dry sobs.

'Mr Samuels,' Ashworth said gently, 'do you feel up to answering a few questions? I know this is highly distressing for you, but we need to establish where you bought the contaminated spirits.'

'I'm all right . . . really. It's just when I think about my wife . . .' He took a deep breath and attempted to compose himself. 'The booze came from the supermarket. I always get it from the supermarket, and I always pay for it.'

'Yes, of course. So, when exactly did you buy it?'

'The day before the final warning.' He paused, his eyes staring dully into space. 'If only I'd thought . . .'

'And it came from the wines and spirits display behind the counter?'

'Yes, it did.'

'You see, sir, what's puzzling me is how a member of the public could get to that display.'

'The shelves do go a few yards past the counter. It is only a checkout point, after all.'

'True, but it's constantly staffed. I'd have thought it would be near impossible to plant bottles on those shelves.'

'Difficult, I admit, but obviously not impossible, Chief Inspector.'

'Mr Samuels, this does raise the question of your staff.'

'Oh, no,' he said, with an emphatic shake of the head. 'All of my staff are hand-picked. I have complete faith in them.'

'Was any member of the public behind that counter at any time?'

'Chief Inspector, I'm not on the shop floor that much . . .' He frowned, suddenly struck by a thought. 'Well . . . no, it's too ridiculous.'

'Tell us, nevertheless.'

'Well . . . Meg Cowper was.'

'She was behind that counter?' Ashworth asked, glancing urgently at Holly.

'Yes. You see, her sister, Emma, is a very good friend of ours . . .' Pain clouded his eyes for a moment, but he managed to retain control. 'So, when I saw Meg shopping for spirits, I invited her through for a cup of coffee. My office is directly behind the counter.'

'Miss Cowper was buying alcohol?'

'Yes, Chief Inspector, but what you're hinting at is absurd. Meg's not the sort of person who would get involved in anything like this.'

'I agree with you, Mr Samuels, but we do have to investigate every avenue. Now, they tell us you're discharging yourself.'

Samuels hesitated, then said, 'Do you know what I wanted to do when the realization of my wife's death dawned on me? I wanted to get into my car, drive it on to the motorway and crash into a bridge. All I wanted was for my own life to be over too . . .' He looked away from Ashworth and took to plucking at the sheets as if embarrassed by this confession.

'But then the chaplain came to see me. He said I mustn't think that Shirley has gone for ever; I shall see her again and until then she'll be watching over me. He asked me what I could do to make her proud of me. I had to think about it for a long time, but then I saw it was the supermarkets . . . The business had been our whole life . . . I wanted to build it up so it could rival any of the big names but the rest of the board thwarted me at every turn. That's what I'm determined to do now, though. I'll throw everything into the supermarket chain and make it something Shirley can be proud of.'

'And when these people make another demand for money, you're going to pay it?'

Samuels nodded. 'But I'll hand all the information over to you, Chief Inspector, because I want them caught and punished.'

'So do we, Mr Samuels, so do we. Well, thank you, and I'm sorry we had to disturb you at a time like this.'

Ashworth was quiet as they followed the signs back to main reception, and Holly said, 'Meg Cowper's name came up again, then, guv.'

'Yes, I did notice,' he snapped, 'but I still say it doesn't fit.'

* * *

Jason Brent had been involved in petty crime for much of his life, and it was a sure bet that he would continue to court trouble in one form or another, for although aware of the difference between right and wrong, he chose to ignore the distinction. As far as he was concerned, his immediate future was all mapped out: the moment those prison aftercare bastards were off his back he intended to leave the factory and return to his former, more lucrative, occupation. After all, he could pick up as much money from half a day's thieving as he could earn packing soft drinks boxes for a month.

He was in a hurry to get away and was still struggling into his black leather jacket when he passed through the gates of Arnolds at the end of his shift. There was someone he had to meet and, stopping briefly to light a cigarette with fingers that trembled slightly, he continued along with an urgency to his customary swagger.

About half a mile from the factory, Brent slowed and gazed around carefully until he spotted the guy. He was a mysterious figure loitering on a corner, his outfit made entirely of black leather, wearing a blue crash helmet, the dark glass of the visor pulled down to hide his face. Brent made certain he was not being watched and then, flicking his cigarette into the gutter, he ambled across to the man, coming to a halt a good two yards away, unsure of the reception he was about to receive.

'I didn't mean to balls it up,' he said, earnestly. 'I'd got the bird, but then this bloke come running into the car park—'

'That doesn't matter now,' the man said, his voice little more than a whisper. 'I want you to do it again tonight — and this time, no mistakes.'

Brent could scarcely believe his ears, and when the man reached into his pocket and passed across an envelope, his eyes widened with astonishment, for he had expected strong censure and here he was being given another chance.

Pocketing the envelope quickly, he said, 'Thanks. Tonight, then.'

'Just tell her if the police interfere, she's dead,' the man said, his voice hissing through the visor.

'Yeah, okay, like I said, it would have been all right the last time if that bloke hadn't interrupted me.'

'Just make sure she gets the message. Mark her if you have to.'

Brent grinned as the man turned and walked away.

'Oh, I'll mark her,' he said to himself. 'I'll mark her, all right.'

* * *

'They've made contact,' Ashworth said gruffly as he strode into CID and settled behind his desk, 'but they haven't made any demands for money, as yet. It was the woman's voice again. She's going to ring back tomorrow with the exact details.'

'Do you mean to say they rang Samuels?' Holly said. 'After what they did to his wife?'

'Yes, we're dealing with extremely callous people here. We'll have to be very careful in the way we handle them.'

'Anything else happening, guv?' Josh asked.

'Nothing, apart from the fact that Emma Cowper's still shouting her mouth off, demanding to know what we're doing. That woman is beginning to get on my nerves. She actually had the effrontery to tell me that we should be checking all those with access to oxalic acid . . .' His mouth flicked up into a savage smile. 'I had the pleasure of informing her that we were doing just that, and her sister was one of the people we were looking into. That shut her up . . . for at least two seconds.'

* * *

Holly spent the evening alone in her small two-bedroomed semi-detached, and after a couple of drinks and *News At Ten*, she showered and got ready for bed. She slipped, naked, beneath the duvet and, thanks to the alcohol and the hot shower, was asleep in no time at all.

Jason Brent waited a full thirty minutes after the house lights went out before he snaked across the road and in through Holly's front gate. Skirting around the Micra, he approached the front door where he delved into his pocket and withdrew a plastic credit card. Inserting it into the crack between the door and its outer surround, he skilfully worked it up until contact was made with the Yale lock. Concentration wrinkled his forehead as he manoeuvred the card until the lock slipped back. He tried the handle and when the door swung open, he stepped inside and closed it quietly behind him. For many seconds he stood in the hall, listening for any sounds from above. When all remained quiet, he replaced the card in his pocket and, pulling on the brown balaclava, mounted the stairs. Within the confines of the mask, his breathing sounded awfully loud and he could smell the fumes of tobacco and alcohol.

A stair creaked beneath his foot. He stopped, silently cursing, and strained his ears for any movements from the bedroom, but only Holly's rhythmic sighs pierced the silence. Testing the next stair gingerly, Brent sank his foot into the soft pile of the carpet and continued up to the landing. His eyes were now accustomed to the darkness, allowing him to work his way around the linen chest positioned ahead of him. The door to her bedroom was slightly ajar, and he peered through the crack to where Holly was turning on to her back, the quilt slipping down to expose her breasts.

Drawing a knife from the waistband of his jeans, Brent hungrily ran his tongue around his lips and pushed the door, which swung noiselessly open on its well-oiled hinges. He approached the bed stealthily, his excitement growing with every step and Holly, lost in a dream world, murmured softly in her sleep.

* * *

Although he had enjoyed his usual three measures of malt whisky, Ashworth was finding it impossible to relax and he surprised Sarah by suggesting that they take the dog for a walk. That was the last thing she wanted to do at 11 p.m. on a chilly autumn evening, but sensing her husband's disquiet, she readily agreed.

They walked briskly to where their road narrowed into little more than a winding lane with fields at either side while the dog, ever glad of exercise, pulled excitedly against the restraints of her lead. Away from prying eyes, Ashworth linked hands with Sarah and eventually they stopped by the entrance to a field, both leaning on the five-bar gate. A full moon hung above the horizon, and Ashworth stared up at it for many minutes, studying its dark shapes that created the illusion of a face while his mind grappled with the few facts that they had amassed on the case. Then he turned to Sarah, his expression earnest.

'Tell me,' he said, 'Jean Churchman and Emma Cowper . . . why is there so much bad blood between them?'

'I told you, dear.'

'Yes, I know about the affair, but surely that should have died down by now.'

'I don't think so, Jim. Jean might be a rich woman, but before the divorce she was positively dripping with money — she had to give half of her fortune to her husband, and that still rankles.'

'And she blamed Emma for enticing him away in the first place?'

'Exactly, and now Jean never misses a chance to do Emma a bad turn whenever an opportunity shows itself.'

'What do you think of Meg Cowper?'

'I think she's very nice.'

'No, go deeper, Sarah . . . what's she all about behind the mask?'

'Jim, I hardly know the girl.'

'That's it . . . she's thirty-eight years old, and yet you called her a girl.'

'Someone of thirty-eight is a girl to me,' she said with a rueful grin.

'But that's how she comes across to me, too. I feel she's repressed, as though she hasn't been allowed to develop as a person.'

'Yes, I see what you mean. Of course, Emma does dominate her dreadfully. I've never really given it any thought.'

'Do you know if she's had any boyfriends?'

'She's had a few, Jim, but I don't think any of them were serious.'

'Do you think she's capable of having anything to do with the murder of Shirley Samuels?'

'What?' Sarah threw back her head and laughed, startling the little dog at their feet. 'You can't be serious, Jim.'

'She does have a supply of oxalic acid.'

'Even so, I can't see Meg as an extortionist, or a murderer.'

'That's my opinion, as well, but as Holly pointed out, serial killers get away with their crimes for so long because in most cases society regards them as harmless.'

'That may be true, Jim, but in Meg's case I really can't see it.'

'I can't either . . . Oh, come on, let's get back. I thought the fresh air might clear the cobwebs, but I still feel as if I'm chasing shadows.'

* * *

Holly quickly surfaced through thick layers of sleep to find the point of a knife once again pricking her neck. Opening her eyes, she calmly stared up at the ceiling, unwilling to allow the man to see the panic which was churning her stomach.

'Keep still, you cow,' Brent breathed. 'Just keep still and do what I tell you.'

'What do you want?' she whispered, glad that her voice sounded steady.

'I've got a message for you. You've got to tell the filth to keep out of it, or you're dead.'

He was now slowly steering the knife down towards her breasts and Holly gasped, her Adam's apple appearing to stick in her throat.

'Push the cover off. Go on, push it off and let's see what you've got.' His voice held a slight tremor and he seemed to start, as if taken unawares by this new development.

With the knife pressing into her breastbone, Holly threw the quilt to one side and Brent's breathing quickened as the eyes behind the slits scanned her naked body before finally coming to rest on the thatch of dark hair at her crotch. Bringing the knife back to her neck, he climbed on to the bed and ordered Holly to open her legs. She meekly complied, all the while waiting for a chance to strike back.

'If you make a sound, I'll kill you. I mean it,' he snarled, pressing the sharp blade against her windpipe. 'Do you understand me, cow?'

'Yes,' she said, attempting to nod despite the pressure on her throat.

While Brent kept his wild eyes on her face, Holly heard the ragged rasp of his zip as he struggled with his flies.

CHAPTER 11

The sleek Ford Escort pulled up behind Meg's ancient Volkswagen in the pub car park. James Dallington killed the engine and turned to look at her.

'This is it,' he said. 'Do you think you can go through with it?'

She nodded. 'Can you?'

'Oh yes,' he said, smiling. 'I most definitely can.'

They kissed, her arms encircling his neck, her lips eager, and when they parted Dallington cupped her face, his eyes warm with affection.

'I'll phone you in the morning with the final details,' he said.

'Yes, all right.' She climbed from the car, their fingers still touching. 'Ring me. Don't forget.'

Pulling up her coat collar against the chill night air, Meg waited until the car had pulled out on to the main road, its tail lights glowing red in the darkness. Her steps were slow as she returned to the Volkswagen, for she was contemplating the enormity of what they had planned for the following night.

* * *

Holly inhaled deeply and forced her body to relax. The pressure on her throat eased a little as Brent fumbled with his underpants. Seizing the opportunity, she pushed the knife away and in the same movement pulled back a leg and smashed her foot into the face of the hooded figure kneeling between her thighs. Brent howled with pain and fell backwards on to the floor, freeing Holly to scramble from the bed. They came to their feet at the same moment, Brent still clutching the knife in his right hand. He made a wild swing with it but Holly, perfectly balanced on the balls of her feet, swayed back and felt the blade whistle past her face. Keeping her eyes fixed on the slits in the hood, she circled him.

'Come on, then, you bastard, stick me. Come on, where's your bottle gone?'

She continued to goad him, almost willing him to attack so that she could retaliate. He lunged but she had caught the intention in his eyes and, side-stepping, she grabbed his wrist with one hand, his elbow with the other, and twisted his arm up behind his back. He tried to kick out but she was pushing herself close, forcing her knees into the back of his, all the time driving his arm higher, enjoying his pain, thrilling at his screams.

'Drop the blade, you bastard,' she yelled. 'Drop it, or I'll break your bloody arm.'

A cold shiver travelled the length of her body as the knife slid over her stomach and fell to the floor. Grabbing the back of his neck and still gripping his arm, she pushed him across the room and smashed his skull against the wall, the thud on impact hugely satisfying. Then she let go and watched him sink slowly to the floor. He tried to rise almost immediately, but Holly was standing over him and before he could get very far she kicked out at his face, sending him sprawling.

'Oh God, stop it . . . just leave it, will you?' he squealed, trying to crawl under the bed as she advanced on him again.

'Let's see who you are, shall we?' she said, grabbing the hood and snatching it away. 'Well, bloody hell, if it isn't Jason Brent. I should have known.'

He started to snivel, continually shouting for her to pack it in while he tried to edge away.

'On your feet,' she said, grabbing a handful of his hair and yanking him upright.

With Brent yelping and complaining that his hair would be pulled out at the roots, she dragged him towards the telephone on her bedside table. Lifting the receiver she pushed him into a corner where he collapsed in a heap, and with her features distorted by a snarl she aimed another kick at his ribs.

'I owe you that one, you bastard,' she spat.

Brent was curled up into a tight ball, whimpering softly while Holly punched out the station's number.

'Central control.' It was PC Gordon Bennett's voice in her ear.

'Gordon, it's Holly Bedford. Could you get a patrol car to my house? I've got an attempted rape.'

'On its way. Are you all right, Holly?'

She looked at the young man cowering in the corner. 'Yes, Gordon, no sweat.'

* * *

Jason Brent had to be taken to hospital, which held things up considerably. There was little the matter with him apart from a few cuts and bruises, but when the patrol car arrived and he was delivered into the custody and comparative safety of the uniformed officers, his bravado resurfaced and he straight away faked injury, collapsing onto the floor and holding his ribs. The arresting officers showed no signs of sympathy but were nevertheless obliged to call in the police doctor, who in turn was forced to send Brent to the hospital. By the time two superficial cuts to his face had been dressed and X-rays had showed that no bones were broken, it was 3 a.m. and his cocky disposition was restored to the point where he was demanding a brief. It soon became obvious to all concerned that an interview would not be possible for a few hours yet, so he was ushered into a police cell and told to keep quiet for the night.

Ashworth arrived at the station at 8 a.m. convinced that Brent's arrest was the breakthrough they had been waiting for in the supermarket case, and his step was brisk on the way to CID. His team of three was already in.

'Are you sure you're all right?' he asked Holly, an edge of concern to his voice.

'Of course I am.' Her tone implied that Ashworth was not the first to ask, and she was fed up with giving the answer. In all truth, the previous night's events had left her badly shaken, but she would never have admitted to it.

Ashworth was settling into his chair when a knock came on the door and Superintendent Newton marched in.

'Good morning,' he said, straight away turning to Holly. 'I trust you're all right?'

'Yes, sir,' she said tersely.

'I understand this Jason Brent is claiming that you beat him up—'

'Sir . . .' Holly cut in.

'Superintendent,' Ashworth barked, 'this man broke into Holly's house. He was carrying a knife . . .'

'I'm not disputing the facts,' Newton said stiffly. 'I'm merely trying to ascertain whether DS Bedford's report will confirm that all of his injuries occurred while she was disarming and subduing him. That way we shouldn't have anything to worry about.'

He strode to the door and turned to the chief inspector. 'I'm not totally bereft of understanding, you know.' The door was gently closed.

'My God,' Ashworth exclaimed. 'He is human, after all.'

That remark dispelled the tension and they all laughed just a little too loudly.

'Right, then, let's get on with this chap, Brent. Bobby, I want you to conduct the interview with me.'

Bobby was on his feet, eager for this new challenge, and he hurried after Ashworth who was already striding along the corridor.

'Guv . . .' he ventured. 'You said you'd call me Bob.'

'No can do, I'm afraid,' Ashworth said cheerfully. 'You're Bobby — that's the only way I can think of you. Sorry, son.'

CHAPTER 12

The uniformed officer stationed to the right of the door in number one interview room kept his eyes fixed on a point midway between the ceiling and the floor on the opposite wall. He refused to be riled by Jason Brent who, despite repeated admonishments from his solicitor, continually flicked cigarette ash at the constable's feet and grinned widely at what he obviously saw as a highly amusing and clever stunt.

The solicitor, Jonathan Lawson, newly qualified and hoping to build up a solid reputation, was already showing signs of impatience with his young client and he gave a thankful sigh when Ashworth strode purposefully into the room, coming to a halt at the table.

'Mr Brent,' he said, directing Bobby to the tape recorder, 'I'm Chief Inspector Ashworth, and that is Detective Constable Adams.'

Brent smirked. 'Charmed to make your acquaintance.'

'Do you know why you're here?' Ashworth asked, pulling up a chair.

'That bird beat me up, that's why I'm here,' he replied, his tone petulant. 'I'll have her for that, you see if I don't.'

'It's my duty to tell you, Mr Brent, that your threat has been recorded and may be used against you,' Ashworth retorted. 'Now . . . you broke into Detective Sergeant Bedford's house, threatened her with a knife and tried to rape her. Because she objected to that — at the same time taking measures to protect herself — you feel you have grounds for complaint about the way you were treated. Is that what you're saying?'

Confusion clouded Brent's face and he shot a glance at his solicitor, who motioned for him to answer the question.

'Yeah, that's about it,' he said, stabbing out his cigarette. 'She banged my head against the wall . . .'

'Well, it didn't knock any sense into you, son. What were you doing in the house in the first place?'

'You don't have to answer that,' Lawson interjected.

Ashworth glared at the man, and then returned his attention to Brent. 'You're in trouble, son. You were arrested inside the house — we know you broke in.'

'I don't want to say nothing.'

'All right, but you're going to be charged,' Ashworth said, getting slowly to his feet.

'With what?' Lawson demanded to know.

'Murder, extortion, and attempted rape,' he stated flatly.

'I ain't killed anybody,' Brent said, his face suddenly a pale grey.

Ashworth leant across the table. 'Shirley Samuels was murdered. The people responsible were trying to extort money from the Save U Supermarket. Their threat was that if the police interfered, DS Bedford would be killed . . . and you threatened to kill her, didn't you?'

'You don't have to answer that,' Lawson cut in.

'No, he doesn't, because we've already got enough to charge him.'

Brent thought for a moment, then whispered urgently with his solicitor.

Lawson cleared his throat. 'My client will admit to certain things, if you drop the murder charge.'

'How can I do that?' Ashworth argued. 'Until I've heard what he's got to say?'

The whispering became frenzied and then Lawson, looking slightly embarrassed, said, 'My client claims that he was paid to put the frighteners on DS Bedford. You'll find that means—'

'I know what that means.' Ashworth sat down again and studied the sticking plaster over the young man's right eye, the tiny cut and bruising on his upper lip. 'You didn't do a very good job, did you, son?'

Brent flushed, his fists bunched in a threatening gesture, and straight away Lawson put a restraining hand on his shoulder.

Ashworth exhaled sharply. 'Stop this game of charades and talk to me, Jason. Any way you look at this, you're in trouble. How much is up to you.'

'Okay,' Brent said, slumping back in his chair. 'Somebody paid me three hundred pounds to put the frighteners on the bird.'

'Who, Jason?'

'I dunno. This guy approached me outside Arnolds and asked me if I wanted to do a job.'

'You mean, he just walked up to you in the street? Why would anyone do that?'

Brent shrugged. 'Everybody at the factory knows I've done time, so I suppose word just got about.'

'And what did this man look like?'

'I dunno.'

'Someone approaches you and offers you a job, and you've no idea what he looks like? Oh come on, son, you don't expect me to believe that?'

'I couldn't see his face, honest. He was wearing a crash helmet with the visor pulled down.'

'How tall was he? What sort of build?'

Brent considered this. 'I'd say about six foot, and he was slim.'

'Yes, go on.'

'Like I said, he offered me three hundred quid just to frighten this bird. He gave me the number of her car, told me where she lived, so I just watched till I knew who she was.'

'Did you attack her in the multi-storey car park?'

'Yeah. I was supposed to say if the police got involved I'd kill her, but before I could, some guy comes rushing up saying he's a police officer.'

'And what happened then?'

'I ran off.'

'I don't mean that. Did the man approach you again?'

'Yeah. He was waiting for me yesterday after I finished my shift. I thought he was gonna try to give me a slapping for fouling up, but he just give me another three hundred quid to do it again.'

'And he had a motorbike?'

'I never saw it, but he must have done. He was kitted out in black leathers and, like I said, he had a crash helmet on.'

'What colour was the crash helmet.'

'Dark blue and white. It'd got ACE wrote across it in light blue.'

'Good,' Ashworth intoned. 'Now tell me what happened last night.'

'I went to the house and got in through the front door — I was supposed to give her the message again, see. The bird was asleep upstairs so I woke her up and threatened her with the knife, and then she attacked me.'

'Did you try to rape her?'

Brent shook his head, and said earnestly, 'No, I never touched her.'

'Are you sure? You have to tell me the truth, you know. This is a murder investigation and you're calling one of my officers a liar. That could make me doubt everything else you're telling me.'

'All right, I did,' Brent mumbled, resignedly.

'What was that, Jason? Speak louder, for the benefit of the tape recorder.'

'I said, all right, I did it. She hadn't got nothing on and I fancied her. I didn't plan to,' he added hastily, 'it just happened.'

'You're saying you attempted to have sexual intercourse with DS Bedford against her will?'

'Yeah.'

'Right,' Ashworth said. 'I'm satisfied that you had nothing to do with the murder of Shirley Samuels, or the attempted extortion.'

Brent immediately perked up, but the smile was wiped from his face when Ashworth continued, 'But you'll be charged with attempted rape, threatening to kill, and breaking and entering. See to it, Bobby,' he said, marching towards the door.

* * *

On the way back to CID, Ashworth became aware of the smell of cigarette smoke clinging to his suit, and his nose was still wrinkling with distaste as he hurried into the office.

'Oh, guv,' Holly said, 'we didn't want to disturb you, but not long ago the organization made contact with Richard Samuels.'

'Did they now?'

'They want the money tonight. He's to take it to Aldridge Farm on the Old West Road at ten p.m.'

Ashworth skirted around his desk and considered the map of Bridgetown on the wall. 'Hmm, a good choice. This is the Old West Road . . .' His finger followed a red line on the map. 'And this is the road that used to service Aldridge Farm when it was there.' This time he traced a horseshoe line that left the road and rejoined it about a mile further on.

Josh said, 'But that leaves the extortionists in a lousy position, guv. There's only one road in and out. If we seal both exits—'

'Don't you believe it, Josh, all this is open country,' he said, indicating the surrounding areas. 'They could cut across it on foot and link up with any number of major roads where they could have a car waiting. And don't forget, they're probably banking on us not having a presence there.'

Holly had remained silent, and Ashworth noticed her impatient expression. 'Oh, sorry,' he said, 'you want to know what happened with Brent.'

'Yes, guv.'

He filled them in on the results of the interview, pleasing her immensely.

'And you believe him about the man in the biker's gear?' she asked.

'I've no reason not to. I don't think the lad's got enough intelligence to lie.' He paused for thought. 'No doubt you two have realized that the death of Shirley Samuels has altered things considerably. This is now a murder investigation and we can't allow private security personnel to monitor the handing over of the money. We have to be there. So, as much as I sympathize with Richard Samuels's plight, I'm going now to have a word with Newton about this.'

* * *

It was late afternoon when Superintendent Newton breezed into the office, coming to a stop in front of Ashworth's desk.

'How are you on compromise?' he asked hesitantly.

'To tell the truth, it's not one of my strong subjects, sir.'

Newton perched on the edge of the desk; it was an action he had seen performed by many and he hoped it would make him appear matey, more at ease with the lower ranks.

'As I thought,' he said with an uncomfortable smile. 'Now, I've spent most of the afternoon talking with Emma Cowper, who has chosen to mediate with Samuels. She's very aware that we can't just sit back and let the security people handle this, so what she's suggested is that Samuels keeps in touch with you on his car phone, and once he's handed the money over—'

'We can move in?' Ashworth asked hopefully.

'That's right.'

'And we'll be allowed to watch from the Old West Road?'

‘Yes, as long as your vehicles are off the road, parked in fields, no one will know you’re there.’

Ashworth glanced at the map. ‘Yes, sir, I think I can live with that.’

* * *

At 9 p.m. Holly was waiting with Ashworth in his Scorpio, hidden in a field opposite the entrance to the farm road, while Josh, with the lights dimmed on his Nissan Sunny, was making his way with Bobby to watch the exit. The night was still, quiet, and a full moon bathed the fields and lane with a pale lustre. A thin layer of frost was already forming and the chill had penetrated into the Scorpio’s interior.

‘There’s a car coming down the farm road, guv,’ Holly said suddenly.

Ashworth checked his watch. ‘It’s only nine p.m. Samuels isn’t due until ten, but we’d better take the registration number.’

She opened the car door, allowing colder air to circulate, and Ashworth shivered as he watched her sprint the twenty or so yards to the gate and crouch down just as an arc of headlights swept across the field. The car turned left on to the Old West Road, giving Holly a clear view of its illuminated rear plate. She scribbled down the registration number then hurried back to the Scorpio, her breath fogging the crisp air.

‘It was a small car, guv,’ she said, scrambling in. ‘Just the driver — female, I think.’

He grunted and pushed his hands deeper into the pockets of his waxed jacket. Waiting around had never been easy for Ashworth and over the next hour he consulted his watch at least thirty times. At last, it was 10 p.m.

‘Samuels should be on his way,’ he said.

‘I can see a car now, guv, and it’s turning into the farm road.’

The car phone started to buzz at that moment. Ashworth snatched up the receiver.

'This is Richard Samuels.' His voice was taut, nervous. 'I've just turned into the road leading to the farm . . .'

'Right, Mr Samuels,' Ashworth said. 'I want you to keep in contact all the way until you see signs of life.'

Holly was relating developments to Josh via her police radio and Ashworth cupped a hand over his ear to block out the noise as Samuels said, 'The road's really narrow and very uneven. I'm having to crawl along. I can't see any movements yet.'

'Just let us know when you do.'

Static crackled on the line while precious seconds ticked away, then Samuels's voice was again in his ear.

'There's a man standing in the middle of the road, Chief Inspector. He's wearing a crash helmet . . . Hold on, he's waving me down. I'm going to have to ring off . . .'

'Make contact as soon as you've handed the money over,' Ashworth said hurriedly, just as the line went dead.

'Hadn't we better get on the road, guv, ready to go?'

When he gave the nod, Holly was out of the car and running towards the gate, waving Ashworth on the moment it was open. He started the engine and eased the car out of the field, coming to a stop on the grass verge. Holly was busy radioing Josh as she closed the gate.

'Okay, lover boy, we're on the road and ready to go,' she said, climbing into the passenger seat.

'We're doing the same, Holly,' Josh responded.

'Good. Stand by.'

They waited. Finally, Ashworth glanced at his watch. 'It's fifteen minutes since Samuels went past,' he muttered, tapping the steering wheel. 'I don't like it, Holly. We've got to go in.'

He slammed the Scorpio into gear, and Holly called into the radio, 'Go, Josh, stop anything that's moving.'

The car wheels hit the untreated road with a vengeance, throwing Holly forward, and pain shot through her neck when the seat belt jerked her back.

'Hang on,' Ashworth advised.

'Too late, guv,' she mumbled, rubbing at the discomfort.

The car ploughed along the road, lurching from side to side on the increasing gradient. A slight bend lay up ahead and when he manoeuvred the car around it they were met with another turn, behind which could be seen the glow from headlights. Ashworth felt a rush of adrenalin and, putting his own lights on to full beam, he reduced the Scorpio's speed and waited for the vehicle to emerge from around the bend. The moment it did, he accelerated, his headlights dazzling, then hit the brake pedal and brought the car to a skidding halt, blocking the road and forcing the advancing driver to brake and pull up only inches away. They tore from the Scorpio, only to stop in their tracks when Josh and Bobby tumbled out of the other vehicle. The four of them stood facing one another.

'What the hell . . . ?' Holly exclaimed.

'Didn't you pass anyone coming in?' Ashworth snapped.

Bemused, Josh shook his head. 'No, guv.'

'So where the hell's Samuels?' Holly wondered aloud.

CHAPTER 13

The uniformed division was called in to help with a search of the area, and it was during that search that the escape route came to light. An old cattle grid was uncovered, beyond which lay the road that the farmer would have used to drive his herd along to market; it joined up with what was now a dual carriageway. Although the tarmac had long since given way to weeds and grasses, concealing its existence, it was still solid enough to support a car.

Ashworth stood with Holly at the cattle grid and even in the moonlight they were able to trace the path of churned-up grass and flattened weeds left in the wake of the vehicle.

'Well, we really made a mess of that,' he said.

'We weren't to know, guv. But if you think about it, that woman who drove up here earlier must have had something to do with this.'

'I agree. She must have dropped off the man in the crash helmet. Are you sure there was no one else in the car?'

'Positive, guv, but he could have been crouching out of sight. Anyway, in the morning we should know who she is.'

'But until then, we've got some flak to face,' he said wearily.

* * *

At 2.15 a.m. the following morning, the station master at Bridgetown Railway Station noticed a vehicle in the otherwise deserted car park. Although it was unusual for anyone to park there overnight, he wasn't particularly disturbed at the time. He did, however, walk around the vehicle to check that it was secure and that nothing of value was open to display. Satisfying himself that there was nothing to tempt the town's steadily growing criminal fraternity, he wandered back to his office and promptly put the car out of his mind.

* * *

The flak which Ashworth was confidently expecting failed to materialize. Indeed, most ranks knew better than to antagonize him when a case was not going well; and even Superintendent Newton showed his concern by keeping Emma Cowper's ravings well out of his earshot. After hasty consultation it was decided that they would conceal Richard Samuels's disappearance on the grounds that his abductors could well effect his release once they were clear.

Holly put her head around the office door. 'I've traced the owner of the car registration number, guv, and you're not going to like it.'

'Give me the bad news,' he growled from his desk.

'It's Meg Cowper.'

'What?' He tossed down the report he was reading and glared at her accusingly. 'I do not believe this.'

'We've got to look into it, guv.'

'I'm well aware of that, Holly, but thank you for pointing it out,' he snapped, the strain beginning to show on his face.

* * *

If Meg Cowper had anything to hide it was not betrayed in her welcoming smile, although Holly did notice dark smudges under her eyes and a general lack of sparkle in her appearance.

'And what can I do for you two today?' she asked, dropping her paintbrush into a jar.

'Meg, I'm sorry I've got to bother you with this . . .' Ashworth began haltingly, 'but could you tell us what you were doing in the vicinity of Aldridge Farm last night?'

A livid crimson rushed into her cheeks and, with hands on hips, she said sharply, 'Does that have anything to do with you?'

'No, I'm sure it doesn't. It's just that we're looking into an incident that took place near there last night and we wondered if you saw anything.'

'I saw nothing,' she flared. 'And in any case, how did you know I was there?'

'Your car registration number was taken.'

'What? But, why?'

'It was just a routine check,' he said lamely.

'Chief Inspector, you seem to be asking me a lot of questions lately, and I'm starting to feel my privacy's being invaded. So, if you've no further questions to ask, I'd like you to leave.'

'But you were seen near Aldridge Farm last night,' Holly persisted. She was acutely annoyed by Ashworth's apparent inability to view the woman as a suspect, and thoroughly pissed off by her high-handed manner.

'That's got nothing to do with you,' Meg said, opening the stable door. 'Now would you please leave?' No sooner were they outside than the door was forcibly slammed behind them.

'Whether you like it or not, guv, I'd say we touched a raw nerve there.'

'I must admit, it looks like it. I just wish Samuels would turn up, Holly, then we could really start to ask questions.'

* * *

When the car was still there on the second night, the station master rang the police and was rather surprised by the quick response to his call. He had hardly replaced the receiver and was preparing for the arrival of the 1 a.m. train for Euston when a patrol car arrived with tyres screeching.

It took the attending officers only seconds to confirm that the vehicle was the property of Richard Samuels and the subject of an all stations alert. Forensic were informed immediately, and the patrol car stayed until their arrival.

* * *

Ashworth had elected to be the CID member on permanent call and he was summoned to the station as soon as the car was brought in for forensic tests. To relieve the tension while awaiting the results, he decided to join Sergeant Dutton, on night duty in reception, for a cup of tea.

'Feelings are running high in the town, Jim,' Dutton remarked. 'On the supermarket case, I mean.'

'Mine are too, Martin,' Ashworth retorted.

'Funny really, though. I know Shirley Samuels died, but do you know what's really upsetting people out there? It's the fact that a baby could have been killed.'

'What kind of person does these things?' Ashworth asked, rubbing at his tired eyes.

'Not the likes of you or me, Jim. I reckon society's gone the wrong way you know. People have got so used to having everything provided for them — housing, money — that when it's not, they feel they're quite within their rights to just go out there and take it.'

Although he basically agreed with Dutton's views, Ashworth was in no mood to discuss them.

'Meg Cowper . . .' he said, deliberately changing the subject. 'Do you know anything about her?'

Dutton frowned. 'Emma's little sister? A couple of my lads have taken her out — mind you, that was a few years ago.'

'And?'

'I don't think they had any complaints,' he said with a knowing wink. 'But she comes on strong with the hearts and flowers bit, apparently. They found that a bit off-putting.'

'What would you say if I asked you whether she could be tied up with this supermarket business?'

'I'd say put more water in your whisky, Jim,' he laughed. 'You *are* pulling my leg . . . ?'

'No, I'm not. I find it as ridiculous as you do, but there are a lot of things beginning to point in that young lady's direction.'

The sergeant put down his mug, shaking his head in disbelief. 'I could see Meg doing a lot of silly things, but getting involved in this sort of caper, well . . .'

'Do you think she might if she was infatuated with a man?'

'What you've got to ask yourself, Jim, is — would a nice girl like Meg get herself involved with a man who'd do this sort of thing?'

'When you said you could see Meg doing a lot of silly things, what did you mean, exactly?'

Dutton swallowed the last of his tea while he considered the question. 'She does have a romantic turn of mind. I could see her getting involved in lost causes, that sort of thing.'

The telephone rang. It was Forensic for the chief inspector. Dutton passed the receiver across and tried to read Ashworth's expression while he listened to a summary of their findings.

'Thank you,' he said, hanging up. 'For nothing.'

'No joy?' Dutton asked.

'The car's as clean as a whistle. They found absolutely nothing that could help us in any way.'

Their attention was distracted by Police Constables Bennett and Baker breezing in through the swing doors.

'Oh, hello, sir,' Bennett said, catching sight of Ashworth. 'We've taken a statement from the station master.' He removed his notebook from the breast pocket of his tunic and flicked to the relevant page. 'He first spotted Samuels's car at midnight the night before last, but he can't recall seeing the owner. Although around that time he did spot a man wearing a black leather jacket and a crash helmet. He remembers thinking it was funny because he couldn't see a motorbike in the car park.'

'Did he watch the man?'

'No, sir, apparently a train came into the station so he had to go on to the platform.'

'Thank you, Gordon. Leave a copy on my desk when it's typed up.'

As they watched the young constables head off towards the canteen, Ashworth suddenly felt very tired.

'I don't know, Martin, I feel as if I'm banging my head against a brick wall.'

'They'll slip up, Jim. They always do.'

'Let's hope. Anyway, I'm off home. I might just have time for a shower at this rate.'

At 8 a.m. he was back at his desk, but strain and lack of sleep were beginning to show on his face. As very little was happening on the supermarket case, Josh and Bobby were despatched to deal with routine matters elsewhere and Ashworth was alone in the office with Holly.

'Why don't you go and have a cup of tea?' she suggested. 'Get away from the office for a while.'

'Where can Samuels be?' he muttered, running impatient fingers through his hair.

'I wish we knew, guv. But uniformed are out there combing the area—'

'But what was the point in taking him?'

He exhaled sharply, then gave her a penitent smile. 'Yes, all right, I think I will go and have a cup of tea.'

She watched him leave, tension showing in his every step, and wished that something would break for all their sakes. She was about to start on a pile of burglary reports when her desk phone buzzed.

'DS Bedford.'

'You must be the good-looking one,' a cheerful male voice said.

'Who is this, please?'

'You don't know me. My name's Dale Spicer. I'm an associate of Jerry Townsend. We've been going through the security tapes from the supermarket and we've come up with something you've missed. Would you like to come round and have a look?' His voice was deep and throaty with an attractive quality about it.

'This isn't a variation on you flashing your etchings, is it?'

He laughed. 'A policewoman with a sense of humour . . . how unusual.'

'A police person to be politically correct. Now, come on, what have you got for us?'

'We'd rather you came and saw it for yourselves. It will interest you, I promise.'

'Okay, give me the address.' She jotted it down, her mind visualizing the expensive apartment block. 'Thanks, we'll be there some time this morning.'

'I'll look forward to it,' he said graciously.

* * *

The address that Dale Spicer had given to Holly turned out to be Jerry Townsend's penthouse apartment on the edge of Bridgetown. Ashworth's step was heavy as they headed for the lift, stopping awhile on the top landing to marvel at the view of Bridgetown and its surrounding countryside.

They wandered along the plush corridor and rang Townsend's bell. The door was promptly opened by a tall, dark and very attractive man somewhere in his thirties.

'Hello, sir, I'm Chief Inspector Ashworth,' he announced in that clipped tone he adopted when things were not going well. 'And this is Detective Sergeant Bedford.'

'Hi, I'm Dale Spicer.'

'You rang me this morning,' Holly said, unwilling to make eye contact.

'I did. Please come in.' He stood aside and let them pass.

The hall was large, and impressive. Spicer led them through a door on their left and into a modern lounge with plain white walls and expensive black leather furniture. Townsend was reclining on one of the chairs, his legs draped over its arm.

'Hello, again. Take a seat,' he said, waving towards the huge settee.

Holly hardly dared walk on the deep-pile white carpet and felt a strong urge to remove her shoes.

'Can I offer you anything?' Townsend asked. 'Tea? Coffee? What about a drink?'

'Nothing, thank you, sir,' Ashworth replied shortly. 'I'd rather see what you've got to show us.'

Surprised by the chief inspector's frosty manner, Townsend's smile faded. 'Right, then, I'll hand you over to Dale.'

'If you'd like to watch the monitor,' Spicer said, 'I'll run the tape through in its original form.'

He pressed a button on the remote control and the screen flashed and flickered until an image came up of an aisle in the Save U Supermarket. There was a woman pushing a trolley, her back to the camera. She wore tight jeans, a loose-fitting tee shirt, and the minute Ashworth saw the white sun hat an uncomfortable feeling began in his chest.

'Do you recognize her?' Townsend asked.

'It's Meg Cowper,' Holly replied.

'That's right. Now, watch this bit. See? She stops to make a call on her mobile telephone . . .'

'She's receiving a call,' Ashworth corrected him. 'She only pressed one button, so she couldn't have been dialling a number.'

'I must admit I didn't notice that,' Townsend said, shooting a sideways glance at Spicer. 'Anyway, keep watching.'

They stared at the screen. Meg continued to walk along the aisle, still pushing her trolley, until her image was little more than a dot.

'There it is,' Townsend exclaimed. 'Can you see it? She stopped and took something from one of the shelves.'

'I can't see anything suspicious in that,' Ashworth scoffed.

'But I can. She took too long.'

'That's when Jerry called me in,' Spicer explained. 'I enhanced and enlarged that part of the tape.' He withdrew the cassette and replaced it with another. 'And this is what I got.'

Spicer pointed the remote control and straight away they saw the enlarged image of Meg. This time they could clearly see her come to a stop by the mixer drinks.

'This is the bit,' Townsend said excitedly.

The detectives leant forward and waited. Meg took two bottles from her trolley and returned them to the shelf then, after idly scanning the display, she chose two more and placed them beside the rest of her shopping.

'What's the date of this tape?' Holly asked.

'It was the day before the mild poisoning cases caused by the ginger ale,' Townsend answered.

Ashworth exhaled. 'We'll have to take that tape.'

'Okay,' Townsend said, removing the video cassette. 'Come through into the kitchen, and I'll get you a box.'

They left Holly with Spicer, who was appraising her in that confident way that attractive men do.

'Nice place,' she remarked, strolling across to a pair of sliding doors leading to the balcony. The view was breathtaking and, she surmised, would have added a few thousand pounds to the price of the apartment. She was about to turn away when her eyes settled on a powerful black motorcycle in a corner of the car park. Her breath quickened.

'It's not bad,' Spicer replied, his smooth voice directly behind her left shoulder.

'Do you ride a motorbike?' she asked, lightly.

'No, I drive a Porsche.'

She turned and gave him a satirical smile. 'I've got a Nissan Micra.'

He chuckled. 'You are indeed a police person with a sense of humour.'

'Who does the motorbike belong to?' she asked, trying hard to sound casual. 'It seems so out of place near an expensive block of flats like these.'

Spicer peered down at the car park. 'Oh, that's Jerry's. He's at an age when he's trying to be eighteen again.'

'But you're not?'

His dark eyes twinkled. 'I'm enjoying being the age I am . . . and I'd like you to have a drink with me.'

Holly's gaze returned to the motorbike. 'Okay. Yes, I'd like that.'

'Tonight, then?' She nodded. 'I live in the apartment directly below this one, and you'll be perfectly safe, I can assure you.'

'I know,' she retorted with a grin. 'The last man who tried to force his attentions on me ended up in hospital.'

Spicer evidently thought she was joking, and he laughed obligingly. 'Shall we say eight p.m.?'

'All right. I'll be there.'

CHAPTER 14

Holly was preoccupied as she followed Ashworth back to the car. Dale Spicer was a very good-looking man, but she had no intention of starting an affair — her interest in him was purely academic. She was eager to find out more about Jerry Townsend; there was something about the man which disturbed her, but she was having difficulty in pinpointing what it could be.

'Townsend owns a motorbike,' she informed Ashworth.

'I don't see what relevance that has,' he answered. 'What possible motive could he have?'

'Don't know, guv, but I may find out tonight. I'm having a drink with Spicer.'

He shot her an old-fashioned look. 'Are you sure that's strictly in the line of duty?'

'Yes,' she snapped, skirting round the Scorpio. 'It may have escaped your attention, guv, but a few days ago I came within seconds of being raped. Now, I know I'm supposed to be game for—'

'Hey . . . hey . . . now, come on, what's all this about?'

'I just don't feel in the mood for any of the nudge-nudge-wink-wink jokes — okay?' She climbed into the car and slammed the door before he had a chance to speak.

'Yes, I think that's plain enough,' he mumbled, opening up the driver's side.

* * *

It was late afternoon, and already the light was fading as Jed Summers went to round up his flock of one hundred and fifty sheep grazing in the long meadow, prior to steering them back towards the farmhouse where they would be less likely to attract the unwelcome attention of sheep rustlers.

Clambering from his Land Rover, Jed ambled to the rear and released his two dogs, Bonnie and Chap. They bounded off in front while he crossed the pasture, noting its long swaying grasses. The flock would have to be brought back for a good few days yet if he were to keep it down.

The sheep were uncomfortable, having picked up the dogs' scents, and were huddled together in groups, bleating warningly. Jed blew the signal for his dogs to spread out and bring them into one group. Chap, a black and white male Collie, ignored the command and stood still, his ears pricked.

Jed sounded his whistle again. 'Chap, go on, boy, get 'em together.'

At the sound of his master's stern tone, the dog started rounding up the sheep, pushing them into one tight pack. But every so often he would stop, paw the ground and bark in the direction of the old cottage while the sheep broke ranks and spread across the field.

'Damn that dog,' Jed muttered. 'Chap, bring 'em together.'

Reluctantly, the dog obeyed, although it kept on looking back towards the cottage. The sheep milled around in the centre of the meadow until one broke away and hurled itself in Jed's direction. The rest soon followed, their hoofs pounding on the hard ground. The dogs ran along the flock's flank, keeping it together, but then Chap stopped again and looked back briefly before continuing his work, wary of his master's wrath.

Jed was a man who had immense love for his dogs, and he also understood them. If Chap was behaving strangely, then there was good reason. Perhaps he'd better give the dog its head and see what came of it.

* * *

Ashworth's instincts might not be infallible but over the years they had proved to be right more often than not. Those instincts were now urging him to temper his actions with caution in the case of Meg Cowper. More and more incriminating facts were piling up against her and Ashworth was at a loss to know why. There was no motive as far as he could see, and certainly no concrete evidence. None of it made any sense.

He had tried earlier in the day to use Holly as a sounding board for his thoughts but she was still in an uncooperative mood and the other two, sensing the strained atmosphere, were keeping their heads down so he was left very much to his own devices.

As far as he could see there were two likely scenarios. Either Meg was involved — and if that was the case then she was making their job very easy — or the real perpetrator was deliberately setting out to point all the clues in her direction. But who would do such a thing?

By five p.m. he had developed a gnawing headache and was looking forward to having the office to himself. Josh and Bobby left spot on five but Holly seemed to be delaying, making much of checking the contents of her shoulder bag.

'Guv,' she said, as soon as they were alone, 'do you think somebody could be setting Meg Cowper up for this?'

'Two minds with but a single thought,' he said, smiling. 'But who, Holly, and why?'

She frowned. 'That's really why I want to find out about Townsend.'

'I still can't see what motive he could have.'

'All roads lead to Meg at the moment, and what possible motive has she got?'

'Yes, I see your point.'

She was hovering by her desk, staring down at her feet. 'Guv, I'm sorry about this morning, but the incident with Brent shook me up.'

'I should have realized that . . . Holly, if there's anything either Sarah or I can do, just say. We'll always be there for you, even if you just want someone to listen.'

'Thanks, guv, but just give me a couple of days and I'll be back to my old self.'

The door was knocked on briskly and a grinning Martin Dutton hurried in. 'Good news, Jim. Richard Samuels has turned up in a derelict cottage on Long Meadow. He was handcuffed to the stair rail. He's in hospital now, none the worse for wear, but they're keeping him in overnight.'

'Now, that is good news,' Ashworth said. 'Thank God he's turned up alive.'

'He's ready to see you at any time.'

'Thanks, Martin.'

As the door closed on the sergeant, Holly glanced at her watch. 'Shall we go, guv?'

'What time's your date?'

'It's not a date, I'm simply going there to find out about Townsend, and it's at eight p.m. but as I won't be making any elaborate preparations for it, I'll have plenty of time.'

* * *

Samuels was sitting up in bed, drinking a cup of tea, when a nurse ushered them into his private room.

'Every time you see me I'm in hospital,' he said wearily.

'How are you, Mr Samuels?' Ashworth asked, pulling up two chairs.

'I'm fine physically, but mentally . . . well, I'm not so sure. What with Shirley's death, and then spending two days in that shell of a cottage.'

'I can understand how distressing that must have been for you, sir. Do you feel up to telling us what happened?'

Samuels nodded and returned his cup to its saucer. 'As I told you on the car phone the night I took the money, there was a man in motorbike gear standing in the middle of the road. He was waving me down—'

'I believe you said he was wearing a crash helmet?' Ashworth cut in.

'Yes, he was.'

'Now, I know it was dark but did you get a close look at it? Did you notice the colour, any motifs on it?'

'I think it was black and white, or blue and white. And it definitely had the letters A, C and E on it.'

'Good. Go on, then.'

'Well, the man got into the passenger seat and shoved a knife in my ribs. He wanted to know if I'd brought the money. When I said yes, it was in a carrier bag on the back seat, he checked that it was all there and then told me to drive on. The road was very bumpy, and it led to the dual carriageway. Anyway, when we got onto it, the man told me where to go next. I'm sorry, Chief Inspector, but I can't remember what the directions were.'

'Don't worry about that. What happened then?'

'He told me to stop the car on a country lane, and then we walked across a field to a tumbledown cottage. He took me inside and handcuffed me to the bannisters in the hall. Then he left me there with a bottle of mineral water and some chocolate bars.'

'Did he say anything, apart from giving you instructions?'

'No, nothing.'

'Would you be able to recognize the voice, do you think?'

'I doubt it. It wasn't very clear — almost as if he had something around his mouth to disguise it.'

'Was the visor on the crash helmet pulled down?'

'At all times.'

'Did you see anyone other than him?'

'No, but after he'd chained me up I heard him outside talking on a radio to a woman. He told her everything had gone according to plan, and he was taking the car to the railway station and he would meet her there.'

'Did you hear the woman's voice?' Ashworth quizzed.

'Plainly, yes. It was the sort of radio you people use.'

'Did you recognize the voice?'

Samuels looked away, and Ashworth noted his slight hesitation.

'Did you recognize the woman's voice, Mr Samuels?'

'No, I think the accent was local, but I wouldn't be prepared to say any more than that.'

'That's a strange turn of phrase to use,' Ashworth remarked. 'Am I to take it that you think you may have recognized the voice?'

'I told you,' Samuels said flatly. 'I've no idea who it was.'

'I see. What about the money? Did that remain on the back seat all through this?'

'No, he had it with him when he took me into the cottage. Before he left, he transferred it to a black briefcase.'

'Do you remember anything about the briefcase?'

Samuels's brow knitted into a frown. 'It was black leather, I think, and quite old. Oh, and there was a tear in one of the bottom corners.'

'Well done,' Ashworth said, checking to see that Holly was getting all relevant details down. 'So, he spoke to a woman on a two-way radio — what happened then, sir?'

'He drove off in my car. I must have been in a state of shock because I can't remember much of what happened after that. There was one terrible moment this morning, though, when I knocked over what was left of the water. I really could see myself dying in the ruins of that cottage, but then a shepherd came to collect his sheep and I started yelling for help.'

Ashworth got to his feet. 'Our forensic team are going over the scene with a fine-tooth comb, Mr Samuels, so let's hope they come up with something. In the meantime, we'll leave you in peace.'

'I don't think I'll ever find peace again, Chief Inspector . . .'

In the corridor they faced each other, both with the same thought.

'I know, Holly, he did recognize the woman's voice, or at least he thought he did.'

'Shouldn't you have pushed him, guv?'

'No,' he said, glancing back at the door. 'That man's been pushed to the edge as it is. But we'll have to bring Meg Cowper in tomorrow and ask her some questions . . . and this time we'd better get some answers.'

'That could be a bit sensitive,' Holly ventured.

'Because of her sister, you mean? Well, too bad, we've got enough to seek out some sort of explanation.'

'I'd better be off, guv,' she said, looking at her watch. 'Let's see what I can find out about Townsend — it might have escaped your notice but the voice Samuels thought he recognized doesn't necessarily have to be Meg's, it could have been Jean Churchman's. In either case he probably thought he was mistaken, which is why he's reluctant to mention it.'

'Or he thought it so ridiculous that he was unwilling to tell us for fear of a slander suit.'

'Anyway, guv, I'd better be going.'

'Be careful,' he said sternly.

CHAPTER 15

Dale Spicer's flat was tastefully decorated in neutral tones which complemented its rust-coloured lounge suite and light ash-wood furniture. Holly chose a chair to the right of the fireplace and surveyed the room while Spicer poured the drinks. So far, he had proved to be the perfect gentleman and she felt able to lower her guard a little. He passed her a glass of dry sherry then sat in the armchair opposite, studying her over the rim of his glass.

'Something tells me you're here on business,' he said.

'And what makes you say that?'

He shrugged. 'Maybe it's in your body language. There you are, sitting bolt upright on the edge of your seat, knees tight together . . . You forget, I'm in the security business so I have to be observant.' He paused to sip his Scotch, a teasing light in his eyes. 'I'd say that you want to know something about Jerry Townsend.'

'And would you be willing to talk, if I did?'

'Why not? As far as I know he hasn't done anything criminal.'

'Is he as successful as he appears?'

Spicer let out a laugh and swirled his drink, the ice cubes clinking against the glass. 'Poor old Jerry doesn't have any delusions of grandeur, but he does aspire to a lifestyle that's way beyond his means.'

'But I thought he had a security business.'

'He has, but he's only just started it, and although he calls himself Arnolds's security consultant, he's actually only on their payroll.'

'So, why the pretence?'

Spicer placed his glass on the carpet and sat back, obviously enjoying the back-stabbing content of the conversation. 'I don't suppose Jerry sees it in that light. He's struggling to get his business off the ground.'

'What's his relationship with Jean Churchman?'

'They do what men and women instinctively get up to . . .' He gave her a playful smile. 'If they spend enough time together, that is.'

Holly looked away. Although the room was pleasantly warm from the heat of the coal-effect gas fire, she was finding it increasingly difficult to relax.

'Their relationship is sexual, then?' she asked, her voice taut.

'That's the polite way of putting it.' He leant forward, and she immediately flinched. 'Now, now, there's no need to be nervous. I was only reaching for your glass.'

'Please, don't,' she said hurriedly. 'Look, it's still half full.'

Scolding herself for coming across as a witless female, Holly directed her mind back to the line of questioning.

'When I asked you about Mr Townsend's relationship with Jean Churchman, your expression indicated that you wouldn't want to change places with him. Why is that?'

'You're very astute,' he said, taking his glass to the drinks table. 'Jean's attractive enough, but she's not my type. A little too horsey, I suppose.' He replenished his Scotch, and then returned to his seat. 'And I don't think she's Jerry's type, either.'

'Then why is he having a relationship with her?'

'This may put Jerry in a bad light . . . You see, Jean lent him the money to start his business. Some fifty grand of it.'

'Fifty thousand?' she echoed.

'That's not a great deal of money to Jean, and I'm not saying that's the sole reason he's going to bed with her.' He sipped his drink. 'But if you owe money and the lender fore-closes on the debt . . .'

'The piper calls the tune.'

'You've got it,' he said, raising his glass. 'You don't actually suspect Jerry of being involved in the supermarket thing, do you?'

'Could you see him doing it?'

He considered the question for longer than Holly would have expected, and then shook his head. 'No, if Jerry had planned it, he would've gone for the big pot. Forty thousand pounds wouldn't interest him.'

'It would clear his debts.'

'You're still not understanding Jerry. He borrowed that money to build a future.' Spicer's dark eyes were alive with devilry as he considered her openly. 'He fancies you, you know.'

'Well, he's wasting his time.' She put her unfinished drink on the carpet and stood up. 'I'd better be going.'

'Holly,' he said, thoughtfully, 'I haven't come onto you in any way, but the distance you're putting between us makes me suspect you think I'm going to attack you.'

She relented somewhat. He really was a nice guy, and she had been rather abrupt with him.

'It's not personal, I can assure you. It's just something I've got to deal with.'

'So maybe some time in the future we could do this again, in a less formal way, perhaps.'

'Maybe,' she said, flashing him a grin. 'Who knows?'

He escorted her to the front door and let her out of the flat. Alone in the deserted corridor, Holly felt like a helpless female, very vulnerable and very afraid. She walked towards the lift with muscles that were tense, as if her subconscious was expecting an attack at any moment. Holly had suffered many times in her life, but never before had she felt so defenceless. It was a state of mind she found abhorrent, and she resolved there and then to pull herself out of it.

* * *

'Oh, bother,' Sarah exclaimed, when the front doorbell rang.

Ashworth uttered a grunt of annoyance as the dog embarked on an orgy of yapping. 'I'm never going to be able to watch this,' he complained, pointing to the television screen where Kenneth Branagh was rallying the troops outside the city gates.

'It's not my fault, dear,' Sarah snapped, holding the video on pause.

Although hampered by the dog running around his ankles, Ashworth finally managed to open the front door and was surprised to see Holly on the doorstep.

'Hello,' he said. 'What are you doing here?'

'I'm not intruding, am I, guv?'

'No, no, of course not. Come in.'

'The thing is, I think I've got something about Townsend . . .'

Sarah appeared at the lounge door.

'I'm sorry to barge in, Mrs Ashworth . . .'

'Don't be silly, dear, it's nice to see you.' She chased the dog around the hall and scooped her up. 'I'll just put this one in the kitchen.'

'Come on through to the lounge,' Ashworth said, taking Holly's arm.

She settled into an armchair and recounted everything that Spicer had said. Ashworth listened attentively but when she had finished Holly was rather disappointed by his doubtful expression.

'If Townsend does owe Jean a lot of money, I concede that she'd have a lever,' he said.

'Don't forget, guv, he had ample opportunity to plant the tampered goods on the supermarket shelves. *And* he's digging up incriminating evidence against Meg.'

'Well, again I can't disagree, but if Jean was forcing him to do that—'

'Or paying him to,' Holly interjected.

'But what's her motive, Holly? If it was Emma Cowper they were trying to put in the frame, I could perhaps understand it — but why Meg?'

'Maybe it would devastate Emma if her little sister got into real trouble. Maybe Jean Churchman's trying to get at her through Meg.'

'No, I can't see that. Emma regards Meg as little more than a child, someone who has to be guided along life's path — there's no love lost between them — and I can't see her being totally devastated if Meg got herself into trouble.'

Holly gave a defeated shrug. 'Sorry, guv, I'm wasting your time, aren't I?' She got to her feet just as Sarah came in with two glasses of sherry.

'Oh, you're not going already, are you, dear? I've poured us a drink.'

Holly looked undecided, but nevertheless said, 'Thank you, I'll stay for ten minutes as long as I'm not in the way.'

'Of course you're not. Sit back down and keep me company. Jim was just going to feed the dog, weren't you, dear?'

'Was I?' He caught her eye. 'Oh, yes, of course I was. I won't be long, Holly.' He picked up his whisky and soda and left the women together.

'Well, dear, how are you?' Sarah asked, settling back with her drink.

'I'm very well,' Holly replied awkwardly.

Sarah paused, then said, 'Jim told me what happened with that man, Brent.'

Holly took a large sip of sherry, and then blurted, 'It's shaken me, Mrs Ashworth, to be honest.'

'Well, of course it has. It was a terrible thing to happen.'

'I mean, being attacked is one thing — I'm trained to cope with that — but it's the rape part that disturbs me. The guy was paid to frighten me . . . fair enough, ours isn't an easy job. But when he got into my bedroom, I started to wonder . . . oh, I don't know.'

'You wondered whether you were sending out the wrong signals?'

Holly looked up, surprised. 'Yes, absolutely. How did you . . . ?'

'It's common in cases of rape and attempted rape,' Sarah explained. 'I was involved in a Samaritans course once, and during it I attended a couple of talks on the subject. Victims of rape nearly always blame themselves . . . it's for that very reason that a lot of women refuse to report the crime. So, you mustn't blame yourself, dear, because it wasn't your fault.'

'I'm finding it difficult not to.'

'Most men are not rapists, but Brent obviously is — it's as simple as that. It's nothing you've done, Holly.'

'I was sure I'd never go to pieces in that sort of situation, Mrs Ashworth, and I think that's what's frightened me more than anything. Now, I lie in bed knowing that there's only a front door and a few panes of glass between me and anybody . . .'

'It will pass, dear, believe me. It will pass.'

* * *

Ashworth arrived early at the station the following morning and was relieved to find Josh and Bobby already in the office.

'I'd like a word with you two before Holly comes in,' he said, hanging up his jacket. 'Now, it seems that she's taken this attempted rape rather badly. I must admit the possibility of that happening never entered my head. Apparently she's frightened of being in the house alone at night, and she's developed a fear of men. Sarah assures me she'll get over it, but in the meantime, I think we should do everything possible to help her.'

They readily agreed.

'Good. Now that's out of the way, I'll fill you in with some new details on the supermarket case.'

He told them of his interview with Richard Samuels and Holly's meeting with Dale Spicer. Josh sat listening, nodding now and then, but Bobby was taking it all down in a hurried shorthand which he had probably learnt through a postal course.

'Later today,' Ashworth concluded, 'Holly and I shall be bringing Meg Cowper in for questioning, and I want you to deal with all other CID business while we're doing so. That's about it, so let's get on with some work.'

* * *

Meg Cowper was surprisingly passive when they asked her to accompany them to the station to answer a few questions. She was locking the stable door, her face a blank, when Jean Churchman called cheerily from the archway. Meg waited while the woman hurried towards them, her progress hindered by the large bunch of rhubarb in her arms; and in a controlled, steady voice she asked Jean to get word to Emma's office and then strode purposefully to Ashworth's car.

Her demeanour was no different at the police station. She showed not a flicker of emotion on the way to the interview room where she sat patiently waiting for the questioning to begin.

'You do understand that you're here of your own free will?' Ashworth began. 'You're simply helping us with our enquiries, at the moment.'

'Yes,' she responded, staring blankly ahead, 'but I can't think how I could possibly help you. Anyway, I'd like to get this over with quickly. I've had some very distressing news, and I . . .' She faltered. 'Oh, it doesn't matter . . . just get on with it.'

Ashworth waited for Holly to record the time and date of the interview, and then he said, 'We've already talked to you about oxalic acid, but could you reiterate for the benefit of the tape recorder?'

'I use oxalic acid in my work, either to bring out the natural colour of the wood or, as it's a corrosive, to remove ingrained stains . . . Look, Chief Inspector, just ask yourself — if I wanted to go around killing people wouldn't I be silly to use something that could be traced straight back to me?'

'Point taken,' Ashworth said softly. 'Now let's talk about the night before last. You were in your car on the Aldridge Farm road. Can you explain what you were doing there?'

He saw pain flicker in her eyes for a brief moment, and then she said, 'Do I have to? I mean, I was driving on a public road, after all. You've got no right to pry into my private life.'

'You must have been there for a reason,' he persisted.

'I was out for a drive,' she replied in a flat monotone.

'There's something else, Meg. You've turned up on the security tape from the Save U Supermarket. It shows you reaching into your trolley and replacing some bottles on a shelf . . .'

She gave a derisory laugh. 'Are you serious? What does all this add up to?'

'Meg, as you well know certain products in that supermarket have been tampered with. People have been poisoned; an innocent woman has died. Now, in view of all that, we're well within our rights to ask you to explain your actions.'

'What actions?' she yelled. 'Chief Inspector, I'm very pleased that Richard Samuels has turned up okay, and I'm sorry about what happened to his wife and those other people, but I can't for the life of me see what it has to do with me.'

'Then tell us why you were putting those bottles on the shelf . . .'

The quiet of the interview room was abruptly punctured by a commotion in the corridor, and when Emma Cowper's piercing voice could be heard overriding Superintendent Newton's pacifying tone, Ashworth exhaled loudly. He had half risen from his chair when the door flew open and Emma came striding in, the perplexed superintendent following closely behind.

'Would somebody mind telling me what's going on here?' she bawled.

'Calm down, Emma,' Ashworth cajoled.

'Calm down? You drag my sister into the police station—'

'Meg wasn't dragged anywhere. She's here of her own free will — a fact I am sure she'll verify.'

'This is all over the town,' she said, with an accusing glance at Meg. 'How do you think it looks — the sister of a leading councillor, brought into the station like a common criminal? If this has any repercussions, Jim, I'll report you to the Chief Constable.'

Ashworth shot a pleading look at Newton, who was hovering ineffectually on the threshold, and then said, 'Emma, if you don't stop behaving in this fashion, I'm going to charge you with impeding a police investigation.'

'What?' she mouthed, her eyes wide with outrage.

At the door the superintendent shuffled indecisively, fully aware that he should be taking control of the situation, but at the sight of the woman rearing up for another attack he decided to stay where he was.

'I've made this point to you many times in the past,' Ashworth went on, 'but I'll say it just once more — when people are dealing with me, Emma, it'll never be a case of he who shouts the loudest gets his own way, whether those people are criminals or local councillors. Am I making myself clear?'

Emma seemed close to an apoplectic fit as she stood clenching and unclenching her fists, her eyes fixed on Ashworth's forbidding glare; but realizing that on this occasion she would not get her own way, she strove to control her breathing, and asked politely, 'Have you finished with my sister?'

'Surely.' He turned to Meg and gave her a kindly smile. 'Thank you for coming in.'

Immediately they were outside the interview room, Emma turned on her. 'What the hell have you been doing? Can't you understand how embarrassing this is?'

'Oh, shut up, Emma.'

'My God, and to think I'm hoping to be selected as a Conservative candidate for the next election.'

'Oh, for goodness' sake, shut up.'

'Don't you dare tell me to shut up.'

The door at the end of the corridor slammed and the shouting ceased. Superintendent Newton shot a despairing look in the chief inspector's direction and set off to find the women. Ashworth calmly closed the door and turned to Holly.

'And there we have a motive for Jean Churchman to commit a crime and make it look as if Meg was involved.'

'I agree, guv, because that would be the perfect way for Jean to get at Emma.'

'Exactly. I didn't think Emma would've been bothered, but obviously I was wrong. For her to be stripped of the trappings of office and held up to ridicule . . .'

'Jean Churchman would feel her revenge was complete.'

Ashworth smiled. 'Yes, and if we're right, it shouldn't be long before some highly incriminating evidence turns up against Meg, because all we've got at the moment is a lot of maybes.'

CHAPTER 16

When Richard Samuels was discharged from hospital his first call was to the offices of the local newspaper, the *Bridgetown Post*. He was shown at once to the editor's office by a pretty young receptionist who had been instructed that the man must not be kept waiting.

The editor, Kenneth Panting, was tall and heavy, with dark patches of sweat permanently at his armpits and a stomach which hung over his trouser belt. When Samuels was shown in, Panting was straight away on his feet, his hand outstretched.

'Richard, how are you?'

'Hello, Ken,' he said with a melancholy smile.

'Take a seat.' Panting waved vaguely at his desk, which was littered with files and reporters' copy waiting to be accepted, and said, 'I've been reading the police hand-out on what happened to you. It's to be our lead story in tonight's edition.'

'I'm here to beg a favour, Ken . . .'

Panting looked up sharply. 'I hope you don't want us to cut any of the story.'

'No, no,' Samuels assured him. 'In fact, I'm here to offer you another story.'

A calculating glint came into Panting's eyes. 'Really? Now, that's interesting.'

'The Save U Supermarket chain is going into liquidation. This extortion business is totally responsible for the collapse. Our stores have been closed, and there's no way of knowing which way it could go if and when they reopen.'

'I'm sorry to hear that,' Panting said, eager for the man to reach his point.

'The fact is, I've made an offer for the stores. I want to buy out the other directors.'

'Risky . . .'

'It is, but I can get them for a knockdown price. I've mortgaged everything I own.' He leant forward, his expression impassioned. 'This is important to me, Ken. I want to keep the stores open to honour Shirley's memory.'

'That's a good angle for a story, Richard. It could generate a lot of public sympathy.'

'You'll run the story, then? There could be quite an amount of advertising, as well.'

'No need for sweeteners on this,' Panting said with a smile. 'It'll make first-rate copy. Richard Samuels's tribute to his wife . . . one man's determination to rise above the tide of crime.'

Samuels rose from his chair. 'Thanks for being so receptive, Ken.'

'Quite all right. No trouble at all.'

Even before Samuels had left the office, the editor was already scribbling on his pad: I'll keep the Save U Supermarkets open to honour my dead wife's name, vows heartbroken director.

'Yes, nice . . . very nice.'

* * *

On the way home from work, Holly called at Jean Churchman's house in the hope of catching Meg there. She pulled up to find her struggling to fit a coffee table into the boot of her car.

'Hi,' Holly said, with a friendly wave. 'I thought I'd drop by to apologize for this morning.'

'It's okay . . . and I've a feeling I should be the one apologizing for my sister's behaviour.'

'Here, let me help,' she said, when Meg once again tried to get the table into the boot.

They grabbed opposite ends and made repeated attempts to manoeuvre the table into place, but each time they were thwarted.

'Oh, hold on,' Holly said, 'there's something stopping it from lying flat.' She slipped her hand under the table and pulled out a black briefcase which she put to one side. 'There, I reckon you should be able to close it now.'

When the boot clicked shut, Meg turned to consider the detective. 'You're not really here to apologize, are you?'

'Only partly,' Holly admitted. 'Look, this is just a friendly visit, nothing official . . . Can you think of any reason why someone might want to make it look as if you had something to do with the supermarket job?'

'No, I can't. I really can't. And as this is a friendly visit, I'll be friendly too, but you haven't got any evidence to connect me with anything. If you had I'd be arrested by now. All you have is a few coincidences.'

'You're clever,' Holly said, grinning.

Meg's mouth flicked up into a reluctant smile. 'I'm not as thick as my sister would have everyone believe.'

'Do you know what I think?' Holly said, leaning against the car. 'I think you're concealing a boyfriend.'

An angry flush rose up on her freckled cheeks, but when she spoke Meg's voice was without emotion. 'My personal life is none of your business, Sergeant,' she said, stepping round to the driver's side. 'Thanks for helping with the table.'

'That's okay.'

'How's your sex life, by the way?'

'What do you mean?' Holly asked, across the roof of the car.

'Is anybody screwing you? And if so, how many times a week? I bet if I really wanted to know, you'd soon tell me to mind my own business.'

Holly's answering grin was conciliatory and when Meg drove off, she muttered, 'I think I've just been given a bollocking.'

* * *

For the first time since her attack, Holly arrived home without a feeling of dread and realized that she was at last managing to put the incident into some sort of perspective. She was able to take her time in the shower and felt no compulsion to dress afterwards, deciding instead to lounge about in her dressing gown — something she had not done since that night. But dread still jumped into her throat when the doorbell rang a while later. Pulling the dressing gown tight, she went to open the door.

'Hello, Bedford,' Josh said, with an inane grin.

'What are you doing here?' she asked fondly.

He held up a carrier bag. 'I've brought my Chinese round to share with you.'

She giggled. 'I was going to say I haven't got anything on, but that wouldn't make any difference to you, would it?'

'Do I detect a return to your old base self?' he asked, following her through to the kitchen.

'Actually, I am starting to feel better about things. Get the grub out and I'll find some plates.'

'I could stay a couple of nights,' he offered. 'Crash out on the settee.'

Holly reached across and gave his arm a grateful squeeze. 'You're a good mate, Abraham.'

'Oh, Christ, don't go all dramatic on me. I only offered to stay a couple of nights, there's no need to turn it into *Gone With the Wind*.'

She laughed and helped him with the containers.

'Right,' he said, 'it's duck and pineapple, or duck and pineapple. So you'd better like duck and pineapple.'

'I love it,' she assured him.

The plates were piled high, and crispy pancake rolls were on side dishes when the doorbell sounded again.

'Oh, shit,' she exclaimed, eyeing the food hungrily. 'Double shit.'

Josh was biting into a pancake roll, savouring its crispy texture and spicy taste, when he heard Holly say, 'Bobby . . . what are you doing here?'

'I was just passing, so I thought I'd call in and make sure you were okay.'

Josh grinned to himself.

'I'm feeling great — come in. Josh's here.'

'I'll just hang my coat up, if that's all right.'

'Yes, fine,' she said, hurrying into the kitchen. 'Josh, it's Bobby. I'll just slip upstairs and put some clothes on.'

'What for? You didn't put any on when I got here.'

'That's because you're a poof. The sight of my beautiful body wouldn't do anything to you—'

'Oh yes, it would . . . it'd make me feel sick,' he said, ducking to miss her playful slap and dripping hot fat from the roll on to his rugby shirt. 'Oh, no, look what I've done now.'

'Hello, Josh,' Bobby said, standing awkwardly on the threshold.

'Hi, Bobby.'

'We can share the food out,' Holly said, getting another plate. 'I'll just nip up and put some clothes on.'

She was halfway up the stairs when a thought came into her mind, stopping her dead. 'You stupid cow,' she murmured to herself. 'Why didn't you spot it at the time?'

* * *

First thing next morning Meg exploded as soon as Ashworth and Holly walked into the stables.

'Oh, my God, not you two again,' she spat, throwing her paint brush to the floor. 'What do you want now?'

'I'm sorry, Meg,' Ashworth said, 'but DS Bedford was here yesterday evening and believes that she saw a briefcase in the boot of your car which answers the description of one we're looking for in connection with the supermarket case.'

'This is ridiculous,' Meg said, close to tears. 'I feel like I'm being hounded by you.'

'Could we see the case?' Holly asked.

'Follow me.' She pushed between them and flounced to her car. They followed and reached the vehicle just as Meg was throwing open the lid of the boot. 'There it is,' she spat. 'Take a good look.'

Ashworth peered inside and studied the case. It was made of black leather, clearly expensive and quite old; but what excited him most of all was the small tear on its bottom left-hand corner.

'Do you mind if we take this away for examination?'

'Do what you want,' Meg said through gritted teeth.

Taking a handkerchief from his pocket, Ashworth carefully wound it around the handle of the case while Holly ran to the Scorpio and returned with a large polythene bag into which the briefcase was deposited.

'Thank you,' he said lamely.

Meg gave him a withering look, then strode back to the stables.

'Guv,' Holly whispered, 'if she had anything serious to hide, she'd be frightened to death by now.'

'I know. Whatever it is she's hiding — and there is something — it's got nothing to do with extortion. But we'll have to keep on at her because we need to know exactly what is going on.'

* * *

Richard Samuels was in urgent discussion with Emma Cowper when the two detectives were shown into the office at the Save U Supermarket, and Ashworth was not slow to observe that their arrival had startled them somewhat.

Samuels, the first to recover, said, 'I want to put advertising boards on the pavement outside the store, Chief Inspector, and I'm trying to persuade Emma to use her influence with the council.'

'And sympathetic as I am,' Emma said, 'I'm having to point out that should a member of the public trip over one, even through their own stupidity, the council remains liable.'

Ashworth, in no mood to share shallow chat with the councillor, strode to the desk and placed the sealed plastic bag in front of Samuels.

'Is this the briefcase you saw your abductor putting the money into?'

Samuels picked up the bag and peered at the exhibit from different angles. 'It's certainly similar, yes. The tear seems to be in the same place.' He looked from Ashworth to Holly. 'Does this mean you've caught the man?'

Ashworth ignored the question and turned instead to the councillor, his feelings of perplexity plunging to new depths.

'I'm sorry, Emma . . .'

'It's Meg, isn't it?'

'I'm afraid we found the case in the boot of her car.'

Emma's shoulders hunched and she brought her hands to her face, the shock leaving her speechless.

Ashworth turned back to Samuels. 'Sir, I have to put this to you . . . when we asked if you recognized the voice of the woman you heard on the radio at the cottage, you said you didn't. Was that really the case?'

'I'm sorry, Emma, I really am,' he said, his eyes begging her forgiveness, 'but, yes, it did sound like Meg's voice. I wouldn't swear to it in court, mind you, but . . .'

The councillor began to weep softly.

'Don't upset yourself,' Holly said, resting a hand on the woman's shoulder.

'I'm all right,' she said, quickly composing herself. 'I knew something was going on . . . she's been acting so strangely. But I just can't believe she'd get involved in anything like this.' She reached into her pocket for a handkerchief and wiped away the tears.

'We shall have to question her,' Ashworth said. 'All I can promise is that we'll be as discreet as possible.'

Emma turned her dazed eyes to him. 'I won't be causing you any more problems, Jim. I know you're only doing your job.'

CHAPTER 17

The councillor had been granted permission to speak to her sister alone in number one interview room while Ashworth waited outside. He paced the corridor, wincing at every bellowed rebuke. Meg had at first answered with stubborn silence, but now each of Emma's admonishments were met with loud retaliation and the result was a quarrel which was spiralling out of control.

He was on the point of intervening when Holly emerged through the swing doors, chatting to a uniformed officer, a coffee for Meg in her hand. They reached the chief inspector and both frowned quizzically at the raised voices.

'I know,' he said, with an impatient glance. 'When I agreed to allow Emma a few words, I didn't think it would turn into a shouting match.'

They listened for a while longer, and then Ashworth strode forward and rapped on the door. 'Time to break it up, I think.'

Emma opened the door, her expression betraying the hot annoyance so clear in her voice.

'I've tried to talk some sense into her, Jim, but it's like beating my head against a wall. I've said she's to tell you everything and hold nothing back.' She shot a scornful look at her sister, and said pointedly, 'She's only got herself in this position because she's none too bright.'

She pushed past and stood in the corridor emitting exaggerated sounds of frustration while they filed into the room, the uniformed officer closing the door and taking up his position to the right of it. Holly, setting the coffee in front of Meg with a sympathetic smile, moved to the tape recorder and Ashworth took his seat at the table. Meg's eyes were transfixed on the briefcase, still in its sealed bag, sitting accusingly in front of her, the steam from the coffee causing her to blink.

'Tell me about it, Meg,' Ashworth coaxed.

'I've got nothing to tell you,' she replied, her eyes still on the case.

'How did it get into the boot of your car?'

She took a sip of coffee, then said, 'I put it there. It belongs to a friend of mine.'

'Who is he? What's his name?'

'I don't want to tell you.'

'Meg, you must understand, I've already got enough to charge you with murder and extortion.'

She looked up then, and there was an incongruous glint of hope in her eyes. 'Will it be in the papers?'

Ashworth frowned, and she added quickly, 'I don't mean if I'm charged, I mean will it be in the papers that I'm here for questioning?'

'The papers may report that someone is helping us with our enquiries,' Ashworth explained, 'but they won't name you. If you're thinking about Emma . . .'

'No . . . no, I'm not.' She shot him a defiant look. 'I've said all I'm going to say.'

'You're in a lot of trouble, young lady, and this attitude you're adopting isn't going to help you at all. Now, I'm going to hold you here for the rest of today and possibly overnight in the hope that it'll make you see sense.'

She finished her coffee and got to her feet, her movements entirely passive.

'Escort her to the cells,' he ordered the constable.

Meg followed him, a look of utter indifference on her face, and Ashworth let out an exasperated sigh. Holly intoned the concluding details to the tape recorder and turned to him.

'She's covering for somebody, guv.'

'But, why? It doesn't make any sense. That woman may have been hoodwinked into taking part in this crime, but I can't believe that she'd cover for anyone once it was explained in simple language exactly what she'd got herself involved in.'

'I sense something else, guv,' Holly said thoughtfully. 'I think it's just beginning to dawn on her that she may have been conned, and she's searching around in her mind for whoever set her up.'

'This is getting a bit deep for me,' he complained.

'My guess is, she's hoping her lover's going to come galloping to her rescue with answers to all our questions. I bet that's why she asked if she'd be in the papers.'

'But he won't know she's here until she's charged.'

'Exactly. Guv, I'd like a quiet word with her in the morning before she's interviewed again — a little girl-to-girl chat. I'd like to try and build up some sort of rapport with her.'

'All right.' He took a long look at her. 'You seem a bit better today.'

'I am, guv. Brent disturbed me a lot, but I'm over him, now.'

'You know what your trouble is, don't you?'

She sighed. 'No, but I bet you're going to tell me.'

'You think you're a hard case, because you can look after yourself . . .' He scooped up the empty coffee cup and threw it into the waste bin. 'But inside you're a sensitive little soul.'

She grinned. 'Yes, well, don't tell anybody, guv, or you'll ruin my image.'

* * *

Business was slow at the Save U Supermarket. Richard Samuels telephoned neighbouring stores at intervals throughout the morning only to be informed that custom was no better at any of them. However, help arrived early in the afternoon in the guise of a correspondent from a commercial television station. The man telephoned to say that he had heard of Samuels's plight and asked whether he would be allowed to visit the store with his sound and camera crew and conduct an on-the-spot interview.

Samuels wasted no time in agreeing and after the broadcast was screened — in which he was depicted as a man bravely coping with the death of his wife by keeping open an ailing chain of supermarkets as a memorial to her — trade immediately began to pick up; indeed there were long queues at every checkout at all branches. Suddenly Richard Samuels was a sympathetic figure, a hero holding out against crime, and he positively wallowed in the attention and the scores of goodwill messages that poured in with every post.

* * *

'Excuse me, Mr Dallington,' the hotel receptionist called to the tall, handsome man heading for the door.

'Yes?' he said in a cultured tone, returning to the desk.

'Will the young lady be joining you later?' the man asked in a whisper.

'No, not tonight.' He tapped the side of his nose. 'And mum's the word as far as she's concerned . . . eh?'

'Yes, sir, don't worry, I just wondered . . .'

'That's all right.' Dallington opened up his wallet and extracted a ten-pound note which he stuffed into the man's breast pocket.

'Oh, thank you, sir,' he beamed at the departing figure.

* * *

Holly followed Martin Dutton down the stone steps to the police cells.

'I didn't like keeping her in overnight, you know,' he muttered over his shoulder. 'I mean, the girl's got a bit of class.'

'Couldn't be helped, Martin. I just hope a night down here makes her a bit more reasonable.'

'So do I,' he said, leading her towards the end of the block. 'From what Jim was saying, she could be in for the big drop if she doesn't start cooperating.'

'She can be certain of it,' Holly assured him.

'Here, where's my fuckin' breakfast?' a prisoner called on hearing their footsteps. 'Get it here now, or I'll wreck the fuckin' place.'

Dutton straight away opened the hatch in the cell door, and yelled, 'Keep quiet . . . we've got a lady down here.' The hatch was slammed shut.

'Thanks, Martin,' Holly said, giving a slight curtsy.

'I meant Meg Cowper,' he said, hiding a grin.

'Hah, I should have known.'

'That's nothing new to you, Holly, you've heard it all before.'

'And worse, Martin . . . and worse.'

Meg's name was chalked in large letters on a small blackboard attached to the door of the end cell. Dutton selected a key from his belt and noisily opened up.

'DS Bedford to see you, Miss Cowper.' He turned to Holly. 'I'll leave it unlocked. If you could let me know when you've finished . . .'

She nodded and stepped into the confined space. Meg was sitting on the bed looking small and dejected, a pitiful sight.

'Do you want anything?' Holly asked.

She shook her head.

The heavy door creaked on its hinges as Holly pushed it to. 'Hardly the Savoy, is it?' she said lightly.

Meg gazed around the cell, and her 'no' was a tiny sound.

'Do you feel like talking to us? You'll have to sooner or later, you know.'

'I've got nothing to say.'

'Meg,' Holly said, crouching in front of her, 'you're an intelligent woman.'

'Huh, tell that to my sister.'

'You're an intelligent woman, and you know you're in a lot of trouble here.'

'I . . . I can't tell you.'

'You're protecting somebody, aren't you?'

When she remained quiet, Holly decided to get straight to the point. 'He's married . . . that's why you're not talking, isn't it? You're putting yourself through all this to protect him.'

'When he knows I'm here,' Meg said, dreamily, 'he'll come forward. That way his wife won't have to know.'

'But you'll be charged by then. It'll be a far bigger problem for your boyfriend if that happens. We'd have to withdraw the charges for a start, and the press would want to know why. You'd have reporters digging around for ages, believe me, and they wouldn't leave you alone until they'd got their story.'

Meg bit on her lower lip, and tiny worry lines showed on her forehead while she considered Holly's words.

'His wife wouldn't have to know?' she asked eventually.

'Meg, we're not out to spoil anybody's fun.'

'It wasn't fun,' she said dismally.

'It is the way I do it,' Holly grinned.

Despite the awfulness of the situation Meg laughed; only briefly, but it served to lighten the atmosphere.

'That's better,' Holly encouraged. 'Look, Meg, I know you're in love. I understand, and I promise that if your story checks out we'll be so discreet, there's no way any embarrassment will be caused to either you or your boyfriend.'

'I would've liked him to come forward. It would've proved that I wasn't just . . . just . . .'

'A bit on the side?'

She let out a harrowing sigh and looked away. 'That's such a horrible term, isn't it?'

'I've been there,' Holly admitted ruefully. 'I do understand.'

Suddenly Meg turned to her, a new determination on her face. 'I will talk to you, Sergeant, but I don't want to discuss my private life in front of the Chief Inspector. The thing is, I went to bed with James on our second date and . . . well, I wouldn't want him to know that.'

'No problem at all. I'll get someone a little less judgemental. Now, is there anything else worrying you?'

Meg stared ahead for many seconds, her mind in an obvious turmoil, and her eyes were moist with threatening tears when she finally said, 'There is something worrying me, yes. I'm worried that James did have something to do with it all. I'm frightened that he was just using me. And if that is the case I couldn't bear it, Sergeant, I really couldn't.'

* * *

Holly sauntered into CID, highly pleased with herself.

'Right, guv, Meg's in the interview room, ready and willing to talk to us.'

'Good girl,' Ashworth enthused, already rising from his chair.

'There's just one small problem. Apparently the story gets a bit dirty in places and she doesn't think it's fit for your tender ears.'

'What?'

'She feels your presence would inhibit her.'

'I'd inhibit her?' he said, his tone implying that such a fact was beyond belief.

Holly was finding it hard to keep a straight face at the sight of his open-mouthed expression, but she carried on breezily, 'Yes, strange, guv, isn't it . . . really weird. Anyway, I'd like Josh to do the interview with me.'

Ashworth reluctantly agreed and returned to his seat. 'But don't forget, we need to know who she was talking to on the phone from the supermarket, and—'

'Don't worry, guv,' she smiled, leaning across his desk. 'I have done this before — I've got a rough idea how to go about it. Come on, Josh.'

'Cheeky madam,' Ashworth laughed, as they left the office. 'Well, she seems to be back to normal.'

'I think she is, guv,' Bobby said, still watching the door. 'She's a really nice girl.'

Ashworth considered the young man, took in his greased-down hair parted on the left, his fresh young face, and hoped for the boy's sake that he was not nurturing any romantic notions involving Holly. If you are, then forget it, he thought wryly; Holly Bedford would be a baptism of fire for you, son.

CHAPTER 18

'Right, Abraham,' Holly said, on the way to the interview room, 'I've arranged for a WPC to be present, and I want you to man the tape recorder and generally keep a low profile.'

'Yes, sir,' he mumbled.

'I heard that,' she laughed, pointing a finger. 'But, seriously, Josh, if I can get that girl talking the flood gates are just going to blow.'

'Do you think she is involved in it?'

'Meg's either been set up,' she said, pushing open the swing doors, 'or she's very clever.'

'But if she's that clever, she wouldn't have made so many mistakes.'

'True. Anyway, we should at least find out the identity of the married boyfriend, and that has to move the case forward.' They reached the interview room and went inside.

Meg looked thoroughly washed out, and her eyes were large with apprehension now that her predicament had been so graphically detailed. Holly introduced her to Josh, who simply smiled and wandered across to the tape recorder, deliberately adopting an air of complete detachment.

Holly faced her across the table. 'Whenever you're ready, Meg. Just take your time.'

Meg shot a glance at the young policewoman at the door, and said, 'My boyfriend's name is James Dallington. He lives in Morton, and he's a company director.'

'What sort of company?'

'I don't know,' she said, with an apologetic shake of the head.

'And he's married, yes?'

'Yes.'

'Do you know his address in Morton?'

'No.'

'Are you sure? It's important.'

'Honest to God, I don't know his address,' she said a trembling hand rising to her forehead.

'Don't worry, Meg, it's all right.'

'He took me to see his home once,' she said haltingly. 'Only from the outside, of course. He parked opposite.'

'What was it like?'

'Very big, detached. It was painted white. The whole area was really upmarket.'

'Do you remember anything else about it? Any features that would help us to find it?'

Meg frowned, a fingernail between her teeth, and her eyes flicked frantically across the tabletop as she tried hard to remember the slightest detail that might be of use.

'There was scaffolding . . . it was either being erected or taken down, I don't know which.' She shook her head. 'I'm sorry, I can't think of anything . . . Oh, wait a minute, it had a long stained-glass window on the side wall. While we sat opposite, James was telling me how unhappy he was with his wife, and then I saw her. She was walking upstairs and I saw her through that window.'

'What does James look like, Meg?'

'He's tall,' she said with a wistful smile. 'Very good-looking, brown hair, brown eyes, and he's always smartly dressed.'

Holly sighed inwardly. Not much to work on there; any number of men would fit that description.

'Where did you meet him?'

'He came to my workshop looking for some furniture. We got chatting and he asked me out.'

'Did you know he was married?'

'He told me on the first date.' She shrugged. 'I thought, well, that's it, I won't go out with him again.'

'But you did. Why?'

'Even while I was deciding not to, he asked me to make a telephone call for him . . .' She shot Holly a resigned look. 'The call was to book a hotel room for the following night. Do you see? It was a room for two . . . I was arranging my own seduction.'

'Where was the hotel, Meg? What was the name of it?'

'I think it was in Morton, but I can't remember the name. I'm sorry, I . . .'

'It's okay, we can check it out,' Holly said soothingly. 'Go on.'

Meg stole a glance at Josh, who sat with his back towards her, apparently uninterested, and then she leant forward, her voice lowered. 'After that night, I was so hopelessly in love with him, I would've done anything he asked.'

'And what exactly did you do?'

Meg hesitated, unsure of the question, but when its significance became clear she rose up in her chair, and said, 'Not any of the things you think I did.'

Holly realized that she was getting nowhere fast, but afraid of alienating the woman she strove to keep her approach amicable.

'What were you doing in the Save U Supermarket, putting bottles of ginger ale back onto the shelves?'

'Sergeant, I know it looks suspicious,' she said fearfully, 'but it was really quite innocent. I often went shopping for James in my lunch hour and on that day he'd asked me to get some ginger ale. Anyway, while I was in the store he rang me on my mobile phone and told me not to get Arnolds's brand because of what had happened. But I'd already put some bottles in my trolley, so I just took them back and changed them.'

'I see,' Holly said, studying her closely. 'And what were you doing on the road to Aldridge Farm?'

'James feels the same way as I do about our relationship . . .' She faltered on the words, fighting back the tears that were never far away. 'He was going to leave his wife. It wasn't an easy decision — he agonized over it because of his children — but finally he said he couldn't live without me. We . . . we were going away together, and he asked me to meet him on the farm road at eight p.m. that night. When he hadn't arrived by nine I knew he wasn't coming, so I left.'

Tears coursed down Meg's cheeks and Holly had to turn away. She looked so desolate, so hurt, and yet she still believed in the man even though it was obvious that she had been duped.

'Did you see him again after that? After the time you arranged to go away together, I mean?'

Meg balked at the sympathetic note in Holly's voice. 'This wasn't some cheap little affair, Sergeant. James really does love me.'

'Keep calm, I didn't say otherwise.' She waited while Meg pulled a tissue from her sleeve and wiped her face. 'When did you see him again?'

'The next day,' she said, blindly tearing the tissue into shreds. 'He telephoned me at the workshop and asked me to meet him at lunchtime in a lay-by on the dual carriageway leading to Bridgetown.'

'And what happened?'

'He was already there when I arrived. He told me . . .' She suddenly fell forward, her face in her hands, deep sobs rocking her fragile body. 'He told me that his wife had been having tests over the last few weeks and the day before her doctors had diagnosed multiple sclerosis.'

'And because of that he couldn't leave her?' Holly concluded.

She nodded, a hand still covering her face.

'When did he put the briefcase into the boot of your car?' Holly asked gently.

She straightened up. 'I can't remember. I was thinking about that all last night, but I just can't remember.'

'Try, Meg, it's very important.'

'I can't,' she sobbed. 'I can't remember.'

'But it's so important. Can't you see that it's inconceivable that he'd leave it there on the day you were breaking up? — and yet if it is the briefcase we're looking for, then he must have done.'

'I've told you, Sergeant, I can't remember.' The words were slowly spat out, any hope of a continued rapport gone.

'All right, that's all for today,' Holly said sharply.

When she started to leave her seat, Meg glanced up and put out a hand to stop her. 'Can I have a word with you? Just the two of us?'

Holly nodded and signalled for Josh and the WPC to leave them alone. Josh terminated the interview on the tape recorder and followed the woman officer out.

'James has made a fool of me, hasn't he?' Meg said in a faltering voice. 'He's used me, hasn't he?'

'Everything should be a lot clearer when we've spoken to this James Dallington,' Holly replied, her tone deliberately noncommittal.

Meg stood up and crossed to the window, her back to Holly. 'I could see it all when I was telling you. Everything that happened makes it look as if I was involved, doesn't it?'

'Yes, I'm afraid it does.'

She turned, her face etched with misery. 'I can't believe James would do this to me. He told me he loved me.'

'Like I said, things should be clearer once we've spoken to him.'

'Even if James did do those things . . .' She swallowed loudly. 'Even if he did kill Shirley Samuels, demanded money from the supermarket . . . why did he have to involve me?'

'I see what you're getting at,' Holly said, joining her at the window. 'There was no obvious advantage in doing that.'

She thought for a while. 'Meg, is there anyone who has a grudge against you? Anyone who'd enjoy seeing you in trouble?'

'There's no one I can think of,' she said, her lower lip quivering. 'I know I can be a bit silly about men, but I've never hurt anybody.' She broke down then, her face to the wall.

'Hey, stop that now,' Holly coaxed, pulling Meg into her arms.

'Do you believe me, Sergeant?'

'Yes, I do, and my guv'nor's on your side as well. We'll find this Dallington and see what he has to say.'

Meg pulled away, alarm in her eyes. 'But say you can't find him?'

'We'll find him, don't worry.'

'Oh, God, what's Emma going to say?'

'She's the least of your worries, now stop panicking. It's going to be all right — okay?'

'Will I have to stay here?'

'I'm afraid so, at least until we've had a chance to interview Dallington.'

Meg nodded resignedly and Holly prepared to leave. At the door she stopped. 'Oh, Meg, does James Dallington own a motorbike?'

'No, I don't think so. Why?'

'It doesn't matter.'

Holly gave her another reassuring smile, then let herself out of the room. 'Take her back to the cells,' she said to the WPC.

* * *

Josh had already recounted the gist of the interview to the others by the time Holly arrived back at CID; and when she hurried into the office three pairs of expectant eyes were turned in her direction.

'Did you glean anything else from your little chat?' Ashworth asked.

She shook her head despondently. 'No, guv. I'll tell you one thing though, that woman's been fitted up and I can't for the life of me see why.'

'You're forgetting the Jean Churchman angle,' he reminded her. 'Hell hath no fury . . .'

'We've had no luck tracing a James Dallington living in Morton,' Bobby said, tapping the telephone directory on his desk.

'Which means — surprise, surprise — that he might not have been using his real name,' she said, sitting at her desk.

'He might just be ex-directory,' Bobby countered.

'Yes, could be, but there's something else that doesn't fit — if he lives in Morton, why use a hotel in the same town for his bit on the side?'

'I know this may sound unlikely,' Josh said, folding his arms and leaning against the VDU table, 'but do you think it's possible we've just stumbled onto a married man having an affair, and the whole issue's being clouded by a heck of a lot of coincidences?'

'No, too many coincidences,' Ashworth said, dismissing the idea out of hand. 'But there is one detail we haven't given any attention to: this James Dallington is supposed to be a company director — now, what if his company happens to be a supermarket chain? A couple of the major stores have their head offices in Morton.'

'Of course, I hadn't thought of that,' Holly said excitedly. 'Shall we find out, guv? Shall we go to Morton?'

He nodded. 'I've already phoned to let them know we're coming onto their patch. Now, Holly, if you and Josh tour the upmarket estates looking for a large white house, I'll take Bobby around the hotels and try to find a listing for James Dallington.'

'Will Meg be coming with us?' she asked.

Ashworth shook his head. 'I can't see the point in that — she wasn't very helpful in the interview. No, let's see what we can find out and take it from there.'

CHAPTER 19

The town of Morton, some fifty miles north of Bridgetown, dated back to the Industrial Revolution. It was an unattractive place with most of its historic buildings now superseded by ultra-modern monstrosities constructed of breeze blocks and glass. Its sixteenth-century stone cross had survived, however, but was now totally dwarfed by a huge shopping precinct, the type of which Ashworth despised. Numerous clusters of box-like houses bordered the town centre and encroached ever further into the surrounding countryside. They in turn were flanked by more opulent estates — the residences well-designed and substantial — built to accommodate the many wealthy people enticed to the town by jobs in banking and commerce, which were plentiful for those with the appropriate qualifications. All in all, Morton had a depressing atmosphere and Holly, susceptible to such things, soon caught the mood.

'Which way?' she demanded brusquely, bringing the Micra to a halt at traffic lights on the town's main street.

'Left,' Josh snapped back.

When the lights turned to green and the car in front was a little slow off the mark she leant on the horn, her bad mood worsening. Soon, though, the awful uniformity of the streets gave way to open fields, grazing cattle; and in the distance they could see the sumptuous Belvedere Estate spread out on top of a hill.

* * *

Any chance of escape into pleasant open countryside was impossible for the other half of CID. All of the hotels were contained within the town itself, and the two detectives found little enjoyment in tramping from one to the other, the stink of petrol fumes in their nostrils. After visiting the three largest establishments — all of which held no trace of a James Dallington — they made their way by car to the Stag's Head, a twenty-room hostelry with several bars open to the public.

Parking the Scorpio, Ashworth surveyed the building across a traffic-choked main road. From its structure he surmised that it had started life as a coaching inn when transport was of the horse-drawn kind. In those days it would have stood in glorious isolation, a veritable oasis in a desert of green fields. And just look at it now, he thought dismally.

Reluctantly, he motioned for Bobby to follow and picked a path through the lines of traffic, en route to the hotel's entrance. Inside a ghastly foyer were two knights in full armour, positioned as if to greet all comers at either side of the doorway; and Ashworth's disgust spiralled to new heights when close inspection revealed that the figures were made from bonded plastic.

The desk clerk promptly flashed a cordial smile. 'Morning, gents.'

Ashworth nodded an acknowledgement and produced his warrant card. 'Chief Inspector Ashworth, Bridgetown CID,' he said, studying the cheap horse brasses littering the walls. 'And my colleague here is Detective Constable Adams.'

'And what can I do for you?'

'We're making enquiries about a Mr James Dallington. We'd like to know if he's ever stayed here.'

The clerk raised an eyebrow and leant closer. 'What's he been up to, then?'

* * *

There were four large white houses on the Belvedere Estate, none of which had stained-glass windows; and the three houses which did were all covered with a darker rendering. After cruising around for a second time, Holly pulled up and swore hotly. Josh stared out of the side window, equally disgruntled.

The houses were all double-fronted with pillared porches, set behind large front gardens with not a blade of grass out of place. As they sat there, deciding on their next move, it soon became apparent that the residents did not take kindly to strange vehicles parking in the vicinity. Various net curtains twitched and here and there irate householders appeared on their doorsteps to stare openly at the car.

'We're not welcome,' Holly said.

'What are we actually looking for?' Josh asked, shifting in his seat and sighing. 'I mean, if this guy was using an assumed name, we can't just go knocking on doors.'

'No,' she admitted. 'To be honest, I was hoping to find a white house with a stained-glass window . . .'

'But we haven't, so what do we do next? Start knocking on doors, asking if they know anybody who calls himself James Dallington, although that's not his real name?'

'She could have made a mistake about the colour of the house. Think about it, Josh — it was dark and she might have thought it was white.'

'She could have,' he said doubtfully.

'Okay, then, have you got any bright ideas?'

'Nope.'

* * *

'He's stayed here?' Ashworth enquired.

'Yes, he's a regular,' the man confirmed. 'He was here last night, as a matter of fact.'

'Was he now?'

'Yes, there he is.' He pushed the register across and Ashworth studied the tidy signature.

'But he's left now, has he?'

'Yes, quite early. He had breakfast at seven and settled his bill immediately afterwards.'

Ashworth flicked back through the book and saw the signature at regular intervals.

'What's he like?'

'Tall, good-looking bloke. About forty, I'd say. Very smart, well-spoken . . .'

'Is he always alone when he stays here?'

The man peered around, making sure they were not being overheard, and then said, 'No, he's on the nooky run.'

'The nooky run?' Ashworth echoed.

'Yes, married man playing away from home. As soon as some of them get away from the missus, they're at it.'

'And was there a young lady with him last night?'

'No. That's explained by the early start, you see. Appointment first thing in the morning, possibly important . . . Well, you don't want to turn up feeling like you've been through the dishwasher, do you?'

'Is he always with the same lady?'

'Now, that I don't know,' the clerk said, leaning his elbows on the desk. 'You see, in this game you can easily spot the blokes on the nooky run by the fact that they're on their own and yet they book a double room. So then you act as if you're being attentive — Will the young lady be joining you tonight, sir? If you want room service or champagne, sir, just leave it with me . . . you can trust me to be discreet. That lets them know that I know — see? Then, of course, they're always willing to tip a tenner to keep the old mouth shut.'

'I'm in the wrong job,' Ashworth muttered. 'Tell me, is this man local, would you say?'

'No, I wouldn't think so. He's playing a bit close to home if he is. Mind you, with a posh accent it's difficult to say. But if he does come from round here, he'd live in the big houses on the hill, as they're called.'

'Is this Dallington booked in for a future date?'

The man winked at Ashworth. 'Tomorrow night. On his way back, I suppose. Some blokes get addicted to it. Never bothered me that much, but—'

'Thank you,' Ashworth interjected. 'You've been a great help.'

They started to walk away, and the clerk called, 'Shall I tell him you were asking?'

'No, I'd rather you didn't,' Ashworth said, quickly returning to the desk.

'Well, Chief Inspector,' the man said, smiling slyly, 'in this game you have to rely on the tips.'

'I'll give you a tip,' Ashworth said smartly. 'Don't get on the wrong side of me, son, because if you do and I miss Dallington, I'll have the Morton nick watching you day and night. You'd be surprised how many people commit offences without even realizing it.'

'Oh, well, you can't blame a bloke for trying,' he muttered, as they disappeared into the street.

'Well, it looks as if we've got Dallington,' Ashworth said, darting across the road. 'Get Holly on the radio, Bobby, and find out what they're doing.'

'Yes, guv.' For some reason he cast surreptitious glances along the pavement, and then fished out his radio. 'Holly, it's Bobby here. What are you doing?'

'At the moment, Bobby, I'm trying to get Abraham's boxer shorts off, but the prat's still struggling.'

Ashworth tut-tutted and grabbed the radio. 'Put Josh down, Holly, and get back to the nick.'

'Will do, guv,' she giggled.

* * *

Meg looked up hopefully at the sound of keys jangling outside the cell door, and she was halfway off the bed when Emma made a dramatic entrance, her coiffured hair and smart dark grey suit highlighting the dinginess of the surroundings.

'Can I get you a cup of tea?' the uniformed officer asked.

The councillor's nose wrinkled with distaste at the strong smell of disinfectant wafting up from the floor, and she said, 'No, thank you,' with a dismissive wave of the hand.

The officer backed away, leaving the door ajar. Meg stared at the floor while her sister pulled the solitary chair up to the bed, flicking imaginary dust from its seat before sitting down.

'Jim Ashworth can't tell me the whole story,' she said, 'but it seems they've traced your boyfriend.'

'Oh, thank God,' Meg said, hope radiating from her face.

'But they won't be able to interview him until tomorrow night, so that means they'll have to apply to the courts to hold you here for a further twenty-four hours.'

Meg's face clouded over. 'There's no need for them to do that, I don't mind staying.'

'It's procedure, you fool,' Emma spat. 'They have to apply to the courts.'

'I've been thinking, Emma, and I'm sure that once James knows I'm here, he'll quickly clear this whole matter up,' Meg said, a defiant smile on her lips. 'Everybody's trying to convince me that he's some sort of criminal, that he's used me, but I've had time to think it all through and I know that's not the truth.'

'Now, listen,' her sister said. 'I want you to be completely honest with me — do you know anything at all about this supermarket business?'

Meg's mouth dropped open, and a look of incredulity widened her eyes. 'Emma, do you of all people think that I'm guilty?'

'Fair enough, I had to know.' She got to her feet. 'As things are looking so bad for you, I've been talking to Clive Sanderson — he's a top criminal lawyer — so if the worst comes to the worst you'll at least be represented by one of the best legal brains in the country.'

'It won't come to that,' Meg stated confidently. 'James should clear this up in two minutes.'

'Don't be so bloody silly, Meg, use your head. Your beloved James is an extortionist and a murderer. He's been using you.'

'I know when a man loves me,' she retorted.

'Sister, dear, all your feelings are between your legs, but I'm having to use this . . .' She tapped the side of her forehead. 'And I only hope I can pull you out of this . . . this God Almighty mess that you've got yourself into.'

Meg pushed herself from the bed and squared up to her sister. 'That's not fair, Emma, and you know it.'

'It may not be, but if there's any thinking to be done, I'm the one to do it.'

'Oh, no,' Meg shouted, shaking her head. 'I'm so sick and tired of this, Emma. I'll have you know that since I've been in here I've worked something out — the only way you can feel superior is by making me feel inferior. That's exactly what you've been doing all our lives — making yourself look clever by making me look stupid, and it's not going to wash any more.'

Meg's raised voice brought the constable's head round the door. 'Everything okay?'

'Yes,' Emma snapped. He quickly withdrew. 'For God's sake, keep your voice down, you've embarrassed me enough, as it is. Do you realize that even now my fellow councillors are starting to ignore me? If this carries on, my position on the council is going to become untenable.'

Meg recoiled from the hissed rebuke; she would never be able to stand up to her sister. Understanding Emma's ploy was one thing, but having the strength to overcome it was an altogether different matter; a lifetime spent in the psychological grip of another could not be swept away overnight. She sank back onto the bed, all the spirit knocked out of her.

Emma's features twisted into a gloating grin. 'That's more like it. I'm sorry, Meg, but sooner or later you'll have to admit that you're not the clever one.'

* * *

Holly opened a window in the office, listening with only half an ear to Ashworth's post-mortem concerning the hunt for Dallington. Lingering by the window which took up most of the wall, she watched a group of workmen busily erecting scaffolding around a large office block opposite while Ashworth explained that they had tracked the man down to the Stag's Head. Her eyes focused on one workman in particular. He was stripped to the waist, manoeuvring scaffolding poles about, and every so often he would burst into a chorus of 'O Sole Mio' and wave in her direction. Holly smiled to herself as she watched the rippling muscles on his torso.

'What if this isn't the James Dallington we're looking for?' Josh asked.

'He has to be,' Ashworth replied. 'It isn't a common name, and it would be too much of a coincidence if two men calling themselves James Dallington had stayed at hotels in Morton.'

Once again strains of the Italian classic mingled with traffic noise filtering in through the window. Ashworth, with an indignant grunt, marched over and peered across the street. The workman was now two tiers up, very much playing to Holly as he negotiated the planks with ease, serenading her at the top of his voice.

'Why is it that everybody nowadays thinks they can sing opera? Why is that?'

'I think he's quite good, guv,' she said teasingly. 'Don't you?'

He listened for a long moment. 'Never in a million years, son, never in a million years,' he muttered, slamming the window shut. 'Right, Holly, what did you find on the housing estate?'

With one last glance at the man's glistening muscles, Holly brought her mind back to the job. She told Ashworth that they had drawn a blank, at the same time expressing surprise that they had been unable to locate the house.

'I'm with you, guv, at the moment,' she said. 'I think Meg's been fitted up, but if we find that her story's not holding up in places, we'll have to doubt the rest of what she says.'

Ashworth nodded his agreement. 'But let's see what this Dallington's got to say first.'

CHAPTER 20

The following evening James Dallington sat in the dining room at the Stag's Head. His companion was a dark-haired girl, her dress light blue and remarkably revealing. He studied her generous cleavage while topping up her champagne glass. She followed his eye-line and giggled.

'I thought you wanted me for my brains.'

'Those, as well,' he said with a faint smile.

Dallington sank back in his chair, trimming ash from his cigar, and shot her a meaningful look above the rim of his brandy glass.

'Excuse me,' she said, getting to her feet, 'I think I'll go and powder my nose.'

She strolled across the dining room, weaving between the tables, while his eyes rested on her shapely thighs which were hardly covered by the tiny dress, its tight fit showing clearly the outline of her skimpy underwear. Dallington took another sip of brandy and licked his lips, aware of the intense ache in his groin.

* * *

'Right, our man's there,' Ashworth called to Holly as he bounded into CID. 'He's eating dinner with a female companion. The receptionist just phoned. I've been on to Morton nick and they're getting uniformed to keep an eye on him until we get there.'

'Great,' Holly said, snatching up her shoulder bag. 'Let's go and get him, guv.'

* * *

Dallington opened the door of the double room with a hand that was trembling slightly and stepped back to allow the girl to enter.

'This is nice,' she said, looking around eagerly.

He made straight for the ice bucket complete with champagne bottle so diligently positioned at the side of the bed by the mindful receptionist, and poured two glasses. The girl settled on the settee and accepted the chilled drink with laughter in her eyes. Dallington remained standing and lit a cigarette, intent on watching the smoke as it drifted towards the ceiling.

'Why don't you slip into something more comfortable?' the girl suggested, eyeing his formal dark suit, the stuffy collar and tie.

'Yes, all right, I think I will,' he said, hurriedly returning his glass to the bedside table.

He undressed slowly, placing his clothes on a hanger, reluctant to have them creased, and the girl's eyebrows rose as he gradually revealed his well-proportioned body.

'I'll just go and get myself ready. Won't be a minute,' she said, making her way to the bathroom.

Dallington settled on the bed and was reaching for his champagne glass when a sharp knock came on the door.

'Who is it?' he called, irritation showing in his voice.

'Police,' Ashworth barked. 'Open up, please.'

He jumped from the bed and pulled on a black bathrobe which he was still securing around his middle when he opened the door.

'What the hell do you want?' he demanded.

'James Dallington?' Ashworth asked, holding up his warrant card.

The man looked perplexed. 'Yes . . .'

'Can we come in for a minute, sir?' Holly asked.

'No, you can't,' he retorted, glancing from one to the other. 'What is this?'

'I'm Chief Inspector Ashworth, sir, Bridgetown CID, and this is Detective Sergeant Bedford. We'd like to have a quiet word.'

'What about?' Dallington asked, peering worriedly at the bathroom.

Ashworth's patience was wearing thin. He exhaled sharply and said, 'May we come in, sir? It'll make this a lot easier, I can assure you.'

With reluctance Dallington stood aside and motioned for them to enter. Holly suppressed a smile at his neatly folded clothes, while a woman's coat was strewn carelessly across the floor.

'Is the lady in the bathroom?' she said.

'Why do you ask that?' Dallington snapped.

'Well, sir, she's not in here, and we didn't pass a woman on the way up, so the bathroom would seem logical.' She pointed to the discarded coat.

'You people have got no right to be here . . .'

'We've every right,' Ashworth told him calmly. 'Now, I believe you're a very good friend of a lady named Meg Cowper.'

A flicker of panic entered Dallington's eyes, but it was gone in a second. 'I've never heard of her,' he said.

'Our information leads us to believe differently, sir, and I'll have to ask you to come to Bridgetown Police Station to answer a few questions.'

They noticed that Dallington's gaze kept straying to the open door as if contemplating an escape and Holly moved to close it. Then all at once the fight seemed to drain from him. His shoulders sagged, and he said resignedly, 'You'd better give me a few minutes. I do have a guest.'

'We'll have to know the name and address of your friend,' Holly said.

Dallington glowered at her as he disappeared into the bathroom.

'He's frightened,' Ashworth said. 'He's our man.'

'I reckon you're right. I thought he was going to try for the door. Oh, guv, let me deal with the lady friend, eh?'

It was a full five minutes before Dallington emerged from the bathroom. The girl was behind him, a look of absolute fury on her face. Holly straight away guided her to one side.

'I'm sorry, love, having to come bursting in here like this.'

'Piss off,' she hissed.

Holly was taken aback. With her mouth shut, the girl looked elegant and sophisticated — even though Holly thought her dress was too tight. Suddenly, all was clear. 'Wait a minute,' she said, 'are you on the game?'

'No, I'm not,' the girl replied with a haughty sneer. 'I'm an escort.'

'Oh, I see, and do your clients always end up in the buff?'

The girl stared at her with hate-filled eyes and then turned away, her lips firmly together.

'Come on, love,' Holly coaxed. 'I'm trying to be nice here. Just give me your name and address.'

The girl rummaged in her handbag and brought out a gold-rimmed card. 'There . . . it's all on there.'

'Thanks.'

'You're a bastard — did you know that? A bloody bastard—'

'Nice to meet you, as well,' Holly cut in. 'In fact, I hope we bump into each other again — preferably somewhere nice and quiet where there's only the two of us. Then I'll be happy to discuss my parentage in more detail. Now, go on, get out.'

Grabbing her coat, the girl glared at Ashworth and without even a glance in Dallington's direction she flounced from the room.

‘I’d better get dressed,’ Dallington said.

‘We’ll wait outside, sir,’ Ashworth volunteered.

They stood in the corridor, keeping an ear on the man’s movements. There was no escape route from the room, but a desperate man would try anything.

‘The girl wasn’t very pleasant,’ Ashworth remarked.

‘It’s the old escort bit, guv — she’s just a pro. I must admit, though, she had me fooled to start with.’

‘I see.’ He glanced at his watch. ‘I hope we can get this wound up by midnight. I’ve got a loving wife, a faithful dog, and a bottle of malt whisky waiting for me.’

* * *

James Dallington kept tight-lipped for most of the journey back to Bridgetown. He was sitting in the back of the Scorpio, steadily chain-smoking despite the No Smoking sticker adhered to the dashboard. Ashworth let it ride, encouraged by the man’s nervousness, but was still anxious for the car’s interior. He wound down the driver’s window and left the fresh air to do battle with the foul smoke haze. Eventually the dual carriageway fed them onto the first roundabout leading into the town.

‘How much further?’ Dallington asked, lighting up another cigarette.

‘Almost there,’ Holly said, coughing pointedly at the fresh onslaught of smoke. ‘You haven’t asked us what this is all about yet, Mr Dallington.’

‘I’m sure you’ll tell me when you’re ready,’ he replied gruffly.

‘I’m ready now,’ she said. ‘We want somebody to have a look at you. We need to see if the person can identify you.’ Even in the darkened car, she could see a pallor creeping across the man’s face.

‘Now, there are two ways we can do that,’ she went on. ‘We can set up an identity parade which means we’ll have to hold you overnight . . .’ He remained silent but there was definite panic in the way he stubbed out his hardly smoked cigarette. 'Or we can walk you along a corridor with the person there to identify you in one of the offices. That way, they can get a good look at you. It's your choice, Mr Dallington.'

'I can't stay overnight,' he stammered shrilly.

'Fine. So, am I to take that as a request for the latter option?'

'Yes.'

Ashworth reached for the radio and requested that the station staff get ready for the identification.

* * *

Dallington's nervousness became infinitely more pronounced when they pulled into the police station car park, and he was reluctant to leave the car when Holly wrenched open the door and said, 'Right . . . out.'

Light drizzle was falling, and a stout wind blew it into their faces as they hastened across to the building's entrance. Inside, they worked their way through the maze of corridors, Dallington's agitation growing with the turn of each corner. On the fourth floor, they pushed through a pair of swing doors and emerged into a brightly lit corridor, the glass-fronted offices on either side in total darkness. All was quiet, apart from the buzzing of the overhead fluorescent strips.

Holly, with a hand on his arm, could feel Dallington's tension when he was brought to a stop.

'Okay,' she said, 'just walk to the end of the corridor . . . nice and slow.'

He looked straight ahead and stiffly negotiated the twenty yards to swing doors at the far end, with Ashworth and Holly following a few feet behind. Stepping to his right, Ashworth opened a door to one of the offices.

'Right, sir, we'll wait in here,' he said, pressing the light switch. The overhead strips flickered for a few moments while Dallington walked between desks on which stood electric typewriters, and then the room was lit with a harsh light. Ashworth nodded for Holly to get moving and closed the door.

She raced back along the corridor and into an office that was also now fully lit. Meg was sitting at one of the desks, with a woman police officer positioned at each shoulder. In the silence of the room the ticking of the wall clock sounded terribly loud.

'Well?' Holly asked.

Meg looked up, causing tears to spill from her eyes. She slowly shook her head. 'That's not James.'

Holly's jaw dropped. 'Are you sure, Meg?' she said, rushing to the desk. 'That man's name is James Dallington.'

'But it's not James,' she insisted.

Holly crouched before her and adopted a mild tone. 'Meg, you're not just saying that out of misplaced loyalty, are you?'

'No, I'm not,' she yelled, banging a fist on the desk. 'How many times have I got to tell you? That man was not James.'

'All right, all right. Now, listen to me . . .' Holly straightened up and paced about thoughtfully while Meg's tear-stained eyes concentrated on her face. 'That man . . . now you're claiming he's not the James Dallington you were having an affair with — is that what you're saying?'

'Yes. He's not James.'

'Added to that, we've been unable to locate the house in Morton where you claim James Dallington lives.' Holly stared down at the woman, her expression sceptical. 'Your story's falling apart, Meg. Can't you see that?'

'But I've told you everything I know,' she cried.

'Meg, I'm doing all I can to help you—'

'Oh, for God's sake . . . Why won't you believe me?'

'I've got to tell you that I'm beginning to doubt your story,' Holly said abruptly. 'The things you're telling me just aren't adding up.'

'But you said yourself that someone was stage managing this to make it look like me.'

'I'm starting to have doubts about that, too. The fact is, who would want to do that to you, Meg? What reason would anybody have?'

'I don't know,' Meg screamed. 'I don't know. I don't know.'

'Calm down,' Holly said sharply, making for the door. 'This is your last chance, Meg — is that man the James Dallington you had an affair with?'

Holly's blunt words quelled Meg's rage in an instant. She fell back in the chair, staring down at the desk top. 'No, Sergeant, I've never seen him before in my life.'

In the corridor Holly paused and took in several deep breaths then hurried along to where Ashworth was waiting with Dallington. Hearing her high heels clicking on the floor, Ashworth emerged into the corridor the second she reached the door.

'Well?' he asked.

'Sorry, guv, she's saying that's not the James Dallington she was having an affair with.' Disappointment immediately registered on his face. 'I know, guv. I'm starting to feel I've been given the runaround.' She looked through the glass partition to where Dallington could be seen, sitting forward, elbows on knees. 'Anyway, what's his story?'

Ashworth snorted. 'He's a sales rep — biscuits, would you believe? — so he gets around all the supermarkets. He's based in Sheffield. I've checked out all his details — home address, place of work — and they're all genuine.'

'So, we've nothing to hold him on. But he looked so shifty when we were bringing him in.'

'He's already explained that away. He says he uses call girls during most of his visits to Morton, and when we barged in he thought a prostitute had been murdered, possibly one of the girls he'd had in the past. He wasn't worried about being investigated because he knew he'd done nothing, but he was worried about his wife finding out.'

Holly frowned. 'And do you believe him?'

Ashworth peered into the office. 'Well, he became very reasonable when he discovered we were looking into something quite different — almost cheerful, even. It seems he hadn't paid the agency fee for his so-called escort, and he hadn't got round to paying the girl for her extra services, so our intervention saved him in excess of two hundred pounds.'

'It's an ill wind that dries nobody's knickers,' Holly reflected.

Ashworth's watch told him it was two minutes past midnight. 'How you summon up those flashes of poetic genius at this time in the morning always astounds me, Holly.'

She gave him a devilish grin. 'So, he's out of the frame.'

'We're looking for a James Dallington, and we've found one. But without Meg's willingness to identify him, there's little we can do. Holly, I'm beginning to have second thoughts about that woman, and yet I keep coming back to one thing: what could she possibly gain from getting involved in a stunt like this?'

'Love?' she suggested.

'Love's not much use when you're doing twenty-five years.'

'I don't know, guv, a good defence lawyer could easily get her off. The case against her isn't that strong.'

Ashworth gave a doubtful shrug and rubbed at his tired eyes. 'We'd better get a car to take Mr Dallington back to Morton, I suppose, and then we can call it a day.'

CHAPTER 21

The route back to the cells was becoming an all too familiar one for Meg. Sandwiched between the two women officers, she was escorted through the charge room and down cold stone steps leading to the cell block. In just a few days the smell of the place, the disturbed nights with drunks brought in at all hours, the feeling of claustrophobia when the heavy steel door was clanged shut, were becoming major parts of her life. They reached her cell and one of the officers ushered her in.

'Do you want anything?' she asked. 'A cup of tea? Some coffee?'

Meg managed a smile and shook her head. The sound of the key in the lock brought a shiver to her spine as she surveyed the bare essentials around her: the bed, hard and unwelcoming; the two-foot-square table with its solitary chair; but most upsetting of all was the tiny patch of night sky barely visible through the barred window. She leant against the door, the cold from its metal penetrating her blouse and chilling her flesh.

'They'll never prove it,' she mouthed. 'They'll never be able to prove it.'

* * *

Superintendent Newton summoned Ashworth to his office at 10 a.m. the next morning. Fully expecting some sort of rebuke for his department's loss of momentum with regard to the extortion case, Ashworth hesitated at the door, steeling himself for a confrontation.

Inside the office, his gaze went immediately to Emma Cowper sitting before the desk. Newton was standing by the window.

'Well, Chief Inspector,' he said. 'Are you able to tell us the conclusions of your investigation?'

'Yes, sir. We have enough evidence to charge Meg Cowper with murder and extortion.'

'Oh, my God,' the councillor exclaimed, closing her eyes.

'I'm sorry, Emma,' Ashworth said, 'but I really have no alternative.'

'I'm sure you don't, Jim. It's all right.'

'Your investigation in Morton came to nothing, then?' Newton asked, no doubt hoping to demonstrate to the councillor that the enquiry had been a thorough one.

Standing stiffly by the door, Ashworth related the events of the previous night. He also detailed their failure to locate the house in Morton which Meg claimed belonged to Dallington. 'But, of course, we shall pursue all lines of enquiry to their conclusions,' he stated firmly.

'I've hired one of the best criminal lawyers in the country,' Emma told them. 'And I also want to get a private investigator to work on the case. That's if you've no objections, Jim?'

'None.'

'Because if my sister says that Dallington exists, then he does.'

'We'll make any information available to anyone you put on the case, Emma, I can assure you of that.'

She smiled gratefully. 'Thank you, Jim. I shall have to resign as a councillor, of course. Some of my colleagues have already made that abundantly clear.'

Ashworth shuffled his feet, eager to get back to the office. 'Sir, if you'll excuse me . . .'

'Oh, yes, thank you, Chief Inspector. I'm sure you're very busy.'

* * *

Holly glanced through the glass wall. The man working on the scaffolding was waving to her and, peering around to make sure that no one was watching, she waved back. As soon as she did he ran along the planks with a reckless disregard for his own safety, his hands aloft, apparently giving thanks to God. Holly giggled and reached for her shoulder bag.

'I'm just nipping out for a minute,' she announced. Josh looked across at the scaffolding and started to whistle a little too loudly.

Holly raced down the station steps and crossed the road then, having to pass close by the workmen, she entered the newsagent's next door to a chorus of wolf whistles. In the shop she hurriedly glanced around for something to buy, and finally settled for a packet of cheese and onion crisps.

On the way back she was pleased to see the man standing on the fourth rung of the ladder, his back towards it.

'Oh, vision that has come before mine eyes,' he said, with a flourish of his arm. 'Are thee there to torment my very soul? Like veils of sleep that peel away and reveal thee as no more than a passing glimpse of paradise that cannot be touched before it slips away?'

'You what?'

'She speaks, she speaks,' he cried, clamping a hand over his ear. 'But such a regal sound my humble ears are not worthy to receive.'

'You're wasted up there,' she said, laughing.

'I am but a wandering player, a singer of great renown . . .' He shot a glance at the building, pulling a face. 'And a scaffolder.'

Holly grinned, and realizing that she was fiddling with the crisps packet like an overgrown schoolgirl, she dropped it into her shoulder bag.

'No, seriously, I'm an actor,' he said, jumping on to the pavement. 'I went to sign on and they said we've got just the job for you . . . helping some guys erect scaffolding.' He held out a hand. 'I'm Gareth.'

'I'm Holly,' she said, taking the hand, her eyes lowered.

'Holly . . . that's nice.' He smiled and pushed his thick blond hair away from his eyes. 'Well, Holly, how about coming out with a strolling vagabond?'

She looked up at his handsome face and was immediately attracted by his gorgeous blue eyes, alive with good humour, but even so she shook her head.

'I don't think so.'

Then he startled her by grabbing her hand. 'Oh, beautiful no that did pass thy lips. 'Tis worth a thousand ayes from less fairer maidens, for it doth proclaim you know that I exist.'

Holly backed away, giggling. 'You're mad.'

''Tis gazing upon thy countenance that has made me so.'

'You're bloody mental.'

He winked. 'See you tomorrow?'

'Yes . . . okay.' She turned and ran across the road.

In the office Holly was relieved to see that Ashworth was still not back. She threw the crisps onto her desk and sat down, still laughing about the ridiculous encounter. Josh was eager to know what she had bought and craned his neck to see.

'Crisps are cheaper in the canteen than from the newsagent's,' he said innocently.

She let out a raucous chuckle. 'Mind your own business, Abraham.'

'Just trying to be helpful,' he said, turning to the computer with a grin on his face.

Ashworth bustled into the office. 'Right,' he said, 'I want Meg Cowper charged with murder and extortion. Holly, Josh, go and take care of it.'

'That's the end of the investigation, then,' Holly said, getting to her feet.

'Yes,' he replied gruffly. 'We've no further avenues to explore, at the moment.'

* * *

That evening many heads turned as Richard Samuels escorted Emma Cowper into the Travellers' Inn, one of Bridgetown's most exclusive restaurants. The obsequious head waiter straight away showed them to a table already occupied by a distinguished, middle-aged man. He was short, grey-haired, with large horn-rimmed glasses, and was enjoying a pre-dinner Scotch. He swiftly rose to his feet when Emma approached the table.

'Hello, Clive,' she said warmly.

'Good evening, Emma.' His powerful voice boomed around the restaurant and attracted much attention from the surrounding tables.

'This is Richard Samuels,' she said, 'Richard, this is Clive Sanderson, the lawyer.'

The men shook hands and the waiter pulled out Emma's chair for her to sit. Sanderson stared at Samuels with immense curiosity as they took their seats.

'Samuels,' he mused. 'Surely not the Samuels involved in the case?'

'Yes, it's my wife that Meg has been accused of murdering. But I don't believe she did it,' he added quickly. 'Emma's a very old friend of the family and has been most supportive throughout all of this.'

'I see.' Sanderson clicked his fingers at the waiter. 'A drink, I think, before we order dinner.' He held up his glass. 'Cars run on petrol, but good lawyers run on Scotch.'

They laughed as the waiter took the order and he was walking away, still scribbling, when a well-dressed man approached the table.

'Richard,' he said, extending a hand.

Samuels began to rise. 'Hello, William.'

'No, don't get up, I just wanted to say I'm glad the supermarkets are doing so well.' He inclined his head towards Emma and Sanderson. 'Excuse me.'

Samuels watched the man return to his table, a thoughtful look in his eyes. 'That's William Page,' he said, turning back. 'He's a director of Morgan's chain of supermarkets. I'd have thought he'd be anything but pleased that my business has started to do well.'

The lawyer, clearly uninterested, took off his glasses and buffed them up with a startlingly white handkerchief. 'I had a long meeting with Meg today,' he said.

'And what conclusions did you reach?' Emma asked eagerly.

Sanderson said nothing while the waiter served their drinks, placing each before them with a flourish before edging noiselessly away.

'The prosecution haven't a strong case,' he said. 'It's mostly circumstantial, very little evidence.' He turned to peer at Samuels above the rim of his glasses. 'Am I to take it, Richard, that you positively identified the briefcase and Meg's voice?'

'No, and I wish I'd kept my mouth shut,' he muttered. 'I simply said the briefcase was similar to the one used by the man collecting the money, and that the woman had a local accent and could have been Meg.'

'Not particularly damning in itself,' the lawyer remarked, after taking a sip of Scotch. 'Not in confident hands. You will take my lead in the witness box, I hope, when I point out that you cannot positively identify either the voice or the briefcase?'

'Oh yes, of course, Clive, anything I can do to help.'

'There is something else you can do . . . if you want my advice, that is. Now, you've explained that you and Emma are old friends, but I do feel it would be wise for you not to be seen together in public, and I'll tell you why. At the trial I shall portray you as a poor man who's lost his wife, and who's had his own life put in grave danger while imprisoned at the cottage. For you to have suffered in that way and then to state that you can't positively identify the voice or the case will have great influence on the jury. However, if the prosecution can claim that the two of you are friends, they might plant the suggestion that you're lying to get your friend's sister acquitted.'

Emma picked up her gin and bitter lemon. 'Do you believe that Meg is innocent, Clive?'

Sanderson gave a wry smile. 'Everyone I defend is innocent.'

She sampled her drink. 'I'm hiring a private detective to try and trace this James Dallington.'

'Good idea,' Sanderson enthused. 'I shall of course be using this mystery man at the trial, but he won't be named . . . for legal reasons, as they say. If you could come up with him, Emma, it would be an enormous help. As it is . . .' He lowered his voice. 'I think your sister's been used, for whatever reasons. Now, if this man calling himself Dallington was apprehended, he may well clear Meg of any involvement, but he's unlikely to come forward voluntarily to do that.'

'So, what happens now?' Samuels asked.

Sanderson looked around for the waiter; the Scotch had activated his gastric juices and he was ready to eat.

'There will be court appearances for remand purposes, then the Crown Prosecution Service will decide if there's enough evidence for the case to go to trial. I shall argue for a dismissal, but I doubt I'll be successful. So, then we go to trial, and all I can do there is push for an early date . . .' He caught the eye of the waiter and waved him across. 'It's September now, so I'd hope to get a trial date for January or February of next year.'

The waiter was hovering at a discreet distance. 'Shall we order?' Sanderson suggested benignly.

* * *

Holly visited the newsagent's again the next day, and when she returned to the office with a sparkle in her eyes and a preoccupied air, Josh was left in no doubt that she had hooked and landed the young actor-cum-scaffolder. He glanced over at the building and watched Gareth speeding up a ladder, his every movement suggesting that it was good to be alive.

'You poor bastard,' Josh mouthed, before glancing at Holly with an affectionate smile.

'Meg Cowper makes her first court appearance this morning,' Ashworth announced from his desk. The fact annoyed him immensely for he regarded Meg's arrest as an unacceptable conclusion to the case and would not be satisfied until Dallington had been brought to book.

'I asked the Sheffield police to have a good look into the man you brought in last night, guv,' Josh said.

'Good man,' he said absently, tapping a pen on his desk. 'And what have they come up with?'

'Nothing, yet.'

'Now, why aren't I surprised?' Ashworth intoned.

'Dallington's not known to them,' Josh went on, 'but they're going to keep on checking him out.'

'Do you realize how many times Peter Sutcliffe was interviewed before he was finally caught?' Ashworth asked, making his way to the door. 'I want you all to think about that.'

Bobby stared into space for a good two minutes after the door had closed on the chief inspector. 'What did he mean by that?'

'Bobby,' Holly sighed, 'there's an aspect of the guv'nor you haven't seen, yet. He wants enough evidence against Dallington to place him under arrest, and until he gets that evidence he's going to be a real pain in the arse.'

'Oh.'

Holly's telephone buzzed, and she leant across for the receiver. 'DS Bedford.' She listened, all the while scribbling on her note pad. 'Yes, that is interesting . . . in fact, very much so. Yes, all right, thanks for letting me . . . What? No, no, I really don't think so, but it's nice of you to ask. Bye, now.'

'What's so interesting?' Josh asked.

'It seems, lover boy, that Jean Churchman and Jerry Townsend are planning a celebration for this very evening . . .'

'So? What's that got to do with us?'

'It coincides with Meg's appearance in court. Don't you think that's suspicious?'

Josh gave a noncommittal shrug. 'I suppose that was Dale Spicer on the phone?'

'You suppose right, lover.'

'I know what he's after.'

'Well, he's not going to get it,' she assured him. 'But I do think it's interesting that Jean Churchman's finding something to celebrate just as Emma Cowper's political career's hanging in tatters.'

* * *

Meg had already been told that she would be remanded into the custody of a local prison after her court appearance and that knowledge left her dull with shock. So too did the fact that she was forcibly handcuffed to a woman officer prior to being hustled into the back of a police vehicle.

The drive from the station to the Magistrates' Court was a short one and as they approached the small car park at the rear of the courthouse, the accompanying officer asked if she would feel better with her head covered. Meg said that she would, but once the drab prison-grey blanket was draped over her head and shoulders she felt a keen sense of claustrophobia; and every time she inhaled, the air drawn through the dusty material left a strange taste in her mouth.

Presently, the car slowed and she could hear people running beside it. Angry voices called her name, telling her that she was a murderer. She felt the body of the woman officer stiffen just as something struck the vehicle. Meg whimpered.

'It's all right,' the officer told her gently. 'Somebody's just kicked the car, that's all. Nothing to worry about.'

Meg heard the iron gates of the car park squeal open and as soon as the vehicle had passed through they were speedily closed again. Then they were leaving behind the shouting and the name-calling.

'Keep the blanket over your head until we're inside,' the woman officer cautioned. 'There might be reporters with long-range lenses about.'

While Meg was quickly ushered into the building, a policewoman stayed on the steps, speaking urgently into her radio.

'Sarge, we could do with some back-up here. There's quite an angry crowd forming outside the court. Before the prison van can take Cowper away, we'll need a path cleared.'

'Okay,' the sergeant answered wearily. 'I'll get as many helmets there as I can.'

* * *

Holly was alone in the office, eating her cheese and onion crisps and all the time glancing through the glass wall in the hope of catching a glimpse of the athletic Gareth. Now and then he would look in her direction and give a wave. She watched his muscles ripple as he carried pots of paint up to the top of the scaffolding and calculated how long it had been since she'd had sex. Too long, she thought ruefully. Here she was watching a fit male body performing the most mundane of tasks while her lower half reacted out of all proportion. In her mind Good Girl and Bad Girl debated the problem, and Good Girl obligingly agreed to hibernate for the foreseeable future. Holly turned from the window and drank her coffee, hoping to divert her mind away from the hunky Gareth.

'Why couldn't we find Dallington's house in Morton?' she asked aloud. It was a thought which had crept into her mind many times during the past few days.

She pictured again the roads along which they had driven in their search for the white house with the stained-glass window in its side. It wasn't there. But why should Meg make up such a stupid story — one that would crumble the minute they started to investigate? The house had to be there, and yet they couldn't find it.

Suddenly, she crushed the plastic cup in a gesture of jubilation, oblivious to the lukewarm dregs seeping between her fingers and on to the desk.

'Of course it's there,' she exclaimed. 'We just couldn't see it.'

CHAPTER 22

Meg's sense of panic erupted as she was bundled down the courthouse steps between two warders — the blanket once again hiding her face — and into the waiting prison van. When the doors were banged shut the blanket was taken away and she was ordered to sit on the plain wooden bench lining the side of the van. In court she had needed only to confirm to the magistrates her name and address, and was then remanded into custody for two weeks.

The gates of the car park opened and beyond them, on the pavement, a line of policemen were holding back a crowd of about thirty. As the driver brought the van ever closer, the group strained forward, their screams of 'Murderer' bringing a sickness to Meg's stomach. But the blue line held. Slowing to pull out onto the road, the van was swiftly besieged by press photographers holding their cameras to the windows, shutters clicking and flashes blinding, until the driver was able to gather speed and accelerate away.

* * *

Holly hardly noticed the pungent smell of fried food fighting with an acrid tang of cigarette smoke as she worked her way between tables in the police canteen. Ashworth was sitting alone at a corner table, forking shepherd's pie into his mouth and studying the *Daily Telegraph* propped up against the sugar dispenser.

'Guv?' she said, slipping into the chair facing him.

He reached forward for the newspaper and placed it on the chair beside him. 'Yes?' he grunted.

'I know why we couldn't find Dallington's house in Morton.'

A forkful of pie stopped halfway to his mouth. 'Pray enlighten me.'

'You know that building on the opposite side of the road to our office — what colour was it this morning?'

'That's the one with the scaffolding round it?' She nodded. 'It's rendered . . . it's a natural cement colour, isn't it?'

'It was, guv, but now they're painting it white.'

Realization lifted his eyebrows and brought a faint smile to his lips. 'The house that Dallington showed to Meg was white with scaffolding round it, so they could have been about to paint it a different colour.'

'You've got it, guv.'

'Good girl.' He replaced his fork and pushed the pie remains to one side. 'Right then, we've got to be careful here, Holly. We're looking for someone who's been using the name James Dallington, so we can't just go barging in there, because if Meg was telling the truth we could be breaking up a happy home.'

'What we could do is get in touch with the coordinator of the local Neighbourhood Watch,' she suggested. 'Believe me, guv, in that posh area if somebody belched all the neighbours would know about it.'

'Yes, that's a good idea. I'll get the address from Martin Dutton. He deals with all the Neighbourhood Watch schemes.'

* * *

The Neighbourhood Watch coordinator turned out to be Mrs Craddock, a tiny, silver-haired lady who looked like everyone's idea of a favourite grandmother — until she opened her mouth, that is. Her speech was clipped, brisk, and laced with authority.

When the chief inspector knocked at her sprawling bungalow, the door was opened just wide enough to show one pale blue and highly suspicious eye.

'Hello, madam, I'm Chief Inspector Ashworth,' he said. 'I rang earlier.'

'Don't you think you'd better show me your warrant card?' Mrs Craddock snapped.

'Yes, of course.' He fished the card from his pocket and held it up.

'Hmm, that seems to be in order.' The eye turned its attention to Holly. 'And who might you be?'

'DS Bedford,' she said, meekly producing her own card.

Mrs Craddock sniffed and studied the photograph before closing the door. They listened to the rattle of a safety chain and then the door came open.

'You'd better come in — and don't forget to wipe your feet,' she ordered, guiding them across the threshold.

They dutifully did as they were told and then Mrs Craddock was leading them across the hall. 'Come through into the kitchen,' she said.

They were instructed to sit on straight-backed chairs arranged around a wooden table, over which was draped an immaculate red and white check tablecloth.

'So, Chief Inspector, what can I do for you?'

'Firstly, madam, is there anyone living on this estate who answers to the name of James Dallington?'

'Development, not estate,' the woman corrected him. 'And, no, I'm not aware of anyone of that name living here.'

'Over the last few weeks,' Holly said, hoping her smile was sufficiently friendly, 'have any of the houses been repainted? It's the external walls we're interested in. Have any of them been changed from white?'

'Yes, number sixteen, Arch Drive,' she said, without having to pause for thought. 'Changed from white to an awful dull grey.'

'And who lives there?' Ashworth quizzed.

'David Masters. He keeps himself very much to himself. And I'll anticipate your next question,' she said sternly. 'He lives there with a woman. I don't know whether she's his wife, it's difficult to tell nowadays — hardly seems to matter, does it? The woman in question doesn't enjoy the best of health, though. Over the past few weeks, she's taken to walking with a stick.'

Holly glanced at the chief inspector. 'Have you any idea what sort of car he drives?' she asked.

Mrs Craddock snorted. 'No, I do not. If I had my way all cars would be banned. I keep writing to the Prime Minister, urging him to improve public transport to help cut down on pollution—'

'Thank you,' Ashworth said, rising quickly to his feet. 'Thank you very much for your time. You've been a great help.'

'Always pleased to be of service.' Without further preamble, she left the kitchen and showed them out of the front door.

'This looks promising, guv,' Holly said, rushing to keep up with him along the sweeping garden path.

'It certainly does.' He glanced at his watch. 'It's three p.m. now. If this Masters works and I'd imagine he'd have to, living here, we've got at least a two-hour wait. So maybe we'd better go and have a cup of tea in Morton.'

'Or several, guv,' Holly said, climbing into the Scorpio.

It was while Ashworth was starting the engine that Holly remembered the call from Dale Spicer, and even though the information seemed irrelevant in the light of this new line of enquiry, she went on to tell him about Jean Churchman's celebration with Townsend.

'Not much we can do about that,' he said. 'We've got no reason to question them about anything and as far as I can recall, enjoying yourself isn't yet regarded as an offence.'

Holly settled back in her seat and contemplated the sheer pleasure of spending the next few hours drinking tea in a dingy café.

* * *

It was six thirty p.m. when the Scorpio glided to a halt outside number sixteen, Arch Drive. By this time Ashworth was certain that they had caught up with the man calling himself James Dallington. The house was impressive, a four-bedroomed detached with a double garage at the side. A lantern light outside the porch came on automatically as they approached.

Ashworth lightly pressed the bell and its muted chimes could be heard from inside the house. Footsteps sounded in the hall and the front door was promptly opened by a tall man, smartly dressed in a lounge suit. He was holding several sheets of paper and was clearly annoyed at the disturbance.

'Yes?' he said shortly.

'Sorry to disturb you, sir,' Ashworth said, warrant card at the ready. 'I'm Chief Inspector Ashworth of Bridgetown CID. This is Detective Sergeant Bedford.'

'Bridgetown? You're some distance from home, aren't you?'

'Yes, sir. We're looking for a Mr James Dallington.'

'Well, you won't find him here,' he retorted. Ashworth's expression remained resolute and the man, indicating the papers in his hand, said, 'Look, I am very busy—'

'Sir . . .' Ashworth hesitated. 'This is rather delicate, but do you know a woman named Meg Cowper?'

The man looked puzzled. 'That's the woman who's just been charged with murder, isn't it?'

'Yes,' Holly jumped in, 'and she told us that a James Dallington lived at this address with his wife who's suffering from multiple sclerosis.'

'I can assure you that my name is David Masters,' the man told her firmly, 'and I live here with my sister who happens to be severely afflicted by arthritis. Are you suggesting that I was in some way involved with this woman?'

'No, of course not, sir,' Ashworth said, the man's face telling him loudly that they had made a mistake. 'But would you have any objections to giving us your details?'

'I suppose not,' he said resignedly, 'but I hope this puts an end to the matter. Goodness knows what the neighbours will think.'

Ashworth returned to the car while Holly took down the details in her efficient shorthand. She joined him some ten minutes later.

'He's an accountant in Morton, guv. We'll have to check his story about living with his sister, though, eh?'

'I've already asked Morton police to do that,' he said, pointing to the radio. 'They're going to run all the usual checks on him. I'm not very optimistic though, Holly; even his physical appearance doesn't fit that of the man we're looking for.'

'We've fouled up, guv, haven't we?'

'No, we haven't fouled up, we're being deliberately misled. James Dallington is by no means a common name, so either we had our man last night, or we're looking for someone who knows him or has heard his name mentioned, and I'm not going to rest until I find out which it is.'

* * *

Meg's next court appearance saw a very different woman standing in the dock. Her eyes were fixed straight ahead during the whole of the proceedings, her movements slow and lifeless. Two weeks in the remand prison had sapped her will, and the thought of another five months there was beginning to erode it still further.

Outside the courts a crowd had once again gathered, made up of ordinary law-abiding citizens who were so incensed by the deeds for which Meg had been charged that they were quite willing to resort to violence in an effort to demonstrate their anger. When it became apparent that the prison van was moving to leave, the crowd surged forward, its size having grown to over two hundred, and things were looking ominous for the thirty police officers drafted in to keep control. There were many dry mouths and sweaty palms in the thin blue line as the driver of the prison van started its engine. The uniformed sergeant in charge, with the aid of a loud-hailer, appealed for calm but to no avail. Something akin to mob hysteria had gripped the crowd but just when it looked as if reinforcements would have to be called in, Richard Samuels emerged from the court building and swiftly asked the sergeant if he could use the loud-hailer.

He positioned himself on the highest step, in full view of all, and made an impassioned plea for the group to disperse, telling them in a voice packed with emotion that their actions were defiling the memory of his late wife. A hush stole over the listeners, but although the tragic events that had befallen him during the last few weeks had earned Samuels tremendous public support, the situation was uncertain for many minutes. At the sight of the quiet but determined crowd he faltered and almost broke down, then literally begged them to disband, his sobbing voice at times hardly audible.

'Oh, for God's sake,' he said finally, 'I can't even bury my wife until the trial's over. Please, please let her memory have some dignity.'

That seemed to work and at last the group began to break up, most of its members muttering darkly while Richard Samuels, still weeping, was led back into the court building by a uniformed officer. The sergeant waited until he could be certain the crowd would not attempt to regroup and then waved the prison van on. As it reached the road, the press pack made their accustomed pounce, all hoping for the one picture that would make the front page.

Inside the van, while cameras flashed at all of the windows, Meg cowered between two prison officers and wondered if she should tell Ashworth all she knew. But if she did tell, would they be able to prove it?

* * *

The date for Meg's trial was set for the fourth of February, and as new crimes were committed with ever-increasing regularity the priorities in CID shifted rapidly and her plight was pushed to the backs of their minds. Only Ashworth kept her in his thoughts.

At quiet times he would flick through the file on the extortion case and would study the results of the searches of Meg's house and workshop, neither of which revealed anything untoward. The efforts of the police to trace any of the forty thousand pounds paid over by Samuels also proved fruitless, as did the checks on the real James Dallington and David Masters, owner of the newly painted house in Morton. Ashworth even built up a certain kind of rapport with the private detective employed by Emma. The man was a true professional but despite undertaking a wide-ranging investigation, which cost the councillor a small fortune, he had so far come up with nothing new. Every line of enquiry led to a cul-de-sac; each new clue turned out to be a red herring.

Not only was Emma's political career brought to an abrupt end but she had, it seemed, lost all respect from the people of Bridgetown and therefore declared her intention to leave the area once the trial was over. In view of that, and because no attempt was made to extort money from any other supermarket chain, Ashworth's mind repeatedly turned to Jean Churchman and Jerry Townsend. The motive was plain; and Townsend undoubtedly had every opportunity to plant the spiked goods on the Save U Supermarket shelves. He was also sure that Meg was not telling all she knew. A twenty-five-year prison stretch lay before her, and yet she was keeping something back. Whom was she protecting? And why? Why? That tiny word was Ashworth's bugbear.

The Christmas season came and went, and the new year dawned with a landscape lost under four inches of snow. Slowly, too slowly for Ashworth, the days ticked on towards the middle of January.

CHAPTER 23

Ashworth stamped the snow from his shoes before he entered the station, glaring irritably at the web of wet footprints across reception which suggested that most others before him had not bothered to do the same. Martin Dutton immediately gestured to him from behind the front desk and Ashworth sauntered over, thinking that the sergeant wanted nothing more than their usual morning chat.

'Hello, Martin.'

'Jim.' His businesslike nod forewarned Ashworth that the sergeant had more than the general station chit-chat to pass along this particular morning. 'That private investigator's here to see you. He's been waiting some time.'

'Sean Deackon? I wonder what he wants.'

'He says he's got something important to show you; he wouldn't tell me what, but he seemed more than a little agitated. Anyway, I've put him in interview room one.'

'Thanks, Martin,' Ashworth said, already on his way.

* * *

Sean Deackon and the chief inspector shared the same birth year, but that was all they had in common. Whereas

Ashworth was a strapping six-foot-plus, the private detective was small and wiry. Their style of dress contrasted too: Ashworth was always smartly attired, while Deackon's light grey suit was crumpled and partly concealed by an old fawn mackintosh, equally as creased, that suggested his job called for many nights sleeping in his car.

Ashworth pushed open the door to find him sitting at the table and gazing morosely into the polystyrene coffee cup in front of him, the habitual cigarette between his yellowed fingers. When he spoke, his words were warmly coloured by a slight southern Irish lilt.

'Hello, Jim,' he said.

'Morning, Sean. I must say, this is a surprise.' He was eager to hear what Deackon had to say, imagining that it must be hugely important to bring the man into the station.

The investigator read his thoughts. 'It's bad news, I'm afraid. I've unearthed something that's not going to help Meg Cowper's case one little bit.'

While Ashworth's eyebrows arched questioningly, Deackon clamped the cigarette between his teeth and reached into his inside pocket, bringing out a clear plastic container in which could be seen a folded envelope.

'I've handled it as little as possible, but it's sure to have some of my prints on it.'

Ashworth took the container and with great care pulled the envelope from it. He laid it on the desk, eyeing it carefully. It was of good quality, certainly not the type that are two a penny from any stationers. Flipping it over with the help of a ruler, he extracted from within it a single sheet of white paper. That too was expensive, and he unfolded it to find a typed letter which read:

Dearest Meg,
I know how much the woman's death upset you, but I beg you to believe that it was entirely unintentional on my part. If she had been a normal drinker the amount of oxalic

acid in the bottle would merely have made her ill. She must have consumed a large amount of alcohol in a very short space of time. I only hope that you will not let this interfere with our master plan because we are so near now, and I do passionately want us to spend the rest of our lives together. So please, darling, please keep on leading the police astray. You must believe that they will never be able to prove you did it — after all, we planned it all so carefully.

All my love,

James x x x

Ashworth allowed the letter to drop onto the table. 'Well,' he huffed, 'they might as well throw away the keys.'

Deackon lit another cigarette from the one he had just finished, then crushed the stub out in an old throat lozenge tin he carried around for use as an ashtray.

'That was my first thought,' he said. 'I found it in Meg Cowper's workshop. Your forensic lot must have missed it. There were a lot of invoices in a file, and that was lodged between them.'

Ashworth coughed as cigarette smoke billowed his way. 'They either missed it, Sean, or it was planted after we'd searched the workshop.'

'That may or may not be so,' he replied with a shrug. 'All I can say is that it was well concealed between the sheets of a double invoice. I almost missed it myself.'

'What were you doing there in the first place?' Ashworth asked.

'I'd just about wound the case up, but then Emma asked me to go through everything one more time to make sure I hadn't missed anything.'

'And you came up with this.'

'I did.' He nodded sadly. 'That Churchman woman let me in. She was fussing about, saying she wanted all of Meg's stuff out, so I picked up the file to annoy her more than anything else, and that's when I found it.'

'Have you told Emma?'

'I have, and between you, me, and a pint of Guinness, she wanted me to destroy the letter. In fact, she became more than a little unpleasant when I refused.'

'You did the right thing, Sean.'

'I'm not so sure my bank manager would agree with you.' He took one last drag of his cigarette and that too was consigned to the tin. 'Emma still owes me four hundred pounds, but I suppose I can kiss that goodbye now.'

Ashworth's gaze returned to the letter. 'She must have spent a good deal of money, one way or another.'

'She has,' Deackon agreed. 'My bill alone was over four thousand, and a lawyer like Sanderson doesn't come cheap.' He looked into Ashworth's thoughtful face. 'That's all I can do, really. Like I said, I'm off the case now.'

'Thank you, Sean.'

Deackon stood up and stretched. 'If you want access to my notes at any time, you're more than welcome.'

* * *

Although Ashworth had never strayed from the right side of the law, he still shuddered when the iron gates of the prison clanged shut behind him with such a menacing finality. He took Holly lightly by the arm and they followed the prison warder along a covered gully to a second set of barred gates. Beyond those stood the prison proper and once inside they were escorted into a room on their left.

Meg was sitting at a table, her complexion sallow, her hair greasy, and her hands fidgeting constantly as she watched them enter the room.

'Do you want me to stay?' the warder asked in a brisk tone.

'No, wait outside, please,' Ashworth replied.

The keys jangled noisily on the woman's belt as she stepped into the corridor.

'How have you been, Meg?' Holly asked, sitting down to face her.

'How have I been?' she said shrilly, running nervous fingers through her hair. 'How do you think I've been?'

'Meg,' Ashworth said gently, 'something has come to light. That's why we asked to see you.' He withdrew the letter now safely sealed between polythene sheets. 'This was discovered in your workshop.'

She took it from him, and a look of total disbelief spread across her features as she scanned the lines.

'I've never seen it before,' she exclaimed, dropping it on to the table. 'Never.'

'So you've no idea how it came to be in your workshop?' Holly asked.

'None,' she said, her eyes pleading with them to believe her. 'I just don't understand any of this.'

'Please think, Meg. This letter will be produced by the prosecution at your trial,' Holly reminded her. 'Is there anything you can tell us that might throw some light on how it got there?'

'My God, you're unbelievable,' she yelled, the outburst taking Holly by surprise. 'Do you know what it's like to have other women eyeing you up, all the time propositioning you, knowing that sooner or later they're going to get you alone, a gang of them, and then . . . ?' She leant forward, her mouth distorted by a hostile sneer. 'If I knew anything that would get me out of here, do you think I'd be holding it back?'

The warder came quickly into the room. 'Is everything all right?'

'Yes,' Ashworth replied impatiently. He said no more until they were alone again. 'Meg, we're on your side — I want you to believe that.'

She gave a humourless laugh. 'You're on my side? Huh, look where it's got me.'

'Then help us to help you,' he urged. 'If we can find Dallington, it would shed a completely different light on the whole case.'

Meg settled back and seemed to be giving his words a lot of thought. 'What would happen if you did find him?'

'To start with, we'd interview him—'

'No, no,' she interjected. 'What would happen to me?'

The question seemed to take Ashworth off guard, and Holly answered for him. 'You'd be released into police custody to identify him.'

'I'd be taken to Bridgetown, you mean?'

'Yes, that's right.'

'I'd like to see Bridgetown again,' she said wistfully. 'I'd like to see it just one last time.'

'Then tell us anything you know,' Ashworth persisted. 'Anything that might help us to trace Dallington.'

'Have you got a cigarette?' Meg asked suddenly.

Holly rummaged in her shoulder bag and produced a packet of Benson and Hedges and a disposable lighter. Meg took one and accepted a light.

'One of the lovely habits I've acquired since I've been in here,' she said ruefully.

'Dallington,' Ashworth urged.

'Oh, yes.' She drew on the cigarette and watched the smoke spiralling away. 'I really did believe that he loved me, you know.'

Ashworth gave her a long-suffering look. 'Give us something that'll help us find him, Meg.'

His urgent tone seemed to jerk her back to the present, and within the space of a second the dreaminess in her eyes was replaced by a harsh glint. 'I remember there was a little pub we used to go to, about halfway between Bridgetown and Bridgenorton. We never had a drink there, though. James used to go into the bar and collect a package every so often.'

Ashworth frowned. 'If you didn't have a drink, why did *you* go into the bar?'

She gave a regretful smile. 'We went everywhere together then. Always hand in hand. Always together.' She drew on her cigarette. 'I remember that James didn't want me to go in with him; he used to leave me standing by the door.'

'Do you remember the name of the pub?'

Meg considered the burning tip of her cigarette, and said, 'No, but I remember the sign. It used to creak in the wind; it reminded me of a horror film. It had a ploughman on it, I think, stripped to the waist.'

'The Plough,' Ashworth said, with a hint of triumph.

'Yes, that was it, the Plough.'

'Good girl.' He was on his feet and tapping the glass window, motioning to the warder that they had finished. The woman entered the room.

'We're all through here.'

'There's another warder outside, ready to escort you to the main gate,' she said. They nodded their thanks and left swiftly. 'Come on, Cowper, put the ciggy out and get back to the remand wing. Let's be having you.'

There was a grim smile on Meg's face as she put out the cigarette for she had finally made up her mind. If the next twenty-five years of her life were to be spent in prison, then she would make sure that others suffered with her.

CHAPTER 24

The pub sign did indeed creak and groan in the wind. Ashworth stood and watched it while Holly got out of the car. The Plough was situated on a winding country lane, completely surrounded by open fields, the grass now covered by pure white virgin snow. In fact, the pub was so far off the beaten track that it had only survived the introduction of the breathalyser by adapting over the years to become a family pub complete with children's playground, pub grub, and coffee and tea served alongside the beers and spirits.

They made their way between the slides and swings towards the main doors, and once through them their nostrils immediately picked up the rich smell of percolating coffee. The place was empty and the young barman's bored expression suggested that it had been so for some time. He looked up as they entered and gave them a professional smile.

'Good afternoon,' he said. 'What can I do for you?'

Ashworth took out his warrant card and showed it to the man.

'I ain't done nothing, guv, honest I ain't,' he said, grinning. Ashworth's expression remained grave. 'Okay, okay, I know that's a bad joke.'

'We'll let you off,' Holly said, hitching herself on to a high stool in front of the dark oak counter. 'As long as you give us a cup of coffee on the house.'

'You're a cheeky one,' he said, taking two mugs from beneath the bar.

Ashworth gazed around the room; it had a pleasant atmosphere and its countless windows allowed light from the snow-covered countryside to flood in.

The barman wandered over to the coffee percolator, and Holly whispered, 'Leave him to me, guv, he thinks he's God's gift.'

Ashworth nodded, and they waited until he came back with two steaming mugs which he placed on the bar next to a bowl of brown sugar.

'There you go,' he said brightly.

'We're looking for somebody,' Holly told him.

'Aren't we all?' he said, licking his lips and allowing his playful blue eyes to roam down to her breasts.

My God, he can't be any more than twenty, Holly reflected, as she took a photograph of Meg from her shoulder bag. 'Do you recognize this woman?'

He took the picture and studied it, his thumb hooked into the pocket of his floral waistcoat. 'Yeah, I remember her. She's a bit of a looker — past her sell-by date, mind you, but still worth the effort.'

Holly smiled as she spooned sugar into her coffee. 'She used to come in here with a man called James Dallington.'

'James Dallington? Never heard of him. No, the guy she used to hang around with was Clive Davis-Parker, would you believe?'

'Did he collect packages from here?'

'Not as such, no. He stayed here.'

'He stayed here? What do you mean?'

'The landlord lets out a few rooms,' he said, pointing upwards, 'and Clive rented one of them for a couple of weeks.'

'So what were these packages he used to have sent here?' Holly asked, sipping her coffee. 'And who delivered them?'

The barman shrugged. 'Search me. The guests collect their mail and parcels from there . . .' He indicated a pigeonholed rack behind the bar, quite near to the entrance. 'What they are and who delivers them has got nothing to do with me.'

'But would you have taken them in?' Holly quizzed.

'I suppose so. There's nobody else here for most of the day.'

'And what was this Davis-Parker like?' Ashworth asked.

'He was a nice guy, really smooth, had a way with the ladies. He was getting on a bit, mind you — must have been about forty, but the girls seemed to love him. Of course,' he added, tapping the side of his nose, 'that could've had something to do with the fact that he wasn't short of the old dosh.'

'He had plenty of money, then?' Ashworth asked.

'Yeah, and he used to spread it around. He drove a brand new Ford Escort, dark blue . . . that was a nice piece of motor.'

Ashworth pushed his untouched coffee to one side and leant on the bar. 'Does he still come in here?'

'No, he stopped coming quite a few months ago. He got friendly with Janie Munns. She used to be a regular . . . when she could hobble here on her sticks.'

'Are you suggesting she was a bit past her sell-by date, as well?' Holly asked with a laugh.

'And fast coming to the end of her shelf life,' he said, chuckling at his own joke. 'But there you are, if that's what Clive fancies, who am I to judge.'

'Do you know where the woman lives?'

'No idea. Somewhere in Morton, I think. Is this really important.'

'Extremely,' Holly told him.

He sighed and crossed to a large serving hatch. When it was lifted, they could hear the sound of dishes being washed and could smell the stale odours of lunch.

'Al,' the barman called.

'What?' a voice answered above the noise of running water.

'Do you know where Janie Munns lives?'

'Stroll on,' he jeered. 'You must be hard up.'

'No, come on, Al, I've got the law here, they want to know.'

'Tell them to try the upmarket estate at Morton.'

'Did you hear that?' he asked, slamming the hatch shut. They nodded and the man came sauntering back.

'How long ago did this Clive form a relationship with Janie Munns?' Ashworth asked.

'Form a relationship?' he mocked. 'When did he start knocking her off, you mean?'

'Perhaps I do,' Ashworth said lightly.

'Let's see, must have been the back end of last September . . . something like that, anyway.'

'Thanks,' Holly said, finishing her coffee. 'You've been a great help.'

He flashed her a cheeky grin. 'I'll help you any time, sweetheart.'

'You're too young, kid,' she said with a wink.

'Don't you believe it,' he called good-naturedly.

In the playground an icy wind bit through them, its edge more cutting after the warmth of the pub. They were in the car, pulling on their seat belts, when Holly said, 'It looks like Clive Davis-Parker is our James Dallington — eh, guv?'

'Yes,' he said, inserting the ignition key. 'And the estate at Morton is in the frame once again. This man must have been going out with Meg while he was having some sort of affair with the Munns woman. That's why he knew the estate well enough to point out a house and pretend he lived there.'

'The same thought struck me, guv. So, now we have an extortionist and murderer with a very tangled love life, and that doesn't make any sense.'

Ashworth started the engine. 'Either he can't concentrate on one thing for any length of time,' he said with a wry smile, 'or there's a reason he befriended the women.'

'That was good, guv, about not being able to concentrate on any one thing. Very nearly droll, that was.'

He shot her a scathing glance, then pulled out into the lane.

* * *

The single set of tyre tracks through the snow in Phenbrook Drive suggested that the road was very quiet and little used. Central Control had supplied the address of Janie Munns in order to save Ashworth the ordeal of tangling again with Mrs Craddock of the Neighbourhood Watch. He pulled up outside number ten and saw a woman poke her head around the drawn curtains at the lounge window.

'Looks like we've been spotted,' he remarked to Holly.

'Yes, I noticed.' She unhooked her seat belt and sat looking at the house. 'I don't think our Janie would have much trouble finding a couple of pennies to rub together.'

'Hmm, that house must be worth a fortune. Right, Holly, let's go and meet Mrs Munns, shall we?'

A pathway had been cleared on the drive, and frozen snow lay piled high. They negotiated the route gingerly for the dusk was bringing with it lower temperatures, making the tarmac treacherous. The house was similar to others on the estate — double-fronted, tandem garage on the side — but with added improvements, such as the impressive double-glazed porch which they now approached. Ashworth lifted the heavy lion's head knocker on the expensive double-glazed door but before he had chance to rap, it was opened by the woman they had seen at the window. She was quite tall, elegantly dressed, and possibly in her fifties. Her hair was dyed a youthful shade of blond which only served to highlight the lines etched deeply into her face.

'Can I help you?' she asked in a cultured voice.

'Mrs Munns?' Ashworth enquired.

'Ms Munns,' she hastily corrected him. 'And who might you be?'

'Chief Inspector Ashworth, madam, and this is Detective Sergeant Bedford.'

She studied their warrant cards with surprise, and said, 'What can I possibly do for you?'

'May we come in for a moment?'

'Well, yes, I suppose so.' She reluctantly stood to one side. 'I'll show you to the lounge.'

As they followed her across the large hall, Holly assessed that the woman's designer label beige suit must have set her back at least a thousand pounds; she also noticed the scent of aftershave which she thought might be French. The lounge had been tastefully designed along the lines of a country cottage, with beamed ceiling, huge inglenook fireplace, and floral three-piece suite.

'So, how can I help you?' Janie Munns asked.

'We believe you know a Mr Clive Davis-Parker,' Ashworth said.

'Yes, I do,' she replied, nodding tentatively. 'He's a business acquaintance.'

The answer took Ashworth by surprise. 'And what line of business is he in?'

'Fashion — the rag trade, as it's called.'

They had not been invited to sit and Ashworth wandered over to the window while Holly stayed near the doorway.

'Do you know his whereabouts at the present time, Ms Munns?'

'No,' she said quickly. 'As a matter of fact, I haven't seen him for quite a few weeks. I think it was Christmas when I . . .' She stopped and frowned worriedly. 'You're not enquiring into his business ventures, are you?'

'No, we're not,' he assured her. 'It's a small matter which I'm sure Mr Davis-Parker will be able to clear up in a matter of minutes once we've found him. Do you have his address?'

'No . . . no, I don't,' she said, clearly relieved.

'Rather strange,' Ashworth ventured. 'I mean, if he's a business acquaintance . . .'

'Clive moves around, I believe. Rented properties . . . that sort of thing.'

'I see.' Ashworth scrutinized the woman, who refused to meet his gaze.

'Excuse me,' Holly said. 'I wonder if I might use your loo?'

'Loo?' Janie said with a haughty sneer. 'You may use the bathroom, yes. It's at the top of the stairs.'

Holly gave her a sweet smile, and said, 'Thank you.' Her high-heeled shoes made no sound on the thick Wilton stair carpet, and she hurried into the bathroom hoping that Ashworth would keep the woman talking for the few minutes that she needed. The suite was of Victorian design, with dark wood panelling on the bath and matching accessories. She made straight for the cabinet over the wash basin and looked inside. Satisfied with what she had found, Holly flushed the lavatory and returned to the lounge. Janie Munns was about to show Ashworth out.

'Thanks again,' Holly said.

'You'll let me know if he gets in touch?' Ashworth asked.

'Of course,' she said, ushering them quickly through the front door.

'Well, what did you find?' he asked Holly as they walked back to the Scorpio.

'Unless Ms Munns wet shaves every morning and uses expensive French aftershave, he's there, guv.'

'How do you know he shaved there this morning?'

'The brush was still damp.'

Ashworth chuckled and let her into the car. 'Good girl,' he said. 'Now all we have to do is work out a way to keep an eye on the house without Mr Davis-Parker knowing we're here.'

* * *

Janie Munns raced up the stairs and hurried along to the front bedroom. When she flung open the door, a man spun round from the window.

'Why are the police looking for you, Clive?'

‘Calm down, Janie.’ He turned and peered around the curtain to where Ashworth’s car was still parked. ‘What did they say?’

‘Just that they wanted to see you,’ she said, suspicion clear in her tone.

‘It’s nothing to worry about, darling. It’s just that one of my ex-partners has got himself into a spot of bother with some dodgy merchandise. He’s completely innocent, incidentally, which is why I want to dodge the police.’ He turned to her, a warm smile on his face. ‘You know what they’re like — they’ve no real proof against the man, but they’ll keep hounding him. I’m certain they’ll have to let the matter drop, so I’d rather not see them in case I inadvertently land poor old Terence in it.’

She still appeared wary. ‘Are you sure that’s all it is? I do have a lot of money tied up in your company.’

He started towards her, a pained look on his face. ‘Do you think I’d . . . ? Oh, Janie, darling, how could you?’

‘I’m sorry,’ she said, giving him a penitent smile. ‘It was just the shock of them calling.’

‘I wouldn’t do anything like that to you,’ he said, reaching forward to cup her breasts. ‘You mean too much to me.’

Janie’s hands came up to cover his and she sighed as he gently rubbed her nipples. ‘I’m being silly, I know, but you’re so attractive, Clive. I don’t know what you see in me.’

He pulled her to him, his hands slipping down to her buttocks as their lips met. Janie flung her arms around his neck and pushed hard against his erection.

‘There,’ he said soothingly when the kiss ended. ‘You can feel the effect you have on me.’

She glanced towards the bed, then turned hopeful eyes to his face. ‘Please?’ she murmured.

With his mind still on the police car outside, he pushed up her skirt and reached between her legs, forcing his breathing to become heavy until it matched her own.

CHAPTER 25

The problem they had with keeping an eye on Janie Munns's house was solved with a little help from the Neighbourhood Watch coordinator. Ashworth spotted Mrs Craddock in the rear-view mirror; she was hastening towards them with determined strides, totally impervious to the icy conditions.

'Oh dear,' he muttered, when she skirted round the car and tapped on his side window. He wound it down and gave her a smile.

'It's you two, is it? I'll have you know, you're parked outside my sister's property and she's just reported that fact to me.'

'We are the police,' he argued reasonably. 'And besides, Mrs Craddock, anybody can park on the road.'

'I'm sure you're correct, I'm not disputing that, but you have no right to go around alarming innocent members of the public—'

'Mrs Craddock . . .' Holly interjected. 'Do you know anything about Janie Munns who lives at number ten?'

The woman scowled. 'Mutton dressed as lamb,' she said. 'That type of person should never be allowed on a development like this one.'

'Is there a man living there?'

'Yes, there is,' she said, sniffing with disdain. 'And he's a lot younger than that . . . woman.'

Ashworth had a thought. 'I wonder . . . would your sister allow us to park a car on her drive, so that we can watch number ten without being too obvious?'

'Well . . .' She smiled, evidently flattered that they should be seeking her help. 'I can't see why not.'

'But, guv,' Holly whispered, 'we can't just reverse into the drive. They'll see us.'

'I know, but I was thinking — say I leave you here and send Josh back with the Vauxhall from the police pool, the one with the tinted windows. That way, you'll be able to look out without being seen.'

'But what would I be doing while I was waiting for Josh?' she asked warily.

'Again, I was wondering,' he said innocently, 'whether Mrs Craddock's sister would let you wait in her house. You could keep an eye on number ten from in there.'

'There's no reason why she should object to that,' the woman beamed. 'In fact, I could wait with you. Two pairs of eyes are better than one.'

'But, guv, it could be over two hours before Josh arrives,' Holly said pointedly.

'I know,' he replied, hiding a smile. 'Is that a problem?'

'Thanks a lot, guv, I owe you one.' Ashworth chuckled mischievously as Holly climbed out of the car.

'Come along, dear,' Mrs Craddock said, glancing up and down the road. 'We'd better get under cover before we're spotted.'

* * *

By the time Josh arrived in the Vauxhall, Holly knew the names and addresses of all the residents on the development, knew which couples were married and which were merely cohabiting, was told of any suspected affairs being conducted behind the prim net curtains, and was brought up to date about the serious case (in Mrs Craddock's view) of the Yorkshire terrier from Stamford Drive which had allegedly fouled the footpath on numerous occasions. As her sense of humour had not yet re-established itself, Josh was leaving her well alone. The night sky was clear, the temperature was bitterly cold, and a full moon was casting a bluish tint over the crisp white snow.

'It's bloody brass monkeys,' Holly complained, pulling the tartan rug tighter around her legs. 'If this prat doesn't show soon, I'm going in there after him.' Josh said nothing. 'Is there any coffee left?'

'In the flask,' he muttered.

She swivelled round and lifted the thermos flask from the back seat. Balancing its cup on her knee, she poured the coffee and swore irritably because it was only lukewarm. Just then, the outside light came on at number ten.

'We could have action,' Josh said.

'Oh, bloody great timing,' Holly spat through clenched teeth as she returned the flask to the back seat and threw the car rug aside.

The security light had a strong beam and fully illuminated the driveway, which glistened with a thick layer of frost. A man stepped out of the porch and cast furtive glances right and left before dashing off along the pavement.

'Let's go,' Holly said, spilling coffee in her rush to put down the cup and open the door.

The man from number ten was halfway along the road and when their car doors slammed he peered back to locate the vehicle then hesitated slightly, unsure of what to do. When he realized that they were heading for him, however, he turned tail and bolted, disappearing along an alleyway between two houses.

'Cut him off, Josh,' Holly said, pointing to a side road that ran parallel with the alley.

High privet hedges lined either side of the gully which was perhaps a yard wide. Holly came skidding to a halt at its entrance and, trying to keep up a running pace, she followed the man's footprints in the deep snow. They led her away from the street lighting and onto a park area, completely dark and still. She looked around blindly, unable even to keep to his footprints for the path here was well-trodden, the snow turned to packed ice. She started off and immediately lost her footing, landing on her back.

'Oh, bollocks,' she exclaimed, struggling to her feet.

Holly kept to the path, all the time checking the surrounding snow in case the man had turned off at any time. After about two hundred yards of squinting into the dark, her night vision was sufficient to make out a small lake with an island at its middle. Her breath fogged the chilled air as she stopped and looked around. She could see no signs of the man, no footprints, no sudden movements. Her attention returned to the island in the middle of the frozen lake.

'Oh God, no,' she muttered.

Holly knew full well that she should radio for help so that the Morton police could seal off the area but still she hesitated; before she did anything she would need to check the island. Taking a deep breath, she placed a tentative foot on the ice. It seemed thick enough. She slowly moved her other foot forward and put her full weight on the frozen water. It held. With tiny steps, she edged forward and made her way towards the island. Her heels chipped noisily into the ice, and the cold from it seeped through into her shoes, chilling her to the bone.

As she neared the centre the ice beneath her feet began to move, to crackle, and fissures appeared every time she bore down on it. A wave of terror sucked the colour from her cheeks when she realized that the ice was thinner on that part of the lake because it was well protected by the overhanging branches of numerous evergreen trees at the perimeter of the island. With every muscle tensed, Holly backed away until the ice felt more solid. Standing still for a moment she became aware for the first time that her legs were badly trembling, both from fear and cold.

'I'm pissed off with this,' she mouthed, negotiating another path. 'Why the hell didn't I go into nursing?'

There was a small part of the island which was free of vegetation and with great caution Holly made her way towards it. The ice gave way slightly but this time she refused to turn back, choosing instead to ignore the thin layer of water soaking through her shoe leather. In desperation she ran the last few yards and scrambled breathlessly onto dry land. She took a minute to compose herself and then started to pick a way through the dense thicket, cursing softly whenever a thorn tore at her flesh. She found the man standing in a clearing at the centre of the island, his back towards her.

'Okay,' she said, approaching him boldly. 'You're nicked.'

He turned around, and Holly stopped dead in her tracks. 'Jesus Christ,' she uttered. 'It's you.'

* * *

Josh found her just as she was bringing her prisoner off the island.

'Where the shit have you been?' she bawled. 'I nearly bloody drowned out there.'

'It was a dead end,' he responded angrily. 'You sent me up a dead end.'

'Look who we've got,' she said, pointing to the man's face.

'Surprise, surprise,' Josh said. 'We'd better get him back to the car and radio the guv'nor.'

* * *

Holly watched through the car window as Josh tried to pacify a distraught Janie Munns.

'Holly . . .' Ashworth's voice jumped from the radio in her hand.

'Guv, you're not going to believe who James Dallington turned out to be.'

'Enlighten me, then.'

'The man I've got is none other than our friendly con-man, Vincent Blakewell.'

'Blakewell?' Ashworth was silent for a long moment. 'Has he said anything?'

'Nothing, apart from suggesting that my parents weren't married when I was born,' she said, casting a blithe grin at the man.

'You fucking bitch,' Blakewell snarled.

Holly released the radio button and kicked him hard on the shin. Blakewell cried out in pain.

'You can't do that—'

'Just shut it,' she hissed. 'If you give me any more verbal, you're going to get damaged — understand? I can always claim you resisted arrest, so just keep it shut.'

'Holly? Holly?' Ashworth sounded concerned.

Blakewell skulked back in the seat, a hurt expression on his face.

'Holly? Holly, what's happening?'

'It's okay, guv, I was just making sure our prisoner was comfortable.'

'Bring him in.'

'Will do.'

* * *

It was way past 10 p.m. when they got Blakewell back to Bridgetown Police Station. He was taken directly to interview room number one where he was questioned fiercely by Ashworth, but he continually denied any knowledge of Meg Cowper and refused to say anything more. No matter how hard he pressed, Ashworth failed to get answers to his questions so, at ten minutes to midnight, he sent Blakewell to be confined to cells for the night and made his way to reception with Holly and Josh.

'This may well clear Meg of any direct involvement,' he said, still convinced that she was telling the truth.

'I hope so,' Holly said. 'Do we apply to have her released into our custody to identify Blakewell?'

'I've already done that. We collect her in the morning.' They entered the dimly lit reception area, unusually quiet for that time of night, and Ashworth glanced at his watch.

'This case is most definitely cutting back my consumption of malt whisky,' he muttered, as they headed for the car park. And his expression showed that his overall happiness was not benefiting because of it.

* * *

Ashworth sent Holly and Josh to bring Meg in the next morning, and Blakewell was left to stew in the cells until their arrival was imminent. When he was finally led into the interview room, where Ashworth was already waiting with Bobby, the man looked far from confident, and when told by the uniformed officer to stand before the chief inspector he quietly obeyed. The officer retired to his position at the door.

'I trust you slept well,' Ashworth said with heartfelt contempt. 'Sit down.'

He indicated the chair opposite and Blakewell's upper lip curled into a scowl as he settled into it.

'You're not very talkative,' the chief inspector observed.

'I've got nothing to say,' he said, his gaze directed to the floor.

'Pity that. There are a lot of people seeking an explanation from you,' Ashworth said, with a mocking smile. 'Not least, Janie Munns. She wants to know about the twenty thousand pounds of her money that you invested in a company which doesn't exist.'

'But she gave me the money,' Blakewell retorted. 'God, why do women always complain when I want out and they realize how much money they've given me?'

Ashworth chuckled. 'So you'll get sent to prison for swindling them, I would imagine.'

Blakewell ignored the remark and fished into his pocket for a packet of cigarettes. While he lit one, Ashworth said, 'Meg Cowper's on her way here to identify you. Now, we could bring her in here — or would you prefer a formal parade? It will of course take time to arrange . . .'

Blakewell leant back, exhaling smoke. 'What's the point?' he said, looking directly at Ashworth for the first time.

'Am I to take it that you'll see her?' He nodded. 'Good . . . very good, Mr Blakewell.'

There was a knock on the door and the uniformed officer went out into the corridor. In a matter of seconds he was back and he crossed to Ashworth and whispered in his ear.

'Meg Cowper's here,' he announced, his chair scraping as he got to his feet.

Blakewell's eyes flitted nervously towards the door, and then he bowed his head.

'Okay, Holly,' Ashworth called.

Meg was the first to appear, guided by Holly who had a firm grasp of the woman's upper arm. When her gaze fell on Blakewell she lunged forward but Holly's grip held fast.

'Steady, Meg, don't be silly,' she cautioned.

'Meg, I'm sorry,' Blakewell stammered. 'I can explain everything.'

'You bastard,' she cried, finally breaking away. 'You lying bastard.'

Before Holly could stop her, Meg was at the table, smashing into Blakewell's face with her clenched fists. He screamed, both with pain and surprise, bringing up his hands to block the blows. Holly dashed forward and grabbed her flailing arms, but not before Meg had managed to land two more heavy punches. Eventually, she was wrestled away from the table and Blakewell fell back in his chair, a trickle of blood escaping from his left nostril and running down his face on to his shirt collar.

'I'm all right, now, Sergeant,' Meg said softly. 'There's no need to hold me so tightly.'

Holly glanced at Ashworth, who nodded for her to be released. Meg's eyes never wavered from Blakewell's face as she stood trembling with anger.

'I would have walked through fire for you. I loved you,' she whispered, with tears coursing down her cheeks. 'How could you do this to me?'

He turned away, a hand to his nose in an effort to stem the blood.

Holly gently took her arm and pulled her towards the door. 'Come on, Meg, let's go.'

She allowed herself to be led from the room, all the time staring over her shoulder at Blakewell and frowning with disbelief.

'I want a doctor,' he whined, as soon as the door was closed.

'Oh, shut up,' Ashworth snapped. 'In my time, I've had worse knocks than that dancing with girls.' He settled into his seat. 'Are you going to talk to me?'

Blakewell stared at him. 'You're not going to believe me.'

CHAPTER 26

Holly took Meg to the canteen where she gave her a cup of tea and a shoulder to cry on. They talked for a long time and Meg wept constantly, but at last the tears stopped and Holly started to think about getting her back.

'Do you have to take me straight to the prison?'

'Well, I should really.'

'Please, Sergeant, could I take one last look at the workshop and my house?'

'Oh, I don't know,' Holly said doubtfully. 'I've already given you more freedom than I should have done. You're supposed to be handcuffed to an officer at all times.'

'Please,' she begged, placing a hand on Holly's arm. 'There's so much of my life tied up here, and I know it's going to be a long time before I see it all again.'

Holly hesitated. 'Oh, all right, then. But don't do a runner on me, okay?'

'There wouldn't be much point in that, would there?'

* * *

'You're right, Mr Blakewell, I don't believe you,' Ashworth said firmly. 'You're admitting that you planted the first jar of baby food with the glass in it, but say you know nothing about anything else.'

'Yes, and that's the truth,' he said, his eyes pleading first with Bobby and then with the officer by the door. 'Can't any of you see? I've been set up for this.'

Ashworth looked highly sceptical. 'Why did you plant the jar of baby food?'

'I got the idea the last time I was inside. One of the other prisoners told me that Arnolds baby food didn't really have tamper-proof lids. So I thought if I came here and did one simple hoist on a local supermarket that didn't have the funds to withstand a boycott by the public, I could walk away with an easy forty grand.'

'How did you know it was forty thousand? The sum of money paid was never made public.'

Blakewell gave an exasperated sigh. 'Because that's the amount I was going to ask for. Look, I planted the jar on the shelf, and all the way back to that doss house I was staying at, I had a funny feeling that I was being followed but I couldn't see anybody. Then, that night I had a telephone call, and a woman's voice told me I'd been spotted planting the baby food on the security tapes. She said if I didn't do exactly what I was told, they'd go to the police.'

'So, it was a woman's voice,' Ashworth said thoughtfully.

'Yes, and when you and Bedford turned up the following morning, I thought they'd shopped me. Then I realized you were just making a routine enquiry. Just after you left I received another telephone call. It was the same voice, and she instructed me to go to Meg's workshop, turn on the charm and ask her out.'

He caught Ashworth's cynical frown. 'I knew you wouldn't believe me — but anyway I said hold on I haven't got any cash, and the woman said don't worry about that. She said I was to go to the multi-storey car park opposite the supermarket and somebody would meet me there, give me some cash and supply me with a car. When I asked how I'd recognize this person, she told me to look out for a man in black leather, wearing a crash helmet.'

* * *

Holly followed Meg through the arch at Jean Churchman's cottage. She was gazing around her, hungrily taking in the views, her eyes sweeping down the long garden to the orchard, its bare plum and apple trees draped in frost, to where the rhubarb patch lay dormant beneath the snow. Finally, they came to the stables.

'Can I go in by myself?' she implored.

Holly gave her a pained look. 'I'll have to search you when you come out, you know.'

'I'm used to that by now,' she said with a hollow laugh.

'Yes, all right, go on, then.'

Meg went through the door and closed it silently behind her. Holly heard the light switch click on as she leant against the wall and delved into her shoulder bag for a cigarette. Although only an occasional smoker, she always carried a packet in case she needed one. And, God, she needed one now. She felt an almost overwhelming sympathy for Meg Cowper; after seeing her reaction to Blakewell, Holly was one hundred per cent certain that the woman was innocent. Lost in her thoughts, she flicked the cigarette away and it sank into the snow as the stable door opened and Meg emerged. It was plain that she had been crying.

'I had so many dreams, Sergeant,' she said, standing before Holly, her arms held away from her sides.

Holly expertly ran her hands over the contours of Meg's body, feeling for the tell-tale bulge of a concealed object.

'You're clear,' she said. 'I'd better look in the bag, though.'

Meg took the canvas holdall from her shoulder and opened it. Holly checked the purse which contained a small amount of change, the cigarette packet with eighteen still remaining, and the lighter. The only other object in the bag was a white plastic container designed to hold two tampons. She removed the lid; there were two inside.

'That time of the month?' she sympathized, replacing the top.

'Yes,' Meg sighed.

* * *

'You know about the crash helmet because you were the one wearing it,' Ashworth yelled.

'That's not true,' Blakewell insisted. 'When I met the guy, he gave me a thousand pounds and the keys to the latest model Ford Escort that was parked there. He told me to move out of the doss house and into the Plough, under the name of Clive Davis-Parker. He said for all other purposes I'd be using the name James Dallington and it was really important that Meg went to the Plough with me.'

'Why use a different name at the Plough?'

'He said it would muddy the trail if things went wrong.'

'Did he say where he got the name James Dallington from?' Ashworth quizzed.

'Yes, he said he found it in a hotel register. He said he wanted me to use it because it sounded respectable and also if the police got onto the case, it would confuse them because it was a real name. He also told me to show Meg the house in Morton, the one where I was supposed to live with my wife.'

'This doesn't have the ring of truth to it,' Ashworth scoffed. 'Why should they tell you where they got the name from?'

'Because I asked. Don't forget, I use a lot of aliases, and I usually like to choose my own.'

* * *

Emma Cowper was not at home when they reached the house, and Meg seemed relieved to have the place to herself. She wandered around the downstairs rooms, touching various objects, and then returned to the hall and gazed up the stairs.

'Do you want to have a look at your bedroom?' Holly asked.

'You couldn't do me one enormous favour first, could you?'

'If it's possible, yes.'

'Would you ring the station and find out what James is saying?'

'He's Vincent Blakewell,' Holly corrected her gently. 'Your James Dallington doesn't exist.'

'Please, Sergeant, there are so many things I need to know.'

Holly reluctantly agreed. 'But my guv'nor's not going to be very happy about being interrupted.' She reached for the telephone on the hall table.

* * *

Holly was right; Ashworth was not at all happy about having to break off his questioning of Blakewell. Josh had the dubious honour of fetching him from the interview room and listening to his ravings on hearing the reason.

The moment he picked up the receiver he exploded, but Holly soon calmed him down after explaining in hushed tones that she was certain Meg was holding something back and Blakewell's explanation of events seemed to be of vital importance to her. Ashworth told her all that he had gleaned and when pushed had to admit that if the man was inventing the story, then it was the worst defence he had ever heard.

'You think he's telling the truth, then?' she pressed.

'Yes, I do, but there's still the briefcase and the letter to question him about. At the moment, though, I'd say some very clever people have orchestrated the whole thing to make it look like the pair of them are guilty.'

'Thanks, guv.' Holly hung up and went into the lounge where Meg was waiting in an armchair.

'Well?' she asked.

Holly told her everything that Ashworth had said, and when she was finished Meg looked doubtful. 'So, it was a man and a woman?'

'That's what Blakewell's claiming, and that does fit in with Richard Samuels saying it was always a woman who made contact with him.' She hesitated. 'Does that mean anything to you?'

Meg gave a secret smile, but shook her head. 'Can I see my room, now?'

'Yes, go on.'

* * *

Ashworth breezed back into the interview room and Bobby activated the tape recorder.

'Right,' he said to Blakewell, 'you're saying the whole thing was scripted. You were told to get Meg into certain areas at certain times.'

'Yes,' he sighed. 'I had a telephone call instructing me to ring Meg on her mobile when she was in the supermarket and ask her to change the ginger ale. I had to tell her to meet me at Aldridge Farm so that we could go away—'

'All right, that's enough, we've been through all that.' Ashworth sat down and stared at the man across the table. 'So, when all the poisoning started, and Richard Samuels was held captive at the cottage, you didn't tie any of that in with what you were doing?'

'Yes, of course I did, but I was hardly in a position to do anything about it, was I? Look at it from my point of view: I wasn't breaking the law, and I was drawing a thousand pounds a week. The money was being left at the Plough . . .'

Ashworth exhaled loudly and snapped his fingers for Bobby to bring the briefcase and the letter across. Both were sealed in their protective polythene.

'First of all, the case,' Ashworth said. 'Have you seen it before?'

Blakewell examined it carefully. 'Yes, that was given to me in the car park at the Plough by the man in the crash helmet, and I was instructed to leave it in the boot of Meg's car.'

'When was that?'

'I can't remember.' He glanced at Ashworth's impatient expression and thought harder. 'No, I'm sorry, I've no idea when it was.'

Ashworth took the case and pushed it to one side. 'Have a look at the letter,' he said, placing it in front of him.

Blakewell read the contents and then looked up, horrified. 'I didn't send this. Check it for fingerprints — you won't find mine on it.'

'It hasn't escaped my notice that you're a con-artist. You wouldn't be foolish enough to leave fingerprints on something that could be used as evidence.'

'Honest to God, I didn't send that letter.' A fearful look crept into his face, and he said, 'How much trouble am I in?'

'About twenty-five years' worth, at the moment . . . and the situation worsens every time you open your mouth.'

Blakewell closed his eyes, and a grey pallor swept over his features.

* * *

During the ten minutes Meg was alone in the bedroom, the only sound that Holly heard was the lavatory flushing in the en suite bathroom. Meg came out holding a pile of underwear.

'Can I put these in a suitcase to take back with me?'

Holly nodded and followed her into the bedroom, where she checked the suitcase and the garments as they were put into it.

'Look at that,' Meg said, holding open her wardrobe. 'Two bottles of gin left. Do you know, that was full when I was arrested. I used to nip over to France every so often to stock up. Emma's stolen it — she was always doing that. You'd think somebody with her money would buy their own.'

'She's suffered a lot because of this business, you know.'

'I realize that,' Meg said, as she came and sat on the bed. 'It's funny, but now I know that James — I'm sorry, but I'll always think of him as James — now I know that he wasn't setting me up—'

'Meg, he was setting you up in a way, although he may not have been aware that he was.'

'That's what I mean. I'm certain now that when we were together . . .' She nodded towards the bed. '. . . he really meant it. Can you understand that?'

'I think I can, yes.'

'My sister may think I'm stupid, Sergeant, but there are some things I know.'

Holly considered her openly. 'I've a feeling there's something you're not telling us.'

Meg shot her a smile that was tinged with sadness. 'Do you know what I cling to when I'm locked in that cell? The fact that they didn't do it to get at me personally. I just happened to be convenient. I was in the wrong place at the wrong time.'

'Who, Meg?' Holly asked, crouching beside the bed. 'Who are they?'

'You wouldn't believe me, Sergeant, and even if you did, you'd never be able to prove anything.'

'We might. Why not give us a chance?' Holly urged. 'If you know anything, you must tell us.'

'That's exactly what I can't do. My lawyer's trying to do a deal. If he's successful I could spend less time in prison — and there'd be a chance that I could serve the final part of my sentence in an open prison. To you, that may not seem much to hope for, but it's all I've got. So I'm not going to start making accusations I can't prove in case I jeopardize my lawyer's negotiations.'

Holly could see the sense in that. 'Okay, I can't force you,' she said, 'but can't you just point us in a direction?'

Meg stared thoughtfully at the opposite wall for a long time. Then, in a voice that was hardly audible, she said,

'Look for someone who has access to a supply of oxalic acid. Perhaps not as obvious a supply as the one I had, but nevertheless someone who has access.' Holly's brow creased in concentration and Meg stood up.

'Right, let's get the search over with, then you can take me back to jail.' She picked up her bag and opened it. 'I've used a tampon,' she said, withdrawing the holder and placing it on the dressing table.

'I'd still better check it.'

Holly picked up the container and flicked open the lid. There was one tampon left. The canvas bag was looked over next, and finally she conducted a body search. Then, with one final glance around, Meg followed her back to the car.

CHAPTER 27

Vincent Blakewell had the look of a desperate man. Having always prided himself on being able to talk his way in or out of any situation, he was now forced to accept that this time he had been manoeuvred into a position from which there was no avenue of escape. He was chain-smoking, and a hazy smog hung over the interview room.

'Are you going to charge me?' he asked Ashworth.

'I shall have to, but for the moment I'd like to hold you here for further questioning.'

A glimmer of hope appeared in Blakewell's eyes. 'Does that mean you believe me?'

'Yes, I do,' Ashworth answered gruffly. 'Despicable as you are, I don't think you did this.'

'You certainly don't mince words, do you?' he said, managing a smile.

'No, I never have.' Ashworth rose wearily to his feet. 'Now, I'm going to have you taken to the cells where you'll be held for the twenty-four hours allowed to me. After that I shall have to charge you, because if I don't I'll be answering questions myself.' He stopped by the door. 'You know what you're facing, don't you, Mr Blakewell?'

He drew on his cigarette. 'No, you tell me.'

'If you could prove your story, you'd get five years for planting the first jar of baby food, plus time for whatever charges Janie Munns brings against you. If you can't prove it, well, you're looking at twenty-five to thirty years minimum.'

Blakewell let out a long breath as he demolished the cigarette. 'Okay . . . thanks for being frank with me.'

'I'd suggest therefore that while you're sitting in your cell, it would be wise to try and remember any detail, however small, that might help to substantiate your story.'

* * *

Back in CID the frown on Ashworth's face was becoming a permanent feature. He was sitting at his desk while Bobby paced about, hands in the pockets of his jacket.

'There's not much we can do, guv, is there?'

'No,' Ashworth agreed. 'I'll tell you what's going to happen now — the prosecution will claim that Blakewell and Meg were in this together, and about the only defence she can offer is that she was so infatuated with the man that she allowed herself to be talked into going along with it.'

'But, guv, the fact that Jason Brent told the same story about the man in the crash helmet must help her.'

'No, it doesn't. In fact, it has the reverse effect by making it look as if Blakewell was the man in the crash helmet. Did uniformed come up with anything when they searched Janie Munns's house?'

Bobby crossed to Josh's desk and sorted through some papers. 'No. There was no crash helmet and no motorbike gear, just a few personal belongings.' He grinned. 'It seems that Miss Munns took exception to them searching her house because of the neighbours and she took a pop at one of the officers.' There was no answering smile from Ashworth, and Bobby continued to riffle through the papers.

'This is interesting, guv. Holly phoned in and left a message — something about Meg Cowper saying they didn't do it to get at her and we should be looking for somebody else who has access to a supply of oxalic acid.'

Ashworth snorted. 'Instead of stating the obvious, I just wish Meg would tell us where to look.'

* * *

Blakewell came up with nothing new during the time he was held for questioning and became quite distraught when formally charged with murder and extortion. The fact that Janie Munns had decided not to press charges because the court case would show her to be a rather silly middle-aged woman seemed of little importance. He was taken before magistrates and remanded until the middle of the following week.

Holly, meanwhile, with a doggedness that matched Ashworth's, was wrestling with the task of finding someone with access to an alternative supply of oxalic acid. Jean Churchman and Jerry Townsend surfaced repeatedly in her mind, but there seemed no possible link between them and the poison. Her intellect kept telling her that the answer was there, staring her in the face, but the solution was proving to be elusive.

* * *

It was Tuesday when Meg's lawyer, the eminent Clive Sanderson, called on her at the prison. He was shown into the visitors' room by a large warder with a tart expression souring her face, who announced in an almost threatening tone that she would be waiting outside. Sanderson dismissed her with a brisk thank you, and then moved to where Meg was seated at the table.

'And how are you this morning?' he began heartily.

'Never better,' she spat, toying aggressively with her cigarette packet.

He chose to overlook the scornful rebuttal and busied himself with retrieving papers from his briefcase.

'Now, Meg, as you know I've been involved in a lot of discussions over the past few days and I think I've come up with a package that's acceptable to both of us.'

She looked up hopefully and waited while he settled himself in the chair.

'Plead guilty,' he said.

'What? Plead guilty?' she yelled. 'Is that your idea of a package acceptable to both of us?'

Sanderson glanced over his shoulder to where the warder was peering in through the window, and said, 'Calm down, Meg, and just let me explain.'

'But I haven't done anything,' she said, slowly enunciating each word.

He gave her a tight smile. 'The question of guilt or innocence doesn't come into this. You see, we simply cannot mount a credible defence — that's all there is to it. The minute that letter from Dallington turned up in your workshop, any hope of a jury finding you not guilty went out of the window.'

'Has anybody stopped to consider that the letter could have been planted?' Meg flared.

'Of course, and Blakewell denies having sent it, but none of that matters. As far as a jury is concerned, it's just one more piece of evidence pointing to your guilt. And, believe me, there's more than enough evidence against you to make the outcome of the trial a foregone conclusion.'

'Okay, so what's this fantastic deal you've got for me?'

'If you plead guilty, that will save the court's time.'

Meg sneered as she took out a cigarette.

'If you do that, Blakewell will have no choice but to do the same—'

'Saving even more of the court's time,' she interjected bitterly.

'Precisely.' He shrugged. 'I'm afraid that's the way things work.'

'And what exactly do I get for saving all this time for the court?'

'Simply this,' he said, leaning back in his seat. 'You get a life sentence . . .'

Meg felt her heart miss a beat as a coldness gripped her stomach. 'This is really cheering me up,' she murmured.

'A life sentence, but without any recommendation as to how many years you should serve. Which means that in fifteen years you'll be eligible for parole.'

'Fifteen years? Oh, my God . . .'

'Meg, I know that sounds like a long time but you're a young woman. You could be out by the time you're fifty, with enough years in front of you to start a new life.'

She huffed and tried to light the cigarette, but her shaking fingers were unable to coax a flicker from the lighter. Sanderson gently took it from her and held out the flame.

'And there are other pluses,' he went on. 'As I've already told you, if your behaviour is good you could be moved to an open prison for the last five years of your sentence. Those establishments are like holiday camps, take my word for it.'

'What's the alternative, Mr Sanderson?'

'Grim,' he said. 'The judge could recommend that you serve at least thirty years and of course that would mean you'd be almost seventy when you came out.'

Meg drew on her cigarette and exhaled thoughtfully. 'What does Emma think about this?'

'At first she was very much against the idea,' he said, unwilling to meet her eyes. 'But, to be honest, I had to tell her there was no way I could offer a defence and I advised her to contact another lawyer.'

'So, that's it, bottom line?'

He leant forward earnestly. 'Meg, my job is to do the best I can for my client. Now, what I've offered may not sound like a good deal, but it's the best you can expect under the present circumstances.'

'Can I have time to think about this?'

'Of course. The trial is next week, so I'll need to know by then, but I'm sure that once you think about it, you'll see there's no alternative.' He studied her slumped figure in the chair and cleared his throat. 'Emma's very hurt that you won't see her. Jean Churchman is, as well. As she said, although she and Emma hate each other's guts, she always regarded you as a friend.'

Meg gave a bitter laugh. 'I don't want to see anybody while I'm in here, Mr Sanderson. Mind you, I suppose fifteen years is rather a long time to go without visitors.'

The lawyer bundled his papers together and stuffed them into his briefcase. 'It's a matter of getting your priorities right, Meg. A lot of lifers take degrees, thereby preparing themselves for an exciting new life when they're released.' He fastened his briefcase and moved to tap on the window. 'Think it over carefully, Meg, and come to the right decision.'

'A lifer,' she whispered harshly, as Sanderson was let out of the room.

* * *

Vincent Blakewell lay awake, his worries effectively keeping sleep at a distance. It had been two hours since lights out and his eyes were now accustomed to the gloom. He was due before the magistrates the following morning where he would be remanded for a further week. And after that . . . ? Blakewell was well-versed in the ways of the law and did not need a solicitor to tell him that as things stood his best course of action would be to plead guilty. In fact, if Meg put in a guilty plea, he really had no choice but to follow suit.

The tip of his lighted cigarette glowed in the darkness of the cell as he dragged the smoke into his lungs. In a way he quite admired the people who had put him up for this, but nevertheless he cursed himself for not making sure he'd had some safeguards. If he had followed the man in the crash helmet . . . If he had got clear away from the district after Meg's arrest instead of opting for the easy pickings offered by Janie Munns . . .

'If, if, if,' he muttered, swinging his legs off the bunk and flicking his cigarette end into the ashtray.

Of course, his position was far worse than Meg's in as much as the crime to which he had already confessed held a maximum five-year sentence, then add on the fifteen years minimum he could expect for the extortion and murder charges and he'd be lucky to get out in twenty years — really lucky.

As Blakewell sat on the bunk he went over and over everything that had happened in an effort to find just one thing that would back up his story. What about the man in the crash helmet who had delivered the money to the Plough? Surely somebody there must be able to remember him. He shook his head, utterly despondent. No, they wouldn't remember. Why should they? Quite a number of motorcyclists delivered letters and parcels. So, there was no way he could prove that any money was even delivered there.

Suddenly a thought came into his head and he jumped off the bunk, his heart pounding. Why didn't he think of it before? That would prove he was telling the truth, or at least go a long way towards it. He would see Chief Inspector Ashworth at the courts in the morning. He could tell him then.

* * *

When Holly called at Jean Churchman's cottage the next day to return the keys to Meg's workshop, she was more than a little surprised by the enthusiastic reception she received. Jean opened the front door and smiled warmly.

'I'm just returning the keys,' Holly ventured. 'To the stables.'

'Oh, how good of you. Would you like to come in for a cup of coffee?'

'That would be very nice. Thank you.'

'How is Meg?' Jean asked, as she ushered Holly into the kitchen.

'Not too well, I'm afraid. She's getting really depressed.'

'And who can wonder at that, poor dear. Do sit down, won't you?'

Holly accepted a seat at the table and placed her shoulder bag on the floor at her feet. Jean opened the Rayburn stove and heat from the coke fire immediately warmed the pleasant room.

'Things are looking black for her, aren't they, Sergeant?'

'That's about the best estimate you can put on it,' Holly admitted.

'Poor Meg. I did try to visit her, you know, but she said she didn't want to see me.'

'She's not seeing anybody at the moment. She's really going into her shell.'

'I tried to contact Emma, as well,' Jean said, placing the steaming coffee mugs on the table, 'but I kept getting her answering machine and she wouldn't return my calls.' She pulled up a chair and sat close to Holly. 'Does my trying to contact Emma surprise you, Sergeant?'

Holly shrugged. 'It's none of my business, is it?'

'This whole hate thing between us has been hyped up out of all proportion . . .' She stopped to sip her coffee. 'To be perfectly honest, I was glad to get rid of my husband. Mind you, I didn't like parting with the money after the divorce, and I didn't find it very flattering that he should leave me for someone like Emma.' She chuckled. 'I actually told her that, and I think it offended her more than anything else.'

'She's suffered a lot because of this business.'

'I know, and it's such a shame. I hear her political career has finished, and she's had to sell her travel agent's business.'

Holly savoured the milky coffee, and said, 'Apparently she's moving away from the area when the trial's over.'

'Immediately afterwards,' Jean said knowingly. 'I've heard she's already found a buyer for the house.'

Holly was surprised; she was unaware that the house had even been put on the market. 'How do you know that, Mrs Churchman?'

Jean smiled. 'Oh, Jerry, my boyfriend, knows most of what goes on.' She considered Holly for a long time. 'I suppose Jerry and I must have been your prime suspects at one time.'

'Well, I'll have to admit, we did think of you.'

'Yes, I thought so. What with the feud between Emma and me, and no doubt Spicer told you I put the cash up to start Jerry's business.'

Holly gave a noncommittal shrug, and Jean said, 'You don't have to answer. It's all sour grapes on Spicer's part. He didn't want to see Jerry succeed. Competition, you see. Spicer's had it all his own way for too long, and Jerry's good at his job.'

'We never seriously considered you,' Holly lied.

'No?' Jean laughed. 'Not even with Jerry being at the Save U Supermarket at the time the tampered goods were being planted?'

'You haven't asked if I think Meg's guilty,' Holly said, watching her closely.

'That's because I know she's not.' Jean drained her coffee mug and sat back. 'Word has got around that you have a cast-iron case against the poor girl, but I know she didn't do it.'

'Even so, we're not looking for anyone else. Anyway, Mrs Churchman, I'd better be off. Thanks for the coffee.'

Holly picked up her bag and glanced out of the kitchen window at the vast expanse of garden. A slight thaw had set in and areas of green vegetation were visible through the yellowing snow.

'My pleasure,' Jean said, inclining her head. 'Do call in and let me know how things are going for Meg, won't you?'

She showed Holly out of the cottage and stayed on the doorstep long after the car had disappeared.

CHAPTER 28

Ashworth received a message that Blakewell wanted to see him, and as he made his way down the stairs to the prisoners' rooms in the bowels of the magistrates' court, he speculated that he would have to be very careful with this man who until now had made a successful living out of duping people. Much as he wanted to see Meg walk free, he realized that anything Blakewell might tell him would need to be treated with a great deal of caution. He knocked on the appropriate door and was confronted by a male warder.

'Chief Inspector Ashworth,' he said, showing his warrant card. 'I'm here to see Blakewell.'

'Okay, I'll leave you with him, but be careful, he could talk the paint off the walls.'

'I'll keep it in mind,' Ashworth said, when the door was firmly shut.

Blakewell was sitting on an uncomfortable wooden chair and was, as ever, dressed immaculately.

'You seem to have made an impression on him,' Ashworth remarked, nodding towards the door.

'They don't like con-men,' Blakewell told him. 'We rank just above child-molesters in their book.'

'Right, what have you got for me, then?' he asked, pulling up a chair.

'It's not much. Oh, I don't know, last night it seemed like a lifeline, but now I'm not so sure.'

'Get on with it, man,' Ashworth urged.

'It's the envelopes that the money was left in at the Plough. They should be with my personal belongings you collected from Janie's house. I'd jotted down some phone numbers on them.'

Ashworth considered this. 'Well, if they contained money it should show up on forensic tests, but that's all. There'd be fingerprints, but not much chance of identifying them.'

'No,' Blakewell said dejectedly. 'I don't suppose whoever delivered the money would leave his dabs all over them.'

'We'll have a look, though,' Ashworth said, standing up. 'But I wouldn't hold out any great hopes.'

Blakewell sneered. 'You'd like to see me go down for life, wouldn't you?'

'Believe it or not, no. I'd like to see you get the maximum sentence that's due for what you've done. But my main priority is to apprehend those responsible for the murder of Shirley Samuels.'

* * *

The envelopes were taken from Blakewell's personal effects and passed on to the Forensic department for analysis. The subsequent report made interesting reading. They had indeed contained bank notes at one time; an imprint of the Monarch's head had emerged during one of the tests. Fingerprints were numerous, but mostly smudged and of little use to the investigation, Ashworth had not held out much hope anyway, because along with Blakewell's would have been the prints of all who had handled the envelopes since their manufacture.

One paragraph of the report in particular caught Ashworth's eye and made him sit up; it was found that all of the envelopes carried an identical serial number lightly embossed at the right-hand inside corner — the number indicated that they came from the same batch. Would this information help them to trace the suppliers, Ashworth wondered? And if so, would the suppliers be able to identify the buyer?

'It's an outside chance, but the only one I've got,' Ashworth muttered, dropping the report onto his desk. Josh glanced across quizzically, and Ashworth passed him the document.

'Guv,' he said tentatively, after reading the relevant points. 'The case is officially closed, but it seems to me that neither you nor Holly can accept that.'

'That's because we don't believe the conclusion that's been reached,' he responded shortly.

'Vincent Blakewell's a con-man,' Josh argued. 'Of course he's going to be able to tell a convincing story — it's what he's been doing all his life.'

'I'm with Josh on this, guv,' Bobby cut in, with his new-found confidence. 'I believe Blakewell's guilty. Others may be involved, but I believe the whole thing was his idea.'

'Then why should he involve Meg Cowper?' Ashworth countered.

'In case it all went wrong,' Bobby replied. 'The way I see it, now the envelopes have suddenly turned up and go part of the way to proving his story, even if he's found guilty there'll be grounds for an appeal. So, he could walk away free and Meg Cowper's left to carry the can.'

Ashworth fell silent for a moment; that was something he had not considered. 'Right, we've had the democratic bit, where we've all had our say,' he said with good humour. 'Now let's move on to where we all acknowledge I'm in charge and do our level best to keep me happy.'

Josh shot him a wry grin, and said, 'Just for the record, guv, I think Blakewell was involved with others in this and that makes him guilty as charged.' He caught Ashworth's caustic expression and grabbed his jacket from the back of his chair. 'I know, I know, we'll go and chase the envelopes.'

'Good man,' Ashworth said. 'What I want you and Bobby to do is collect the envelopes from Forensic and visit Manfields. They're the biggest stationers in this area; let's see if they have any record of the serial numbers.'

* * *

Manfields stood in the centre of the high street. The shop itself was a converted crofter's cottage with a thatched roof and black wooden beams decorating the outer wall. Its interior, however, was ultra-modern with glass-topped counters and soft lighting. A pretty young assistant looked up as they entered and a pleasant smile came immediately to her full lips. She was clearly delighted that two attractive men had turned up to brighten her day.

'Hi,' Bobby said, his eyes flirting. 'We're from Bridgetown nick.'

The girl glanced briefly at their warrant cards and then returned her full attention to Bobby's face.

'And what do you want from me?' she asked, an eyebrow raised provocatively.

'I'll get round to that later,' Bobby murmured, leaning on the counter. 'We've got some questions to ask first.'

The girl giggled, and Josh rolled his eyes in despair. Why did he always get partners who were obsessed with their sexual organs?

'Look,' he interjected, 'we're trying to trace the source of these envelopes.'

He withdrew them from his inside pocket and passed them to the girl. She was obviously irritated by his interruption and her mouth fell into a pout as she gave the envelopes her scant attention.

'Can you tell us if they came from this shop?' he asked.

'They do look like our brand.'

'Have you got any idea who they might have been sold to?'

'Are you kidding?' she exclaimed. 'We sell stationery. Customers just come in and buy them over the counter. We don't take their names, you know.'

'What about the serial numbers?' Josh persisted. 'Would they be any help in tracing the buyer — if it was a bulk purchase, for instance?'

The girl shrugged. 'I don't know. You'd have to ask the boss, Mr Peters.'

'And where can I find him?'

'Mr Peters,' the girl called out.

A door to the rear of the shop was pulled open and a short, middle-aged man appeared, his face blighted by a seemingly permanent harassed look.

'What is it?' he asked.

'Somebody here to see you, Mr Peters.'

Josh left Bobby at the counter and strolled towards the man. 'Sorry to disturb you, sir. I'm DC Abraham, and I wonder if I could ask you a few questions.'

'Well, yes, of course.' He directed an impatient glance at his assistant, who was exchanging playful banter with Bobby. 'Youngsters,' he muttered. 'When I was her age we would almost stand to attention when the boss was about.'

'I bet, sir.' Josh handed over the envelopes. 'I want to know if there's any way we could find out who bought these.'

'If they were sold over the counter, then you can forget it,' Peters replied. 'But if they were part of a large order, I might be able to help. Come into the office.'

Josh squeezed into a tiny room which housed a desk and three metal filing cabinets, leaving just enough space for two medium-sized people to stand up in.

'So, Mr Peters, if it's a bulk order, you'd have the name of the purchaser?'

'Not here, no. Manfields is a family firm, you see. They not only own the factory, they also control the outlets. So, for that information you'd have to get in touch with Head Office.' He paused. 'Unfortunately, it's closed down for two days for refurbishment.'

'Great,' Josh huffed.

'The names of bulk purchasers would be on the computer along with the serial number, or batch number as we call it. The orders come into the shop, then I pass them on to the factory and they deliver direct.'

'Does that mean you have a list of bulk purchasers?'

'Oh, yes, I can help you there.' Mr Peters took a green folder from one of the filing cabinets. 'All the names are in here. There's the Local Authority, the Housing Association, the Council, two local law practices, Jerry Townsend Securities, Tom Salter's garage, and a couple of banks.'

'Right, so in two days' time we could find out if the envelopes were delivered to any of those customers.'

'That's correct.' He closed the folder and returned it to the cabinet. 'I'll take the batch number and fax it through, if you like. I'll tell them to contact you directly with the information.'

'Thanks, that would be a big help.'

* * *

Two days later, Clive Sanderson paid another call to Meg in the prison's remand wing. She had lost weight, and dark circles beneath her eyes accentuated the paleness of her face. She hardly glanced up when he entered the visitors' room.

'Hello, Meg,' he said brightly. 'I trust you've reached a decision.'

'Yes, I have,' she whispered. 'I most definitely have.'

'Good.'

A look of apprehension clouded his features as he pulled out a chair and sat down.

* * *

Ashworth had great difficulty in concentrating that afternoon. The call from Manfields's head office was due at around 5 p.m. and, try as he might, he could not give his full attention to the mundane task of writing out reports. The envelopes were the only real clue they had, and if that avenue of investigation came to a dead end then Meg Cowper would have to stand trial.

When Holly joined him in the office at 4 p.m. the atmosphere was fraught with tension. Very few words passed between them, and only the occasional rustle of papers broke the silence as they both made token attempts to finish the reports. At four thirty, Ashworth put down his pen and sat looking at the clock, his eyes following the slow journey of the minute hand.

* * *

Emma Cowper visited Sanderson at his plush high street practice, and anxiety brought a frown to her forehead as his secretary showed her into the main office.

'Emma,' Sanderson smiled. He stood up and waved a hand expansively towards a chair in front of his desk. 'Do take a seat.'

She made herself comfortable and turned her expectant face towards the lawyer. 'Well? Did you talk to Meg?'

'Yes, and it's all right, she's decided to plead guilty.'

'Oh, thank God,' she sighed. 'Though why I should be thankful for the fact that my sister's going to prison for fifteen years is beyond me.'

'It's the best I could do,' he said, sobering somewhat. 'And of course, as I've already explained, it's not a foregone conclusion that she'll only get fifteen years.'

'But it's likely, isn't it? You said it's likely.'

'Oh, yes, I can't see the prosecution pressing for a longer sentence . . . but sometimes one can never tell. The main point in her favour is that this Blakewell character will have little option but to plead guilty as well — it's pointless doing otherwise if Meg's already admitted the offences — and that will be taken into consideration.'

'Clive, be honest with me,' Emma urged. 'What are the chances of Meg only getting fifteen years?'

He pursed his lips and exhaled sharply. 'About fifty/fifty, I'd say. I know you've spent a lot of money, Emma, but it really is the best I can do.'

She gave him a reassuring smile. 'I realize that, and I want to thank you for all your help.' She hesitated. 'Clive, do you think she did it?'

'I usually try to stay completely detached — you know, try not to think about whether my client could be guilty — but to be perfectly honest with you, no, I don't think she did it.'

'And there's nothing we can do about that?'

He shook his head. 'Whoever planned this little caper committed the perfect crime. Not only have they got away with it, but the case will be officially closed because Meg and Blakewell will be serving sentences for it.'

'Poor Meg.' Emma paused for thought. 'Did you tell her I wanted to visit?'

'Yes, I did, but I'm afraid she's still saying no. That's not unusual though,' he added hastily. 'Once she begins her sentence, she'll be only too pleased to see you, I'm sure.'

'Thank you, Clive.' She got to her feet, a hand outstretched.

'Emma, I wish I could have done more,' he said, shaking her hand warmly. 'But it really was a damage limitation exercise by the time it came to me.'

'I know, and I thank you for what you have done.' She turned to leave. 'Oh, Clive, I wonder if I might use the telephone in your outer office?'

'Of course,' he said, skirting round the desk and opening the door for her. 'Please, be my guest.'

'Thank you.' She swept from the room.

* * *

At 4.56 p.m. Ashworth's telephone buzzed and he pounced on the receiver while a hopeful Holly watched from her desk.

'I see,' he said. 'Yes, yes, thank you for letting me know.' He dropped the receiver into its cradle and gave Holly a doleful look.

'Well, guv?'

'That was Emma Cowper,' he said. 'Ringing to inform us that Meg intends to offer no defence.'

'Plead guilty, you mean? But, guv, that's the worst thing she could do. If Meg admits the charges, there'd have to be a heck of a lot of new evidence come to light before we could get the case reopened.'

'I know,' Ashworth intoned. 'This really is a race against the clock.'

'Why didn't you tell Emma about the envelopes?'

Ashworth sighed gloomily. 'Because we've only got an outside chance of finding out who bought them, and I don't want to raise the poor woman's hopes until we've got something definite. If we ever do get anything definite,' he added, glowering at the telephone.

No sooner had he said the words than the telephone buzzed, and he stared at it in astonishment for a moment before picking up the receiver.

'Hello? Yes, this is he.'

His expression darkened as he listened, and after muttering his thanks he sat back, the receiver still in his hand. Holly heard a click as the line was broken at the other end and then the faint purr of a dialling tone.

'Was that Manfields, guv?'

'Yes.'

'Nothing on the envelopes?'

He huffed. 'Would you believe that their computer's crashed? It won't be back on till tomorrow afternoon, at the earliest.'

CHAPTER 29

Emma was in the kitchen, busily preparing vegetables. Brussels sprouts were cleaned and scored, potatoes peeled and broccoli soaked. She was filled with a nervous energy and needed to keep herself occupied. After dropping the sprouts into a saucepan of water, she dried her hands and hurried up to Meg's bedroom where she made straight for the wardrobe. From there she took out a bottle of gin and a bottle of bitter lemon and stood still for a moment to reflect.

'Poor Meg, this is the first time I haven't felt guilty about stealing your booze . . . but where you're going they wouldn't let you drink it, would they?'

* * *

Ashworth was in a particularly cantankerous mood and was likely to remain so until he received a productive call from Manfields. Holly always reacted badly to his sour spells and was therefore making a concerted effort to keep out of his way. It was for that reason that she decided to call at Jean Churchman's cottage the next day on the pretext of relating the news of Meg's intended guilty plea.

By now the snow had thawed completely and huge puddles had to be negotiated as she made her way through the central archway and along to the back door. She knocked sharply and turned to view the large garden. Jean opened the door, her hands covered with flour.

'Oh, hello, you've caught me preparing tonight's dinner,' she said, smiling.

'I'm sorry. Shall I call back later?'

'No, there's no need, come in.'

In the kitchen, warmth from the stove hit Holly as soon as she entered, and she slipped off her jacket.

'Shall I hang that up for you?' Jean offered, wiping her hands on a towel.

'Thanks.'

Holly handed it across and Jean went out into the hall, saying, 'It's nice to see you again. Is there any particular reason for the visit?'

'Only to tell you that Meg's going to plead guilty at the trial.'

Jean's eyes expressed dismay as she came back into the kitchen. 'Oh dear, that is bad news,' she said. 'Still, I suppose it gets it over with quickly. I'll make us some coffee as soon as I've finished this. Sit down.'

Holly pulled out a chair and sat watching Jean swiftly dice a few carrots. 'So you could be besieged by the press after the trial,' she said, pulling a face. 'I knew the Bridgetown poisoner — that sort of thing.'

'I hadn't thought of that,' Jean pondered. 'Well, they won't get much change out of me.' She scooped the carrots into a colander and crossed to rinse them under the tap.

'What's Meg really like?' Holly asked.

'Oh, she's such a sweet woman,' Jean said, leaving the colander on the draining board and returning to the table. 'She'd help anybody. She's a bit silly about men, I suppose, but then again we all are sometimes.' She laughed and started to chop up a cabbage.

'I'd have to hold my hand up to that,' Holly said, grinning.

Jean paused, the knife in mid-air. 'She worked so hard on that business, you know. I suppose she felt she had something to prove.'

'To Emma, you mean?'

'Yes. Having a sister who's always putting you down can't be easy. Do you know, as much as I try, I can't help disliking that woman. Oh, well . . .' She rinsed the cabbage and placed it in a saucepan, then dried her hands. 'If you really pushed me, Sergeant, I'd have to say I feel nothing but pleasure about what's happened to Emma, but Meg . . .' She shook her head sadly. 'When I think of what that poor girl's had to go through, I could cry.'

Holly smiled. 'At least that's honest, Mrs Churchman.'

'You're very easy to talk to,' she said, moving along to the fridge. 'Ah, there it is.' She took out a plastic freezer bag and carried it back to the table.

Holly was enjoying watching someone else work, and she sat back and relaxed while Jean emptied the bag on to a chopping board. Several pieces of blanched rhubarb fell out, about four inches in length and still partly frozen.

'Does this mean that you won't be looking for anybody else in connection with the crimes, then?'

'No, we won't,' Holly said. 'We've charged her boyfriend, as well.'

'Oh yes, I read about that in the papers.'

Jean set about chopping the rhubarb into smaller pieces and Holly's teeth were set on edge as the knife sliced through the fibrous stalks and bit into the board beneath.

Rhubarb . . . Holly jolted when the notion slipped into her mind, her eyes firmly fixed on the knife. Find someone who has access to a supply of oxalic acid . . . perhaps not as obvious a supply as the one I had.

'I'm still hoping Meg will see me,' Jean said.

But Holly was no longer listening. Thoughts were falling over themselves to reach the forefront of her mind. What had Bobby said? You can buy oxalic acid from chemists, or you can make it yourself . . . by boiling rhubarb leaves. There have been quite a few accidental deaths . . . She watched the knife slicing into the pieces, saw Jean push them to one side.

'Are you all right, Sergeant?'

The question startled her, and Holly blinked rapidly to bring herself back to the present. 'Yes, I'm fine,' she said. 'Look, I'm sorry but I won't be able to stay for coffee, I've just remembered something. I'll have to be going. I'm sorry.'

She collected her coat and smiled apologetically as she let herself out by the kitchen door. Jean stared after her while she hastened along the garden path and disappeared through the archway. Muddy water spattered the backs of her legs as Holly strode through the puddles in a hurry to get back to the car. She clambered into the driver's seat, at the same time noticing that Jean was watching her from the lounge window.

'Well, Meg, you said we'd never prove it, but we can give it our best shot.' She started the engine and revved away.

* * *

Back in the office Ashworth was still attempting to clear the mounting pile of paperwork littering his desk. While his pen glided along the pages of yet another meaningless form, he muttered constantly, annoyed as he was by that fairly recent paradox which had crept into the working pattern of the police force — namely that the rise in crime was solely due to the fact that all coppers were having to spend their valuable time filling in forms while they should be out there catching criminals. It was an all too common complaint within the force, and one that served to keep his mind off the real reason for his solemn mood: the call from Manfields which seemed to be taking for ever to materialize.

With a fretful sigh, Ashworth put down his pen and reached for his coffee, the hot liquid burning his fingers through the flimsy plastic of the cup. He considered the telephone in front of him, willing it to ring. When it did, he was momentarily startled and stared at it for several seconds before picking up the receiver.

'Hello? Yes, this is Chief Inspector Ashworth.' He listened. 'That's good, so you can say with certainty who placed the order for the envelopes we're interested in?'

Ashworth frowned as he listened to the reply. 'Are you sure about that? There's no chance at all that you might have made a mistake?' Reaching for his pen, he scribbled a name on a corner of his blotter. 'Yes, of course. Thank you, you've been most helpful.'

He replaced the receiver and exhaled sharply. 'Well, that's a turn-up for the books. You said we'd never be able to prove it, Meg, but I think we've just uncovered the woman's one mistake.'

* * *

He was already in the Scorpio, pulling at his seat belt, when Holly drove into the police station car park. She manoeuvred into the adjoining space and scrambled out.

'Guv,' she said excitedly, as he wound down his window. 'I've discovered who has access to an alternative supply of oxalic acid.'

'So have I,' he replied. 'Get in, and we'll go and ask the woman some questions.'

* * *

Their shoes splashed through the puddles on the approach to the house. Ashworth made his knock forceful and then waited impatiently for the door to open. When no one came after a few moments, he knocked again.

'She's not going to answer, guv,' Holly said, moving to the window and peering through.

'Let's try the kitchen door,' he suggested.

On the way, they both scrutinized the large garden to see if anyone was hiding out there, and then Ashworth banged loudly on the glass. Holly stepped back and glanced up at the bedroom windows. There was no sign of life.

‘She could have gone out, guv.’

Ashworth grunted and stooped down to look through the glass door, but his view was hampered by the net curtain. He shifted his position and peered through the strands that made up the loose border pattern. On the table he could see vegetables prepared for cooking and what looked like a bottle of red wine. He was about to straighten up when something caught his eye. At the far end of the kitchen, through a door leading into the hall, he could see a small portion of the lounge, could see a figure slumped in an easy chair. When she heard his sharp intake of breath, Holly crouched down to take a look, but Ashworth was already trying the door. It was locked.

‘Holly, give me your shoe.’

‘What, guv?’

‘I said, give me your shoe — quickly.’

With a hand on the wall to balance herself, she removed her high-heeled shoe and passed it across. Ashworth took one step back and smashed the thin stiletto into the glass closest to the Yale lock. It shattered immediately and the shards fell noisily onto the ceramic floor tiles. He gingerly pushed a hand through the hole and felt around. With his eyes never leaving the glass dangerously close to his wrist, Ashworth managed to release the lock and the door came open. He handed the shoe back to Holly and she hurriedly slipped it on, then followed him into the kitchen. The broken glass crunched beneath their feet as they made their way to the hall. Holly was curious to know the reason for Ashworth’s urgency, but all became plain when they stopped at the lounge doorway. They viewed the bodies in stunned silence for a moment, and then Ashworth stepped into the room.

‘Right, Holly, get on to the station. I want the police surgeon, the pathologist, and Forensic.’

It was correct procedure for the police surgeon to pronounce that life was extinct, but they both knew that in this case it would be a mere formality. Emma Cowper and Richard Samuels were quite dead.

CHAPTER 30

For the next three weeks the CID department painstakingly unravelled the series of events which ended in the discovery of the two dead bodies. Finally, they had gathered enough evidence to put before a coroner's court. In light of the findings the trial of Meg Cowper was postponed, then eventually cancelled and her release from custody arranged.

Ashworth and Holly went to the prison to fetch her home. Meg was waiting for them in the visitors' room and a broad grin was on her face when the warder let them in.

'Thank you. Oh, thank you,' she cried, rushing from the chair to fling her arms around Ashworth's neck.

'I would've cleared you sooner if I'd known this was the reception I'd get,' he said fondly. Meg laughed and turned to hug Holly.

'You should have told us, you know,' Ashworth said.

Meg sobered immediately and wandered back to her chair. 'I couldn't believe it myself, at first,' she explained. 'I'd known for a long time that Emma was having an affair with Richard Samuels, but I didn't put two and two together until James . . . I mean, until Blakewell was caught and told you his story. Then it hit me like a bolt out of the blue. There was only one person who could have known, without any doubt, that I would fall for Blakewell the way I did. And that person was Emma. She knew the type of man I liked, and she knew how weak I can be when I'm in love.'

'Your falling in love with him was central to their plans,' Ashworth said. 'But why didn't you inform us as soon as you realized?'

Meg sighed. 'I suppose I thought if she'd planned it then there would be no way out of it for me. But even then I couldn't help myself, I had to drop a few hints to the sergeant.'

'And it's lucky you did, my girl,' Ashworth said sternly.

'You have to admit they would have been pretty wild accusations for me to make,' Meg countered. 'Especially as I didn't have any evidence to back them up.'

Ashworth had to agree, and he pulled up chairs for himself and Holly while Meg lit a cigarette.

'So, what really happened?' she asked.

'A hell of a lot of this is speculation,' Holly said, wary of upsetting the woman, 'but we've pieced it together as best we could. There's not much doubt that Richard Samuels spotted Blakewell planting the jar of tampered baby food and followed him back to his accommodation. That was probably when the plan was hatched. We assume that they saw it as a good way of getting rid of Shirley Samuels so that they could be together.'

'And pin the murder on me,' Meg said bitterly.

'We don't know if it was their intention at that point,' Holly quickly replied. 'You were just their insurance policy, in case we got too close.'

Meg lowered her head and stared forlornly at the floor.

'At that stage, they had committed the perfect murder,' Ashworth went on. 'They'd planted enough oxalic acid from your workshop to make two people ill, without actually killing them. And putting lethal amounts of the poison in his own Scotch as well as his wife's gin was a master stroke, because in those circumstances we didn't even consider that Samuels could be the killer. But, of course, he knew his wife's drinking habits, he knew she'd drink far more than he did—'

'He knew she'd die, whereas he would merely be taken ill,' Meg interjected.

'That's about it,' Ashworth agreed. 'Now, we think it was at that point that they became aware of the possibilities. Trade at the supermarket had plunged so they gambled on keeping the extortion threat alive, knowing full well that if the supermarket chain was pushed close to liquidation, Samuels could pick it up for next to nothing. He'd always wanted to modernize it, make it more competitive, but the other directors held him back. So, we believe it was then that they took the decision to . . . to sacrifice you. I'm sorry Meg, but that's the only way I can put it.'

'Cash in their insurance policy,' Meg intoned, as she stubbed out her cigarette.

'That's what it amounts to, yes. There never was a demand for money, of course. Samuels simply took it to Aldridge Farm, left it by the cattle grid road and drove the car straight to the car park at the railway station. To avoid being recognized he put on the crash helmet as soon as he left the car. Emma must have been waiting somewhere nearby to pick him up. It was Emma who took him to the derelict cottage and handcuffed him to the bannister.' He shrugged. 'They must have known that he'd be able to attract the shepherd's attention. So, once again it looked as if Samuels had suffered at the hands of the extortionist.'

'Is that when Blakewell put the briefcase in the boot of my car?' Meg asked, her eyes flitting from one to the other.

Holly nodded. 'Samuels gave us a description of the case, and he even said the woman's voice he heard on the radio at the cottage sounded a little like yours.'

'After you'd been charged,' Ashworth said, 'your lawyer told Emma that the case against you wasn't strong, so that's when they got the idea to really seal your fate. They hired a private detective and then planted the letter that was supposedly from Dallington for him to find. After that it was a simple matter of getting you to plead guilty and the case was over. They weren't even worried about Blakewell turning up; after all, what light could he shed on what actually happened?'

Meg extracted a cigarette from the packet, but then changed her mind and forcibly shoved it back. 'So, by hiring the private detective, Emma made herself look like the loving sister,' she scoffed, 'when in fact she was making sure I got life.'

'It was all very clever,' Ashworth said.

'How did you uncover it?' Meg asked.

He gave a slight smile. 'Holly tells me that Emma used to steal your gin.'

'Hah, she used to steal my gin, my make-up, even my polo mints. She really did have a mean streak.'

'Yes, and it was that meanness that led to her downfall. The envelopes that were used when money was left at the Plough for Blackwell had a batch number on them. We managed to trace that to the local council, and more precisely to Emma herself. They were envelopes she'd ordered in the thousands for a local referendum on whether the marketplace should be resurfaced with traditional cobbles as opposed to more modern paving slabs.'

'Are you saying that if she hadn't been too mean to buy a packet of envelopes, she would've got away with it?'

'Possibly,' Ashworth said quietly. 'Anyway, a search of Samuels's house revealed the black leather motorcycle gear and the blue crash helmet.'

Meg stared straight ahead, her emotions in a turmoil. 'This is the question I've been dreading to ask — what happened to Emma and Samuels?'

Ashworth hesitated. 'We found some bottles of bitter lemon at the house. They were all fine, except for the one they'd been drinking from — that bottle had been spiked with enough oxalic acid to kill. All we can think is that they poisoned the drinks at the house and then Samuels took them to the supermarket. This particular bottle must have got mixed up with their own supply.'

Meg closed her eyes, and for a second it seemed that she would break down. Holly put a comforting arm around her shoulder and murmured encouragingly in her ear.

'If it helps, Meg,' Ashworth said, 'if it makes it hurt any less, Emma was preparing a meal at the time. They must have been celebrating the fact that you were going to plead guilty. If ever there was a case of poetic justice . . .'

* * *

Holly accompanied Meg into the house. She strolled through all of the downstairs rooms, hesitating briefly on each threshold, seemingly unable to believe that she was free. By the time they reached the lounge, Meg was visibly trembling. She stopped by the two easy chairs.

'Is this where . . . ?' Her voice faltered.

'Yes. Look, Meg, are you sure you're going to be okay?' Holly asked worriedly. 'You wouldn't rather stay in a hotel?'

She took in a long breath. 'No, Sergeant, I'm not the soft, gentle, little Meg any more. I've toughened up over the last few months.'

'Are you going to let the sale go through?'

'No,' she said, with a furious shake of her head. 'I love this house.'

'It's a bit big. I mean, now you're on your own . . .'

'I love this house, Sergeant, and I'm going to keep it.'

'Okay, I'll leave you, then.'

'Yes, all right, and thank you, Sergeant, thank you for everything.'

At the front door Holly glanced back. Meg was still standing in the doorway of the lounge, still staring at the chairs. She silently let herself out and joined Ashworth in the car.

'I just hope she's going to be okay, guv,' she said, fastening her seat belt. 'If she starts brooding, she could do something silly in there.'

'She's upstairs now,' Ashworth remarked, glancing up at the window.

Holly leant across. 'That's her bedroom. Guv, I'm really worried about her. She's been through so much.'

Meg looked down at them and gave a tiny wave.

'Oh, well, we've done all we can,' Ashworth said, starting the engine.

* * *

From the window Meg watched the petrol vapour escaping from the car's exhaust as she fingered the tampon holder she had taken from her dressing table drawer.

'I knew what you were doing, Emma,' she whispered. 'All my life you've done what you liked with me, but this time I was determined you wouldn't get away with it.' She chuckled softly. 'When the sergeant took me to my workshop I hid some of the poison under a tampon, then when I got here I tipped it into the one bottle of bitter lemon in my wardrobe. I knew you'd get round to it sooner or later.'

She gave another wave as Ashworth's car pulled away.

'Who's the clever one now, Emma?'

THE END

ALSO BY BRIAN BATTISON

DETECTIVE JIM ASHWORTH SERIES
Book 1: TIED TO MURDER
Book 2: THE PRICE OF MURDER
Book 3: FLIRTING WITH MURDER
Book 4: MURDER IN THE COTTAGE
Book 5: MURDER IN THE LIBRARY
Book 6: THE TASTE OF MURDER

Thank you for reading this book.

If you enjoyed it please leave feedback on Amazon or Goodreads, and if there is anything we missed or you have a question about, then please get in touch. We appreciate you choosing our book.

Founded in 2014 in Shoreditch, London, we at Joffe Books pride ourselves on our history of innovative publishing. We were thrilled to be shortlisted for Independent Publisher of the Year at the British Book Awards.

www.joffebooks.com

We're very grateful to eagle-eyed readers who take the time to contact us. Please send any errors you find to corrections@joffebooks.com. We'll get them fixed ASAP.

Printed in Great Britain
by Amazon

64356829R00158